THE HEROIC GARRISON

Historical Fiction Published by McBooks Press

BY ALEXANDER KENT
Midshipman Bolitho
Stand into Danger
In Gallant Company
Sloop of War
To Glory We Steer
Command a King's Ship
Passage to Mutiny
With All Despatch
Form Line of Battle!
Enemy in Sight!
The Flag Captain
Signal—Close Action!
The Inshore Squadron
A Tradition of Victory
Success to the Brave
Colours Aloft!
Honour this Day
The Only Victor
Beyond the Reef
The Darkening Sea
For My Country's Freedom
Cross of St George
Sword of Honour
Second to None
Relentless Pursuit

BY DUDLEY POPE
Ramage
Ramage & The Drumbeat
Ramage & The Freebooters
Governor Ramage R.N.
Ramage's Prize
Ramage & The Guillotine
Ramage's Diamond
Ramage's Mutiny
Ramage & The Rebels
The Ramage Touch
Ramage's Signal
Ramage & The Renegades
Ramage's Devil
Ramage's Trial
Ramage's Challenge
Ramage at Trafalgar
Ramage & The Saracens
Ramage & The Dido

BY DAVID DONACHIE
The Devil's Own Luck
The Dying Trade
A Hanging Matter
An Element of Chance
The Scent of Betrayal
A Game of Bones

BY DEWEY LAMBDIN
The French Admiral
Jester's Fortune

BY DOUGLAS REEMAN
Badge of Glory
First to Land
The Horizon
Dust on the Sea

BY V.A. STUART
Victors and Lords
The Sepoy Mutiny
Massacre at Cawnpore
The Cannons of Lucknow
The Heroic Garrison

BY C. NORTHCOTE PARKINSON
The Guernseyman
Devil to Pay
The Fireship
Touch and Go

BY CAPTAIN FREDERICK MARRYAT
Frank Mildmay OR The Naval Officer
The King's Own
Mr Midshipman Easy
Newton Forster OR
The Merchant Service
Snarleyyow OR The Dog Fiend
The Privateersman
The Phantom Ship

BY JAN NEEDLE
A Fine Boy for Killing
The Wicked Trade

BY IRV C. ROGERS
Motoo Eetee

BY NICHOLAS NICASTRO
The Eighteenth Captain
Between Two Fires

BY W. CLARK RUSSELL
Wreck of the Grosvenor
Yarn of Old Harbour Town

BY RAFAEL SABATINI
Captain Blood

BY MICHAEL SCOTT
Tom Cringle's Log

BY A.D. HOWDEN SMITH
Porto Bello Gold

BY R.F. DELDERFIELD
Too Few for Drums
Seven Men of Gascony

The
Heroic
Garrison

V. A. STUART

The Alexander Sheridan Adventures, No. 5

MCBOOKS PRESS
ITHACA, NEW YORK

Published by McBooks Press 2003
Copyright © 1975 by V. A. Stuart
First published in Great Britain by Robert Hale Limited, London 1975

Cover painting: *The Indian Mutiny, 1857: Bengal Army Sepoys Rebel against
British Soldiers at Meerut, near Delhi.*
Courtesy of Peter Newark's Military Pictures

Library of Congress Cataloging-in-Publication Data
Stuart, V.A.
   The heroic garrison / by V. A. Stuart.
      p. cm. — (Alexander Sheridan adventures ; no. 4)
   ISBN 1-59013-030-8 (alk. paper)
   1. Sheridan, Alexander (Fictitious character)--Fiction.
   2. British--India--Fiction.   3. India--History--Sepoy Rebellion, 1857-
   1858--Fiction.   4. Great Britain--History, Military--19th century--
   Fiction.   5. Lucknow (India)--History--Siege, 1857--Fiction.   I. Title
   PR6063.A38 H47 2003
   823'.914—dc21   2002012358

Distributed to the trade by National Book Network, Inc.,
15200 NBN Way, Blue Ridge Summit, PA 17214
800-462-6420

Additional copies of this book may be ordered from any bookstore or
directly from McBooks Press, Inc., ID Booth Building,
520 North Meadow St., Ithaca, NY 14850. Please include $4.00 postage
and handling with mail orders. New York State residents must add
sales tax. All McBooks Press publications can also be ordered by calling
toll-free 1-888-BOOKS11 (1-888-266-5711).
Please call to request a free catalog.

Visit the McBooks Press website at www.mcbooks.com.

Printed in the United States of America
9   8   7   6   5   4   3   2   1

For my good friend Jim Schaaf of Concord, California, in the hope that, in the sharing of a mutual admiration for the deeds of brave soldiers, this book may give him pleasure.

⋙ • ⋘

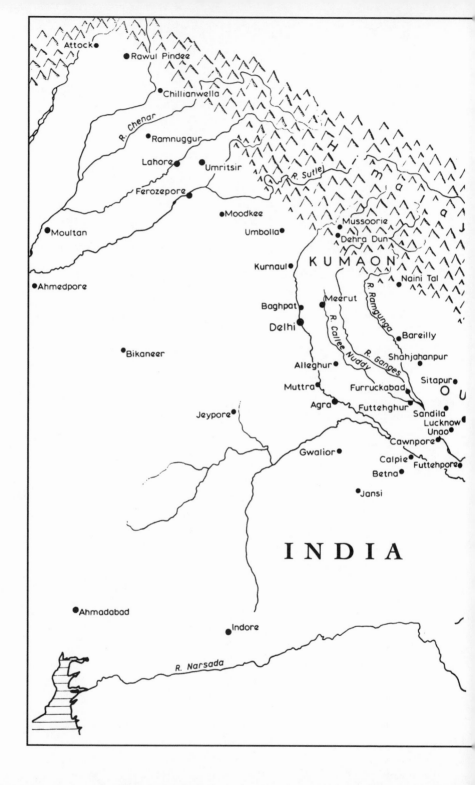

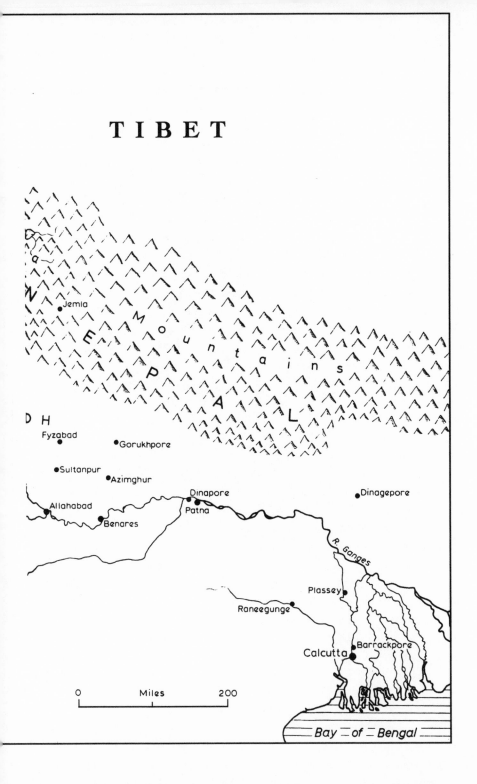

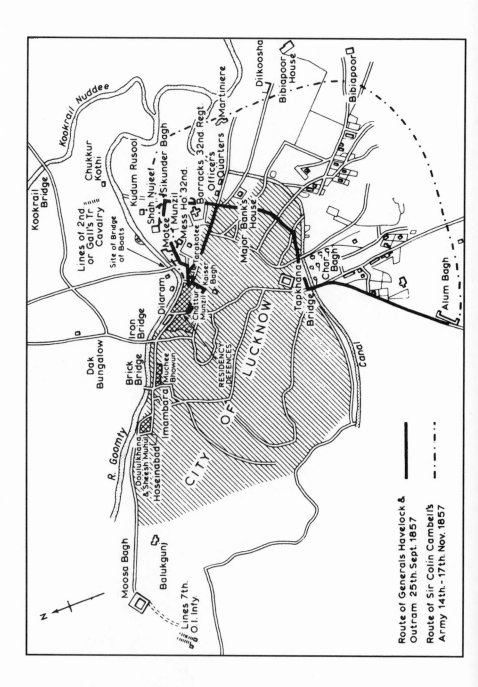

Route of Generals Havelock &
Outram 25th. Sept. 1857

Route of Sir Colin Cambell's
Army 14th. - 17th. Nov. 1857

AUTHOR'S NOTE

❯❯❯ • ❮❮❮

WITH THE EXCEPTION of the final episode—which *could* have happened—everything recounted in this book actually took place.

The only fictional characters are Alex Sheridan and Henri Court; all the others are called by their correct names and their actions are on historical record although, of course, conversations with the fictitious characters and dialogue with each other are imagined. As far as possible, however, such conversations are based on their known views or actions.

Both General Wheeler's two daughters were officially on record as having died or been killed at or shortly after the massacre of the Cawnpore garrison, the elder by her own hand, after she had shot and killed the cavalry sowar who rescued her from the Suttee Chowra Ghat and sought to make her his wife. A strong rumour persisted for many years that the younger had been forcibly converted to the Moslem faith and that, having married a sowar of the Light Cavalry, she was living with him near Lucknow when the Mutiny ended . . . and that she had no wish to return to her father's people. It is possible that rumour confused her with Amelia Horne, whose story—told later by herself—was exactly similar.

Another persistent rumour was of the presence of a European officer with the mutineers during the siege of the Lucknow Residency. His nationality was unknown but it was generally believed that he was French or of mixed French and Sikh blood, and that he held high rank in the rebel army. He was said to have been killed during the siege.

Of the officers and men trapped in what was later known as "Doolie Square," Surgeon Home of the 90th, and Privates Hollowell, 78th, McManus, 5th Fusiliers, and Ryan, Madras Fusiliers, won Victoria Crosses; Captain Becher, Lieutenants Arnold and Swanson and two private soldiers subsequently died of their wounds. V.C.s were not then awarded posthumously, otherwise the gallant Arnold would almost certainly have been honoured. The names of some of the private soldiers do not appear to be on record so that, where necessary, I have given them the names of men noted on the rolls of their regiments as being with Havelock's Force in Lucknow at the time in question.

PROLOGUE

➤➤➤ • ⋘⋘⋘

IN THE WHITE-WALLED palace once occupied by Ali Naqui Khan, prime minister to the deposed King of Oudh, the Moulvi of Fyzabad, Ahmad Ullah, waited with thinly disguised impatience for the arrival of an emissary from the Nana Sahib of Cawnpore, to confer with whom he had been summoned from the battle raging in the neighborhood of the Moti Mahal Palace.

Several hundred British troops—General Havelock's rear-guard—were caught, like rats in a trap, in the Moti Mahal, together with their wounded, their ammunition wagons, baggage train, and heavy caliber guns. Unable to follow the main body into the Lucknow Residency the previous evening, their attempt at first light to smuggle out some of their wounded had resulted in the slaughter of at least forty of them . . . although the rest, due to the bungling of the sepoy officers in command, had been permitted to escape. But one of the heavy guns, which had wrought such havoc with those of the sepoy General of Artillery, Mirza Guffur, was now jammed across a narrow passageway, unable to move and under such heavy musketry fire that the gunners could not use it.

The gun—a valuable prize in itself—could be theirs for the taking, the Moulvi reflected angrily, if only the musketeers' valor were equal to their marksmanship. But none dared risk his

---

For *Historical Notes* on the Mutiny, see page 243, and for a *Glossary of Indian Terms,* see page 255.

worthless life by approaching it, and Mirza Guffur, old woman that he was, had refused to lead a party, with gun-bullocks, to remove it. His own call for volunteers and his promised reward had met with only halfhearted response . . . they were cowards, these miserable dogs of sepoys, reluctant to fight, concerned only with how much plunder they could amass, to enable them to return, as rich men, to their villages. Time and again, they allowed themselves to be routed and put to flight by a mere handful of *feringhi* soldiers who—as they had done that morning, in defense of the laden *doolies* containing their wounded—charged almost contemptuously with the bayonet, aware that no sepoy would face up to them.

It had been the same at Cawnpore and in every battle fought between Allahabad and Lucknow, and the cavalry—even the much vaunted Company-trained Light Cavalry—had acquitted themselves no better. Havelock's puny force of Volunteer Horse—all of them officers, admittedly—had numbered only twenty when they left Allahabad but, even when many of the Irregulars had deserted and come over to the Nana, they had put the whole of the Light Cavalry to shame at Fatepur and again in the battle for Cawnpore. The Moulvi's sallow face suffused with resentful color. Never had he been more humiliated than the day before yesterday, when his own picked body of horsemen had displayed a craven reluctance to engage their British foes, despite the lead he had given them. As a result, instead of taking two of their guns and making the *feringhi* Colonel Sheridan prisoner, he had himself only just contrived to evade capture and his witless followers had allowed themselves to be led into an ambush. Sheridan, even with a lost sword-arm, bore a charmed life—he had survived the Cawnpore massacre and now, presumably, had entered Lucknow with Havelock's force. Indeed, he had been reported as one of a party of cavalry that had made a sally from the Residency during the early hours of the morning, although the identification had not been positive and the promise of substantial reward for proof of his death or capture had, as yet, borne no fruit.

The Moulvi's dark, beetling brows met in a scowl as he crossed to a balcony overlooking the river. The Residency lay a mile to the east, on the opposite bank of the river, but in imagination he saw its battered, shot-scarred walls and the defiant flag, fluttering from its rooftop flagpole in the faint evening breeze. Even at sunset, it was never lowered, and however many times it was shot down, it was never left like that for more than a few hours—one or two of the garrison invariably risked life and limb to hoist it again. The flag was a symbol of the might of the British Motherland, as well as of the Company's threatened Raj. Reminded of this, the Moulvi's lips tightened into a thin, hard line.

So long as it flew, the garrison would not surrender. Half-starved, deprived of all the comforts and luxuries previously considered a necessity by the British if life in India were to be sustained, their women and children dying of dysentery and fever and their wounded for lack of medical supplies, yet they had held out for over three months. Now that they had been reinforced and their casualties made good by the two thousand men of Havelock's column, they would, the Moulvi did not for a moment doubt, fight back like tigers, so long as any hope of relief remained. Havelock had proved himself an able commander in the field, and Outram's record was, perhaps, the best of any of the British generals, his courage second to none. But . . . The Moulvi moved restlessly away from the balcony and started to pace the cool, lofty-ceilinged room, his frown deepening.

If the Nana and Tantia Topi could be persuaded to attack Cawnpore and then, with the Gwalior Contingent, sweep south on Allahabad, to intercept the British troops on their way up-country, it would be a different story. Deprived of their promised relief, the Lucknow garrison could be starved into submission . . . especially if now or within the next few days, they were compelled to dissipate their fighting strength by warding off a series of resolute and well-planned attacks.

Those now surrounded in the Moti Mahal—the original rear-guard and the five hundred or so men sent to their aid from the Residency and occupying two of the adjacent palaces—must on no account be allowed to escape. They were burdened by their camp-followers, their wounded, and by the heavy guns. When darkness fell, they were almost certain, despite this morning's set-back, to make a second attempt to reach the Residency, by way of the river bank and through the gardens and buildings at its edge. If a trap were set for them, the *doolie*-bearers could be counted on to abandon their burdens in panic-stricken flight and then . . . the Moulvi expelled his breath in a long-drawn sigh.

With the loss of a third of his red-coated soldiers, even the redoubtable General Outram would be compelled to come to terms, and the story of Cawnpore, repeated in Lucknow, would strike terror into the hearts of the British. The setting of the trap would require careful timing and firm leadership; he could not trust either Mirza Guffur or the white-bearded old nanny-goat the sepoys had elected as their general, Gomundi Singh. If the plan were to succeed, he would have to attend to the matter himself and lead the attack in person, trusting in Allah to give sufficient courage to his followers to carry out the orders he had given them. His mind made up, the Moulvi ceased his restless pacing and, to the servant who answered his impatient shout, he gave brusque instructions to summon the officers that he had requested the Begum to appoint to his personal staff.

They came, saluted him respectfully and listened in dutiful silence to his orders. He was explaining these in detail when his visitor, the stains of travel now removed from his person, presented himself, accompanied by a tall, slim man in native dress, who took up a position in the shadows at the back of the room. Azimullah Khan came forward, smiling. His greeting was less respectful than that of the sepoy officers had been, but his pleasure in their reunion was, the Moulvi decided, genuine. He had grown in stature and also in arrogance since the days in Cawnpore, when a word or even a gesture had sufficed to bring him running, eager to serve without question . . . But now, as the Nana's envoy and his trusted lieutenant, Azimullah evidently considered himself the equal of his one-time mentor and his opening words reflected his new-found self-confidence.

"Ahmad Ullah, my brother, I rejoice to see thy face again! My thoughts have been often of thee during the past weeks. Dismiss these good fellows"—he waved a graceful hand in the direction of the little group of sepoy officers, who were eyeing him with undisguised curiosity—"I have matters of some moment to speak of, but what I have to say is not for other ears."

"What *I* have to say to my officers is also of some moment," the Moulvi pointed out dryly. "We are at war here." Deliberately taking his time, he repeated the instructions he had given earlier but with more emphasis, and had the satisfaction of seeing Azimullah's eyes widen, as the significance of his carefully chosen words became clear.

"Thou art indeed at war here!" the younger man exclaimed, a note of envy in his voice. He brushed an imagined speck of dust from his *chapkan* and sighed. "But think'st then that the British will simply walk into this ambush? They are not fools."

"They will have no choice," the Moulvi assured him. "They

have many wounded, whom they dare not abandon. If we appear to withdraw our troops when darkness falls, they will make an attempt to break out and reach the Residency. And they will bring their guns with them, as well as the wounded—General Havelock does not like to lose guns, and these are twenty-four-pounders. Such guns are cumbersome and the road is narrow. They will never reach the Residency with them."

"They reached the Residency yesterday," Azimullah reminded him, with conscious malice. "Did they not?"

"Not without loss." The Moulvi dismissed his staff and went on, without troubling to lower his voice as they filed out. "Our men will not stand up to them—the accursed *feringhis* wear a mantle of invincibility in sepoy eyes. Let a *lal-kote* come face-to-face with them and they turn tail—one cannot expect the citizens of Lucknow to do better than trained soldiers of the Company's Army. They fight well enough from behind defensive walls and trenches but in the open . . ." He shrugged contemptuously. "They run like the curs they are!"

"Perhaps they lack the leadership to which they are accustomed," Azimullah suggested. He exchanged a swift, covert glance with the man who had accompanied him, still standing in the deepening shadows beside the curtained doorway, as if anxious to avoid attention. He did not speak, and Azimullah went on, an oddly cruel little smile playing about his lips, "Without their *feringhi* officers to give them orders, few of the Company's soldiers fight well. Could this be because they do not trust their own kind to command them? It was thus at Cawnpore, during the siege and after . . . the sepoy commanders cannot—or will not—enforce discipline. Doubtless it is the same here, Moulvi Sahib, and for that reason—"

"*I* am in command here now," the Moulvi interrupted harshly.

"Thou?" Azimullah was visibly taken aback, staring at him in astonishment. "But we had heard that the Begum placed her trust in sepoy generals!"

"No longer. Hazrat Mahal has appointed me her chief military adviser and I command in her name."

"And the Rajah Man Singh?" Azimullah persisted. "He who once gave sanctuary to British fugitives . . . is it true that *he* is now in alliance with thee and the Begum?"

"It is true," the Moulvi confirmed. "Man Singh has promised his support. He is here with his troops." The Moulvi changed the subject, submitting Azimullah to a barrage of questions concerning the Nana's movements and his plans for the future, to which the younger man replied with boastful confidence. The Nana, he asserted—referring to his master as the Peishwa—had vowed by the waters of the sacred Ganges that he would avenge the defeats he had suffered at Havelock's hands and as soon as Tantia Topi joined him, with the well-equipped Gwalior troops, he would launch an attack on Cawnpore. Tantia could be relied on—he had sent messengers to the Mahratta camp, assuring his master of his whole-hearted loyalty and support. When news reached him that Havelock's column had been wiped out—or, failing this, that both Outram and Havelock were under siege in the Lucknow Residency—he would, Azimullah was certain, march from Kalpi without delay, dispatching part of his force to cut the British lines of communication with Allahabad and Calcutta.

This was the assurance he had hoped for, and the Moulvi nodded his approval. "Thou canst inform the Nana Sahib and Tantia Topi that Havelock's column will no longer pose a threat to them in Oudh, Azimullah. Whilst it is true that Outram and

Havelock are reported to have reached the Residency alive, Neill is dead. The unspeakable defiler of souls was killed in the fighting last night. He fell to a marksman's bullet."

"Neill dead!" Azimullah exulted. "Allah be praised—that is indeed good news!"

"And in the same place, we intercepted a party of wounded this morning," the Moulvi added. "Forty or fifty *doolies,* under escort, were sent from the rear-guard in the Moti Mahal . . . they were cut to pieces. A few escaped but," he shrugged, with pretended indifference, "it is no matter. All in the Residency will die . . . men, women, and children. We shall spare none of them when the time comes."

"We heard from the Peishwa's spies," Azimullah said, a hint of misgiving in his hitherto confident voice, "that Havelock's orders were to evacuate the garrison of the Residency to Cawnpore. These spies are reliable, Ahmad Ullah. Is there a chance that Havelock may endeavor to carry out his orders before Tantia Topi leaves Kalpi?"

"Impossible!" the Moulvi retorted contemptuously. "They have hundreds of wounded and sick, in addition to their women and children—close to a thousand, I would estimate—and they have no carriage in which to convey them to Cawnpore. Besides, they are surrounded—if such an attempt is made, we shall annihilate them. Nothing is more certain, I give thee my word."

"And if they do *not* attempt to reach Cawnpore?"

"Then they are trapped. So long as thy master and Tantia Topi fulfill their promise to recapture Cawnpore and prevent relief reaching them from Allahabad or Calcutta, they are doomed, Azimullah." The Moulvi was smiling, but the smile did not reach his eyes, which remained narrowed and watchful. "The Residency is ringed with guns and their defensive positions are mined.

Oh, they may die at their posts, many of them will, but it is only a question of time before they are compelled to surrender, just as General Wheeler's garrison did. And then they will die, as Wheeler's people did . . . defeated, on their knees and begging for mercy!"

"Not many of Wheeler's garrison died thus," Azimullah was compelled to remind him. "Hast thou forgotten that I was there? I hate all the British, Allah knows I hate them and with good reason, yet . . ." he shrugged and added, with grudging admiration, "I cannot deny their courage, Ahmad Ullah. Those men of Wheeler's were skeletons, scarcely able to hold themselves upright when they left his Fort of Despair. Yet they fought us like soldiers and they died sword in hand. They are not easily defeated. I . . ." he hesitated and then said, frowning, "I heard a rumor that they have taken Delhi by assault. Didst thou also hear it?"

"I heard but did not believe it. Doubtless the British themselves started that hare running."

"Yet it could be the truth, Ahmad Ullah. Indeed—"

"*Nahin!* Three thousand *lal-kotes* against forty thousand sepoys behind fortress walls!" the Moulvi scoffed. "It is inconceivable. In any case, there has been no confirmation, Azimullah. It is mere bazaar gossip and thou art a fool to give it a moment's credence."

"A fool, perhaps," Azimullah conceded. "Yet I wonder . . . The rumor had it that Nicol Seyn himself led the assault, and with such a man, a miracle is always possible."

"It would require a very great miracle," the Moulvi returned tartly, "for three thousand to triumph over forty thousand."

"Forty thousand *sepoys*—dogs of Hindus, most of them, undisciplined and badly led," Azimullah objected. Again he hesitated, biting his lower lip, as if reluctant to engage in argument with the man who, for so long, had been his tutor in the subtleties of mutiny and subversion, but finally he said, with obstinate insistence, "We return, do we not, Moulvi Sahib, to these sepoys— those trained soldiers of the Company who have no stomach to do battle with British bayonets. Thou hast how many of them here, holding the Residency under siege? More, perhaps, than the Shah Bahadur has—or had—in Delhi."

The Moulvi eyed him balefully, resenting the implication. "What is it to thee, Azimullah? We have enough for our purpose. I have told thee, thou canst assure thy master that if he keeps his word, we will keep ours. There will be no escape for the *lal-kotes* in the Residency. Our sepoys will contain them and—"

Azimullah cut him short. "I have brought thee a man who can teach the sepoys their trade, Ahmad Ullah . . . one who will be worth all thy sepoy generals put together. Speak with him, I beg thee." In response to his words, his silent, half-hidden companion stepped from the shadows that had concealed him, acknowledging the Moulvi's presence with a grave inclination of the head. He was tall, and slimmer, even, than Azimullah, dressed in a richly embroidered, gold-laced *chapkan* and the high boots and breeches of a cavalryman, with a turban of Sikh pattern wound about his head and a *tulwar* of formidable proportions suspended from a leather sling at his side. As he moved into the center of the room, the light from the setting sun fell full on his face, revealing that, beneath its coating of tan, his skin was white and the hair of his beard a rich, dark auburn flecked, here and there, with gray.

The Moulvi recoiled from him in shocked surprise.

"Dost thou mock me, Azimullah?" he demanded angrily. "This man is a *feringhi!*"

"*Nahin,* Moulvi Sahib," the stranger denied, speaking perfect Hindustani, with no trace of accent. "I am no *feringhi* . . . nor am

I a lover of the British. I was born in Lahore and my father—whose name, I am sure, will be known to you—was General Henri Court."

The Moulvi recovered from his surprise. Henri Court, he was aware, had entered the service of the Sikh Maharajah Ranjit Singh —the famous "Lion of the Punjab"—some thirty years before. A Frenchman of good birth and a product of the French Military Polytechnic, he had shared with Jean François Allard, Jean Baptiste Ventura, and the Italian general Paolo Avitabile, the distinction of having trained the famous Khalsa army of the Sikhs to the peak of military perfection. Following Ranjit Singh's death in 1839, most of the foreign commanders had either been dismissed or had left the Sikh service, but all had married, and it was, therefore, quite possible that this tall, handsome companion of Azimullah's was what he claimed to be, a son of General Court—half French and half Sikh.

The Moulvi studied him thoughtfully, and—almost against his better judgment—found himself liking what he saw. The newcomer was of good presence; he looked and spoke like a soldier and replied to questions with a fearless frankness that could only stem from honesty. His mother, he said, still lived; she was the daughter of a Sikh *sirdar*, at one time a member of the Durbar. He himself had served his military apprenticeship, under his father and Lehna Singh Majithia, in the ordnance works and later in the field in both the Sutlej and Punjab campaigns, when he had risen to the command of a Ghorchurra regiment, the elite of the Khalsa cavalry.

"Well?" Azimullah prompted, a trifle impatiently, when the Moulvi's questions became less personal and the conversation turned to matters of military strategy. "I would return to the Peishwa's camp tonight, Ahmad Ullah—he is anxious for word from thee and may come to Lucknow himself sometime during the next few weeks, to speak with thee and the Begum. Hast thou honorable employment to offer our friend from Lahore or shall I take him back with me?"

The Moulvi shook his head. "If Colonel Court is willing to remain here I shall very gladly avail myself of his valuable services." He glanced inquiringly at the French general's son and added, smiling, "On my personal staff initially, Colonel Sahib, until I have consulted with the Begum and the Council. But I can promise a command worthy of your achievements." He spoke in Punjabi and Court replied in the same language, as fluently as he had in Hindustani.

"I have one aim, to which I have devoted my life, Moulvi Sahib," he answered quietly. "I want to see the British and their John Company driven from India. For that aim, I would die, not one but a thousand deaths! I ask a free hand in the training of your sepoys and a rank that will spare me from the criticism and envy of your other commanders." Seeing the Moulvi's look of bewilderment, he relaxed a little and explained, "During Ranjit Singh's lifetime, my father had what I have asked for, but, after his death, the jealousy of lesser men drove him back to Europe, bitter and broken-hearted. I am of Hind, Moulvi Sahib, I am born and bred here—for me there is no escape to Europe. Grant me what I have asked and you will have no cause for regret. In return, I will give you an army you can lead to victory."

"So be it," the Moulvi assented. He held out both hands in a spontaneous gesture of goodwill, and his smile widened, for the first time lighting his somber dark eyes as he added, with a flash of wry humor, "I had not thought to call my brother any man with the white skin and the appearance of a *feringhi* but—thou art a man after my own heart! And in very truth, I have need of thee, Henri Court."

"Then I gladly offer my services," Court answered. He took the Moulvi's proffered hands in his and, lowering his turbaned head, touched them to his brow. "But I will take the name of my mother's family. Know me as Kaur Singh, Ahmad Ullah—it will be better thus."

"So be it," the Moulvi said again. "Come," he invited, his smile fading. "The hour approaches when we shall unsheathe our *tulwars* to do battle once more with the enemies of Hind. Havelock's soldiers have been all day under heavy bombardment in the Moti Mahal. When darkness falls, they will rest, believing that we have withdrawn. Then, when the moon rises or at first light, if they see no sign of us, they will make another attempt to break out and save their guns . . . and we shall be waiting for them. In the meantime, some of them are reported to be in hiding, with wounded, in the square where Neill met his end. We will flush them out and enjoy a little sport to while away the time of waiting—wilt thou accompany us, Azimullah?"

Azimullah shook his head. "*Nahin,* as I told thee, I will return to my master the Peishwa, Ahmad Ullah."

"Then *Khuda hafiz,*" the Moulvi bade him, "Allah be with thee." He turned to Court. "Let us go, my brother."

The two went out together and Azimullah Khan watched them go, resenting the Moulvi's perfunctory farewell. But his resentment swiftly faded. His mission had been successfully and diplomatically accomplished, and the Nana, he told himself, would be pleased when he returned to report his success . . . pleased and, Allah willing, also grateful. Court had played his part well— no actor could have played it better. Ahmad Ullah, for all his wary cunning, had failed to recognize his new staff officer for the unscrupulous adventurer he was. But . . . he was a fine soldier, trained in every aspect of war; his professional skill would balance the Moulvi's lack of it and his fanaticism. With Court at hand, neither he nor the Begum would be permitted to make any move that might upset the Nana's plans—they would be held in Lucknow, as securely as the British they were besieging were held, in a state of stalemate, which would leave the Nana free to raise his standard in Oudh. It mattered not that they had crowned the Begum's ten-year-old son, Birjis Quadr, as king; the people of Oudh would know—or be swiftly taught—to whom their allegiance should be given. With the King of Delhi a prisoner, as Azimullah had no doubt that he was, the Nana would indeed be Peishwa, and all the lost Mahratta territory between the Chumbul and the Nerbudda would be restored to those from whom it had been wrested by the rapacious John Company.

And after that, all India, with himself at the Peishwa's right hand, and Court . . . Azimullah was smiling as he moved toward the curtained archway. Court was a soldier and the lives of soldiers were cheap. Cheaper, even, than their loyalties . . .

CHAPTER ONE

❯❯❯ • ❮❮❮

IT WAS BARELY light when the first small party of volunteers left the Lucknow Residency to make their way cautiously through the Terhee Kothee and Furhut Baksh Palaces and from there, along the river bank, to the position held by the rear-guard of Havelock's force in the Moti Mahal.

Alex Sheridan, leading his horse a little way behind the rest, was almost asleep on his feet, stumbling blindly on the rubble-strewn ground, still littered with the debris of the previous day's battle. He had snatched less than an hour's sleep after entering the beleaguered Bailey Guard gate in the wake of the gun-limber bearing Brigadier General James Neill's body, eaten a frugal meal and then—informed of a call for anyone familiar with Lucknow's geography to volunteer to assist in bringing in wounded —had answered the call. For what remained of the night, he had gone, with a surgeon named Greenhow and Lieutenant Johnson of the Irregular Cavalry and twenty of his sowars, as far as the Khas Bazaar, returning with wounded Highlanders and Sikhs slung across their saddles or clinging, limping, to their stirrup-irons.

Lousada Barrow, commander of the Volunteer Cavalry, had also fared forth on a similar mission, along the street leading to the Paeen Bagh and—thanks to the prompt action of the commander of the Bailey Guard, Lieutenant Aitken, who had led a party of his defenders to secure the adjacent buildings—neither party had been fired on by the enemy. Indeed, Alex thought, rousing himself to look about him, the rebels were conspicuous by their continued absence, content, it appeared, to abandon both palaces at the river's edge and their walled enclosures to British occupation. Only ahead of them, in the neighborhood of the Moti Mahal three quarters of a mile away, were the Begum's guns in action . . . and there, according to a report received from Colonel Campbell, of Her Majesty's 90th Light Infantry, who was in command, the position was one of considerable peril. The rear-guard, which consisted of a hundred men of his regiment, was surrounded and under continuous bombardment. Hampered by the column's baggage train and by its wounded—now numbering over two hundred, in *doolies*—and with one of Major Eyre's heavy guns jammed in a narrow passageway and out of action, Campbell stated that he could not advance, although he was so far holding his own. He had asked for reinforcements and, as a matter of urgency, for assistance to evacuate the wounded, many of whom were dying, due to the inability of his handful of surgeons to care for them adequately under such conditions.

The reinforcements—two companies of H.M.'s 5th Fusiliers, under Major Simmons, and a company of Jeremiah Brasyer's Sikhs—had been ordered out by General Outram, Alex was aware, before his own party had left the Residency, but they had been held up by the necessity to clear and occupy the Chutter Munzil garden before proceeding to their objective. When a young civil service officer, Bensley Thornhill—who was well acquainted with Lucknow's tortuous maze of streets and palace courtyards—had offered to guide a party along a path by the river bank, at the rear of the Chutter Munzil, and bring the wounded back by the same route, his offer had been accepted thankfully by General Havelock and agreed to by Sir James Outram.

Havelock's son Harry, deputy assistant adjutant-general to the

Oudh Field Force, had been shot down after the attack on the Char Bagh bridge the day before and he was known to be among the wounded. The little general, despite his stoic efforts not to betray his personal feelings, was beside himself with anxiety on his son's account and Thornhill, who was related to the Havelocks by marriage, was eager to assuage his anxiety. His offer, however, had been confidently made and his route very carefully planned; it was evident to Alex, as the young civilian strode unhesitatingly ahead of his party of volunteers, that he knew the locale as well as he had claimed to know it.

"We're skirting the Chutter Munzil now," he called back softly. "Heads down and keep close to the wall, if you please."

Outside, under the towering wall of the palace, the shadows were deep and the path deserted. To their left, the River Goomti followed its winding course, its murky waters touched with a faint pink radiance as the new day dawned. On the far bank, the lights that had flickered through the darkness like fireflies went out, one by one, but, aside from this indication that the citizens of Lucknow were starting to wake, there was no sign of untoward activity on the part of the rebel troops. All their efforts were concentrated on the destruction of Colonel Campbell's hard-pressed rear-guard, the thunder of cannon and the crackle of musketry bearing witness to the ferocity of their assault.

A guard of Fusiliers, posted in a walled garden overlooking the river, challenged and brought the volunteer party to a halt. Thornhill gave the password of the day and one of the Fusiliers, gesturing ahead with his Minié rifle, told him that the main body of the reinforcements, under Major Simmons, had advanced through the king's stables and the godowns beyond, making for Martin's House. They were retracing the route by which the column had advanced yesterday, Alex's tired brain registered, but this time, seemingly, without meeting anything like yesterday's opposition.

"We'll keep close to the river," Bensley Thornhill said, as they moved forward again. "Until we're opposite Martin's House. Then we'll have to leg it across three hundred yards of dangerous ground, exposed to enemy fire. Perhaps, Colonel Sheridan, as you are mounted, you and your sowars could give us cover?"

"Certainly," Alex assented. He had two native cavalrymen with him, men who had accompanied him on one of his earlier sorties to bring in wounded from the Khas Bazaar area, and he glanced at them inquiringly, wondering if they had understood Thornhill's request, which had been made in English. He was about to repeat it in Hindustani when one of the sowars, who had a *daffadar's* stripes on his tattered uniform, gave vent to a startled exclamation.

"Sheridan Sahib . . . *you* are Sheridan Sahib? Allah forgive me, I was not sure. In the darkness I did not see the sahib's face and, in truth, I believed you dead, Colonel Sahib—in Cawnpore, with all the others!" The man's voice shook and Alex checked his stride, to subject him to a puzzled scrutiny. The lined, dark face, with its graying beard was vaguely familiar and so was the voice but . . . his tired eyes glimpsed the medals pinned to the ragged tunic. Ghuznee and the Sutlej campaign . . . of course, it could be no one else! Pleasure and relief overcame his weariness and he turned, his hand extended.

"Ghulam Rasul—*Daffadar* Ghulam Rasul!"

"The same, Sahib." The old *daffadar* was beaming as he clasped the proffered hand.

"My wits are woolly from lack of sleep," Alex apologized. "I should have recognized you, *daffadar-ji*."

"We have all changed, Colonel Sahib." Ghulam Rasul gestured to Alex's scarred face. "You bear the scars of Cawnpore and
I those of Lucknow."

"Have you been with the Lucknow garrison throughout the
siege?" Alex asked him, resuming his slow, stumbling walk. Ghulam Rasul inclined his turbaned head.

"*Ji-han* . . . since the day when the Colonel Sahib sent me
back from Cawnpore with Partap Singh, the Sahib's orderly. He,
alas, is dead—he was killed many weeks ago, when serving a gun.
But the Sahib's fine horse is yet living . . . the black Arab, Sul-
tan. I have taken the best care of him that I could, Colonel Sahib,
but like the rest of us, he is skin and bone."

Deeply moved by his loyalty, Alex thanked him, his throat
tight. Ghulam Rasul had been one of the eighty-five *sowars* of
the 3rd Light Cavalry sentenced by court martial to ten years'
penal servitude, prior to the outbreak of the mutiny, for refusing
the suspect Enfield cartridges. With the rest of his condemned
comrades, he had been fettered and had his medals and his uniform stripped from him at the infamous punishment parade,
ordered by the obese and senile General Hewitt in Meerut on
May 9. Moved to pity by the plight of the eighty-five—and, in
particular, by that of the old *daffadar*, whose twenty years of loyal
service had earned no mitigation of his sentence—Alex had
picked up his medals from the dust of the parade ground and
had gone to the jail to restore them to their owner. Ghulam
Rasul had not forgotten that small act of compassion. Liberated,
with the other prisoners, when, the following evening, the Native
Infantry regiments and the Light Cavalry had mutinied and broken into the jail, he had ridden with the rest to Delhi but then,
sickened by the orgy of arson and slaughter in which the mutineers had launched their revolt, he had returned. He owed his

life to the *daffadar*'s providential return, Alex recalled. The old man had searched for and found him, in the corn field in which he had been left for dead, and it was thanks to his devotion and gallantry that he had reached Meerut safely, with the orphaned Lavinia Paterson.

"I am too old a dog to learn new tricks, Sahib," the *daffadar* said softly, as if reading his thoughts and Alex smiled, remembering. He had asked the man why he stayed, and Ghulam Rasul had replied with those words, adding in explanation, "I have served the Company for twenty years and I have taken pride in my service. I am too old to learn what I should have to learn, were I to remain in Delhi. The men I commanded have become arrogant madmen, seeking only to kill like butchers, not as soldiers. They rode through the Darya Ganj sabering every white passer-by they could see—women, children, even babes in their mothers' arms. I have no stomach for such slaughter, Sheridan Sahib. I will stay with you, if you will permit this, and serve you. If need be, I will die with you . . ."

He had kept his word. He and perhaps thirty others—native officers and N.C.O.'s—of the 3rd Light Cavalry had remained true to their salt. Alone of the men whom General Hewitt had so savagely punished, *Daffadar* Ghulam Rasul, veteran of Ghuznee and Sobraon, had assisted in the defense of Lucknow and, on this account, could still take pride in his service.

Alex started to tell him so, but the old *daffadar* apologetically cut him short. "We have reached the dangerous ground of which Thornhill Sahib spoke. It is time to mount our horses, Colonel Sahib."

He was right, Alex saw. Ahead he could see the bulk of the Moti Mahal—the Pearl Palace—rising above the trees, dazzling white in the glow of the sunrise, the graceful, pearl-shaped dome, from which it had taken its name, appearing above a pall of black, swirling cannon smoke. It was under heavy bombardment still, with round shot thudding against its walls from a heavy gun battery sited, as nearly as he could judge, in the Kaiser Bagh to his right. Savage volleys of musketry were coming from the Khoorsheyd Munzil—the Palace of the Sun, which had been the mess house of the 32nd Regiment—firing at much closer range, and swarms of rebel infantry could be seen in the loopholed, mud-walled houses to the left and right of it. But from the south side of the enclosure held by the British rear-guard, a spirited fire was being returned, and one, at least, of Major Eyre's twenty-for-pounders was still in action, together with a howitzer, throwing a stream of shot and shell over the intervening trees and buildings, in the direction of the Kaiser Bagh.

"We have to cross a *nullah*," Thornhill warned, having to shout to make himself heard above the uproar. "But there's our objective," he pointed, "Martin's House. We'll keep under cover of its compound wall, halt to get our breath, and then cross over the last forty yards of exposed ground to gain the south-west side of the palace. Major Simmons' force are in position, they're occupying the compound of Martin's House, and they'll give us covering fire when I give the signal." He rose, a torn white handkerchief held above his head, which he waved vigorously. Receiving an answering signal, he said, "Right—off we go!"

The small party—probably because it was small, Alex decided —attracted only a few ill-aimed shots and reached the comparative safety of the Moti Mahal Palace without suffering any casualties. But it would be a very different matter, he knew, when the open ground had to be crossed by a long line of hospital *doolies* containing badly injured men, and when there were several hundred native bearers—of the noncombatant coolie caste

—to protect and control, the majority of whom would drop their burdens and take flight if they came under heavy attack. However, once this first hazard had been negotiated, the rest of the journey along the narrow riverside path would be screened from enemy fire and could be taken slowly, so as not to cause the wounded any unnecessary discomfort.

A harassed ensign, with bloodshot blue eyes and a filthy scrap of cloth serving as a bandage for a head wound, conducted the new arrivals to Colonel Campbell. The rear-guard commander looked even more harassed and exhausted than his subaltern. He was limping from a wound in the right leg, but he received Thornhill's proposals for the evacuation of the wounded with a heartfelt "Thank God!" and proceeded to implement the plans he had obviously prepared earlier.

"I've two surgeons I can send with you, Mr. Thornhill," he said. "Dr. Home and Dr. Bradshaw . . . the third was killed, alas, half an hour ago. As to an escort—dammit, I can't spare any of my men, and, in any case, they're too done up to be of much use to you. Major Simmons' fellows are fresher—we'll see what he can offer you. Preston, pass the word to the major, if you please— he's in the hospital, I fancy, having his hand dressed and—"

"I'll find him myself, sir," Thornhill put in, as Ensign Preston prepared wearily to go in search of the 5th Fusiliers' commander. "I promised the general I'd make sure that his son was safe."

"Harry Havelock?" A smile lit Campbell's smoke-blackened face. "Oh, we've taken good care of him, don't worry. He's taken a musket-ball in the arm, but the surgeons have cleaned and dressed it for him, and they don't think that amputation will be necessary. He's in good spirits." Thornhill went off under the guidance of young Preston, and the colonel, after peering at him uncertainly, recognized Alex. "You're Sheridan, aren't you, of Barrow's Horse?"

"Yes, sir," Alex acknowledged.

"Wonderful fellows, yours," the Queen's officer said, with genuine admiration. "Still, so they should be, with lieutenant colonels serving in their ranks! Tell me, Colonel Sheridan, how did it go with the leading regiments yesterday evening—the Highlanders in particular? We have only heard rumors here but one of the rumors concerned General Neill. It's not true, is it, that he was killed?"

"I am sorry to say he was, sir. I was within a few yards of him when he fell—to a sniper's bullet." Alex gave details of casualties and then, the memory of it still vivid in his mind, described the entry into the Residency. Colonel Campbell sighed when Sheridan came to the end of his recital.

"General Havelock saved the garrison," he said. "But, dear heaven, Sheridan . . . at what cost! It will break the poor old gentleman's heart to have lost so many—and of his beloved Highlanders, too. Still, it had to be done. We could not permit another Cawnpore, and we really needed a force of ten thousand, instead of three, to do the job properly. We—excuse me . . ." he broke off, as his regimental surgeon came toward him. "Well, Tony, how goes it in your department? This, by the way, is Colonel Sheridan of the Volunteer Horse—Dr. Home."

The surgeon bowed in acknowledgement of the introduction, indicating his bloodstained hands with a wry gesture. Like all the rest, he looked tired, and the white coat he wore was torn and filthy, but he listened alertly to Colonel Campbell's instructions and went off to prepare for the evacuation of the wounded, promising that he would hasten his preparations and be ready in half an hour. His estimate of the number of wounded was over two hundred, of whom perhaps twenty-five or thirty were capable of walking. The remainder would have to be carried in *doolies,* with four bearers to each—and they would make a lengthy and slow-moving procession, Alex reflected ruefully, requiring a large escort for at least part of the way. He was about to follow the surgeon to the inner courtyard in which the makeshift hospital had been established, when Colonel Campbell motioned him to wait.

"If you'll lend me your arm, I'll come with you, Sheridan," he said. "I shall have to have a word with Major Simmons concerning the escort. How many men do you think you'll need?"

Alex offered his arm. "It's rather a question of how few we can make do with, is it not, sir?" he suggested.

"Yes, I regret to say it is," Campbell admitted. "But I'm very anxious to get the wounded to safety, for their sake and ours . . . some of the poor devils have been lying in *doolies* since noon yesterday, young Havelock among them. We can't guard them and fight back, Sheridan. But with only the guns to worry about, we'll stand a better than even chance of getting through to the Residency tonight, under cover of darkness, *and* of bringing out Vincent Eyre's guns. You heard that we have a twenty-four-pounder jammed in the passageway across there, no doubt?" He pointed in the direction of the outer wall behind him. "The infernal thing is under a constant fire of musketry. We can't get near it, but neither, of course, can they, and Crump's got some plan for shifting it, as soon as it's dark enough to bring up a team of bullocks without being seen. To return to the question of your escort, though . . . Simmons only brought me 250 men, and they're holding Martin's enclosure, as you know."

"Are you expecting more reinforcements, Colonel?" Alex asked.

Campbell permitted himself a tight-lipped smile. "I'm hoping for more, my friend—Simmons informed me that they'll be sent, under Colonel Napier, as soon as possible. But as you can see, they haven't arrived. Perhaps, when you report to the general, you'd tell him I need them without delay? I . . ." his voice trailed off as part of the palace wall ten yards ahead of them came crashing down under the pounding of a series of well-directed round shot. A gray-haired sergeant, reeling back from the shattered embrasure in which he had been keeping watch, gasped out a warning that the shots had come from an enemy thirty-two-pounder on the opposite bank of the river.

"The bastards just brought it up, sir," he told Colonel Campbell. "Not fifteen minutes ago—there they are, see, in the garden behind them trees?" He spat out dust, cursing luridly. "We can't touch the swine with our rifles, not from here, sir."

"And we can't bring a gun to bear on them," the colonel said bitterly, after a careful inspection from behind the crumbling brickwork of the wall. "But we've got to keep their heads down somehow before you cross that exposed ground with the *doolies,* Sheridan—you won't get fifty yards, if they open up on you with grape."

"The howitzer, sir?" Alex offered, frowning.

Campbell nodded. "Yes, if we can get it into position in time. I'll have to see Major Cooper. Go on without me, will you, and tell Dr. Home he needn't rush his preparations." Leaning now on the sergeant's arm, he limped off in search of the senior artillery officer. Alex continued on his way to the hospital, guided to it by the high-pitched scream of some unfortunate in mortal agony, which rose even above the thunder of the guns and the incessant crackle of musketry. He gave Surgeon Home the colonel's message and found Bensley Thornhill kneeling beside Harry Havelock's *doolie.* The younger Havelock was, as Colonel Campbell had said, in good spirits, but his good-looking face was drained of color and he was clearly in some pain. A stocky young private of the 78th, whom he addressed as Ward, was caring for him with almost womanly solicitude and, leaving them together, Thornhill drew Alex aside.

"Major Simmons has offered us half his force to escort the *doolies,* sir," he said. "And he assures me that Colonel Napier is on his way with further reinforcements. Subject to Colonel Campbell's permission, I feel we should make a start, don't you? The poor devils are dying like flies in here—not only from their wounds but from musket-balls, which ricochet across. The surgeon who died, Robert Bartrum of the Artillery, was shot by a sniper from the roof of the mess house as he was crossing the courtyard." He sighed. "His wife, Katherine, is waiting for him in the Residency, with their child."

Looking across the crowded, evil-smelling palace anteroom in which they stood, Alex echoed his sigh. The bodies of the dead—of necessity, unburied—added to the stench of human sweat and excreta and the awful, sickly sweet smell of gangrene-infected wounds. Both sight and stench were familiar to him; it had been thus in the mud-walled entrenchment at Cawnpore and there, too, in the stifling heat of the Indian hot weather, men had died from their untreated wounds, their bodies burning with fever and racked with dysentery, and the dead had had to be left unburied until, with the coming of darkness, the enemy's fire had slackened.

"The longer we delay," Thornhill was saying, "the more likelihood there is of our . . ." a thunderous crash silenced him. Part of the ceiling above their heads caved in, showering the wounded and the *doolies* with chunks of brick and plaster and filling the room with choking dust. "My God!" he exclaimed, when he could make himself heard above the uproar. "That was from close range, wasn't it?"

"Yes," Alex returned flatly. "The rebels have sited a thirty-two-pounder in the Hazuree Bagh, across the river. That, unhappily, is the reason for the delay. They've got the range of this place and Martin's House . . . we can't cross until the gunners here can draw their fire or put the gun out of action."

"I see. Then we'd better do what we can here, I suppose."

They went to assist in moving some of the *doolies* from the rubble; surgeons, orderlies and walking wounded struggling breathlessly under their weight. Alex heard a faint voice calling him by name as he bent over one of the *doolies,* and he was shocked to see that Corporal Cullmane, one of the original infantry volunteers in his troops, was lying hunched up in the interior of the curtained litter, a soiled and blood-soaked bandage only half-concealing the ghastly wound in his chest. The voice was slurred and indistinct but Cullmane, as always, was cockily cheerful, his bloodless lips twisting into their familiar, gap-toothed grin as he admitted to feeling "none too spry."

Sick with pity, Alex took a small flask of whisky from his pocket and placed it gently between the Irishman's hands.

"Drink it, lad," he invited and added, aware that the hope was unlikely to be fulfilled, "It may ease the pain. And don't worry—we're going to get you to the Residency as soon as we can."

"I'll never make it, sorr. But God bless ye, all the same." With trembling fingers, Cullmane unscrewed the silver-topped flask. "Ah, 'tis a drop av the real stuff," he said, appreciatively. "If ye could lift me head just a moight, sorr, I'll have it drunk in no time."

Alex raised his head, kneeling beside him on the rubble-strewn floor and finding the task an awkward one with his single arm. A few drops of whisky trickled past the injured man's lips, scarcely enough to do more than moisten them, but he persisted and the flask was almost empty when he let it fall from his grasp with a contented sigh.

"They're a foine sight, the Tips, are they not, sorr?" he asked unexpectedly. "Ah, will ye listen to them now . . . hark yez, me beauties, bark to Wanderer! Good bitch, Ranter . . . on, on, on! Sure, dere's de ould dog-fox away up Cool-na-Cappogue from Killenaule Bottom and de whole pack streamin' after him on a breast-high scent! Did ye ever see a foiner sight in all the world, Colonel, sorr, or hear any music the loike o' that?"

His eyes had a faraway look in them, and Alex knew that he no longer saw the battered Moti Mahal Palace, no longer heard the crash of falling masonry or the thunder of the guns. Seamus Cullmane, long-serving private of Her Majesty's 64th Regiment of Foot and one-time whipper-in to the Tipperary Hunt, was back with his "Gallant Tips" in the land that had bred him and, when his head fell back, he was smiling. His eyes were still open, but Alex had seen death too often not to recognize it now. He muttered a brief prayer, closed the staring, sightless eyes and, getting to his feet, called one of the orderlies over. In conditions like these, the living had to take precedence over the dead and empty *doolies* were at a premium, he was fully aware but, even so, he could not bring himself to remove Cullmane's body from this one.

The evacuation of the wounded began half an hour later.

Under the escort of 150 men—made up of walking wounded and a company of the 5th Fusiliers, commanded by Major Simmons—the long procession of laden *doolies* crossed the forty yards of exposed ground to Martin's House without mishap. The rebel thirty-two-pounder on the opposite side of the river had not been put out of action but was being so fiercely engaged by the rear-guard's howitzer that its gunners ignored the target presented by the *doolies,* and covering fire from the Moti Mahal protected them from all but a few random musket-balls.

It was, however, a different story when, after a brief halt, the slow-moving procession emerged from the sheltering walls of Martin's garden enclosure. Throughout the time they had rested there, round shot from a second battery in the Badshah Bagh had been tearing through the scarred walls of the house itself and now this fire was concentrated on the train of wounded. It was at long range but, added to a savage fire of musketry from neighboring buildings, casualties began to mount. When they reached and started to cross the *nullah,* which was three feet deep in water, the thirty-two-pounder opened on them with grape and so many of the unfortunate *doolie*-bearers were cut down that the rear of the line was virtually slowed to a halt.

A number, as Alex had feared they would, yielded to panic. Deaf alike to the shouted orders of the escort and the pleas of the injured men they carried, the terrified natives ran blindly for cover across the rough, uneven ground, slithering and stumbling as they sought to avoid the bounding round shot. To their credit, few of them abandoned their heavy burdens and most headed in the direction they had been ordered to take, running a terrible gauntlet of fire before they gained their objective, to fling themselves down, spent and gasping, behind the outer wall of the

Chutter Munzil garden. Some ran back to the comparative safety of the enclosure they had just left, from which they had to be driven at bayonet point by the escort, and Alex and his two sowars, endeavoring to curb the panic found themselves unhorsed as, for the third time, they galloped back to the *nullah* to be met by a hail of grape. Ghulam Rasul's horse was the only one of the three to pick itself up, but it was seized by two wounded men, one of whom thrust the butt of his rifle into the *daffadar's* face when he attempted to reclaim his mount.

On foot, sweating and shaken, they finally rejoined the rear of the train of wounded on the river side of the Chutter Munzil Palace, escorting two *doolies,* whose bearers had been induced to continue on their way by the threat of Alex's revolver. Once out of the immediate danger of the enemy guns, order had been swiftly restored, and the head of the train was, Alex learned from a sergeant of the escort, already proceeding along the river bank toward the Residency, under the guidance of Bensley Thornhill. Wearily, his whole body aching from the fall he had taken, he set off after them, having given Ghulam Rasul permission to search for his stolen horse.

The worst, he told himself, was over; they were no longer under fire and the rest of the way to the Residency was under cover of the two palaces adjoining it, the Terhee Kothee and the Furhut Baksh, both of which were now in British hands. The *doolie*-bearers were chattering quite cheerfully among themselves, thankful to have survived their ordeal; they picked their way with care, and the poor sufferers, who had endured so much jolting agony during the panic rush across the open ground, were able, at last, to relax, confident that they would not again be flung down or abandoned. Alex paused to speak to one or two in passing, among them Lieutenant Arnold, who had led the Madras

Fusiliers' charge with splendid gallantry on the guns at the Char Bagh bridge the previous day.

Severely wounded in both thighs, the Blue Caps' officer was in appalling pain, but he was conscious and he gratefully accepted the cheroot that Alex took from his dwindling supply and carefully lit for him.

"I'll be damned glad when this is over, sir," he confessed, teeth clamped firmly on the butt of the cheroot. "I shall have to lose my right leg, I fear, but . . ." he grinned wryly, "anything will be better than lying in this infernal *doolie,* never knowing when the blasted bearers are going to fling me out of it!"

"Don't you worry about them, sir," a voice offered from the other side of the curtained litter. "I'll see the bastards keep you on an even keel. They'll get my boot up their backsides if they don't!"

"Ryan, isn't it?" Arnold asked, raising himself with difficulty on one elbow. "Private Ryan of B Company? Come round where I can see you, lad."

"Very good, sir." A bony-faced young Blue Cap stepped across to the open curtain. A bandage, improvised from his shirttail, was wound about his shaven head, on top of which his forage cap, with its pale blue sun-curtain, was incongruously perched. "Mr. Arnold's my officer, sir," he told Alex. "I'll see after him."

Alex left him with the injured Arnold. Despite his weariness. he found himself hurrying, dodging between the straggling line of *doolies* in an effort to catch up with Thornhill and the main body of the escort, who were now some distance ahead, moving too fast for the sweating *doolie*-bearers to keep pace with them. Thornhill, he knew, was anxious to deliver Harry Havelock safely back to his father but . . . filled with a vague uneasiness, he quickened his own pace. The uneasiness became acute anxiety when, reaching the passageway that led from the riverside path to the interior of the Chutter Munzil, he saw that the column had taken a sharp turn to the left. One which . . . he drew in his breath sharply. Dear heaven! Instead of keeping straight on and approaching the Bailey Guard gate of the Residency through the two adjoining palaces as he had planned, Bensley Thornhill was apparently leading them along the route that the relieving force had followed the previous evening.

Yesterday, in darkness, the whole area had been swarming with rebel troops, every loopholed house and rooftop had been alive with armed men. The Highlanders and the Sikhs had sustained their heaviest casualties of the day there and . . . Alex hesitated for a moment, striving to get his bearings and then, like a man waking from a nightmare, he started to run. But, as he opened his mouth to yell at the column to halt, he knew that it was too late. The nightmare became hideous reality as, from a short distance ahead, came the crackle of musketry, which grew to a continuous fusillade, the high-pitched whine of Enfield and Minié rifles sounding above the deeper thud of Brown Bess muskets. Instantly the column was thrown into confusion. Some of the *doolies* turned back, some were abandoned, while others, urged on by the threats of the walking wounded who accompanied them, continued on their disastrous way.

A mounted officer galloped past, with scant regard for any who blocked his path; he caught Alex a glancing blow, hurling him to the ground, the breath knocked out of his body. When he picked himself up, drawing agonized gulps of air into his lungs, he saw that the column was moving forward again, urged on by the mounted idiot who had knocked him down, the wretched *doolie*-bearers cringing beneath the blows he aimed at them with the flat of his saber as he rode on . . . deaf and blind, it seemed, to the battle raging fifty yards ahead of him.

Alex cursed him in futile rage, but the line of *doolies* had come to a standstill by the time he regained his breath, and his order to them to retire was urgently repeated by the younger of the two surgeons who had accompanied the wounded from the Moti Mahal, and then by Bensley Thornhill himself. The young civilian staggered into the passageway, clutching a shattered arm, and the sight of him was enough for the waverers, who turned instantly to retrace their steps. An apothecary assisted Thornhill to an empty *doolie,* and he was borne swiftly away, the apothecary calling out, his voice harsh with shock, "There are thirty or forty poor devils still there! We've had to leave them—the bearers have deserted. For God's sake, send help if you can!"

But there was no help to be sent; all the men remaining in his immediate vicinity were walking wounded. Alex took his Adams from its holster and stumbled on, waving back a sergeant of the 90th with a bandaged head who attempted to join him. Breathless and spent, the blood pounding in his head, he entered the courtyard where, some seventeen hours before, Brigadier General James Neill had been killed by a sniper's bullet only a few yards from him. The courtyard—an oblong square lined on each side by sheds and godowns, with a tall, arched gateway at its western end—was, as it had been the previous evening, seething with white-robed rebels. There were *doolies* scattered about the square and in the street beyond; a few, protected by the escort, could be seen dimly through the dust and smoke, fleeing for their lives in the direction of the Residency, but the majority had been abandoned, their bearers either killed or in hiding.

Apart from a handful of stragglers, the main body of the escort appeared to have fought their way out of the square; within its confines, Alex saw, a terrible slaughter had already taken place. Mutilated corpses lay everywhere, the first to meet his horrified gaze that of the mounted officer who had ridden him down, decapitated and stretched beside his fallen horse. From their loopholed buildings, enemy riflemen and musketeers were pouring a merciless rain of fire onto those who still resisted, and beneath the arched gateway, where half a dozen *doolies* had been abandoned, a party of dismounted cavalry sowars were hacking at the helpless occupants with their sabers. Their hideous task completed, they started to cross the square toward him, seeking fresh victims, and Alex, sickened by their callousness, took careful aim with his pistol and shot their leader through the head. His action brought him to the notice of some of the hidden riflemen. The ground about him was spattered with bullets, but miraculously he was unhit and he ran for cover, finding it in the doorway of a godown, from where he again opened fire on the sowars, who retreated before his onslaught. A wounded subaltern of the 78th waved to him from a *doolie* and, his pistol empty, he covered the thirty feet that separated them and dragged the young officer into another doorway, where they crouched, side by side, to be joined by a number of others. Among them Alex recognized the 90th's surgeon, Dr. Home, whose distress at the brutal butchery of the wounded men he had cared for so devotedly in the Moti Mahal was written in every line of his shocked white face.

Together, supporting several wounded and covered by the accurate fire of two bearded privates of the escort, the small party worked their way around one side of the square, dodging behind doorways and into sheds, until they gained the shelter of a brick house to the right of the gateway. A swift search satisfied Alex that it was empty and, when Surgeon Home pleaded that for the sake of the wounded they should remain there and defend themselves until relieved, he readily gave his assent. Encumbered by men who could barely walk without assistance, it would be madness, he knew, to attempt to reach the Residency by the route the main body of the escort had taken and, with the square now swarming with rebels, their retreat to the river was effectively cut off. Aside from other considerations, in the abandoned *doolies* on the opposite side of the gateway, there were a number of wounded whose pitiful cries and moans indicated that they were still alive and, for as long as they could hold their commandeered house, they could afford these men a measure of protection by shooting down any rebel who attempted to approach them.

CHAPTER TWO

➵➵➵ • ⫷⫷⫷

HAVING REACHED the decision to remain where they were, Alex took stock of their position. The house was strongly built and windowless, with one door leading into the square—the one by which they had entered—and a second, which had been plastered up, apparently leading into a room or courtyard backing onto a street, which ran parallel to one side of the square. A stone pillar, conveniently situated a few feet behind the main doorway, had already been utilized by a private of the 5th Fusiliers as cover and, from behind it, he was firing steadily and with deadly effect on any rebel who came within his sights.

A quick count of heads revealed the fact that there were fourteen of them in the dirty, airless room—Surgeon Home, two other officers who were both wounded, ten soldiers, of whom three were wounded, and himself. Alex set the unwounded men to collecting planks and other lumber, with which to barricade the doorway and provide cover for at least one other rifleman and two loaders and, telling them all to check their ammunition as soon as the barricade was completed, he ducked down behind the pillar.

"You're a good shot, lad," he told the Fusilier approvingly. "What's your name?"

The man did not take his eyes from the square outside.

"McManus. sir," he answered, in a strong Lowland Scottish accent. He added, with conscious pride, "Ah'm the champion

shot o' ma regiment, sir . . . and I canna hardly miss wi' this rifle."
He slapped the butt of his Enfield affectionately.

"Then we're fortunate to have you, McManus," Alex said.
"Can you keep it up until we can get the door barricaded, if I
detail a man to load for you? We've several spare rifles."

"Aye, for as long as ye like, sir," Fusilier McManus asserted.
His finger curled about the trigger of the Enfield, and he grinned
his satisfaction as one of the dismounted sowars emitted a shrill
scream and fell, as if pole-axed, in the dust of the square some
twenty yards in front of him. With the speed and skill of long
practice, he slid a fresh cartridge into the barrel of the rifle and
rammed it home, returning the weapon smoothly to his shoulder, the percussion cap—held in readiness between his
teeth—clipped into position above the nipple with thumb and
forefinger. "I c'n hold the black bastards off, sir. They'll no' gang
past me I promise ye."

Satisfied that he could more than fulfill his promise, Alex
detailed one of the less severely wounded men to load for him
and went to squat down beside the surgeon, who had his case of
instruments out and was searching in it for a fresh bandage. A
handy-looking Colt revolver lay among the scattered instruments
and Dr. Home said wryly, "I can use that in our defense if you
require me to, Colonel Sheridan. But at the present moment, I
think I'll be of more use if I carry on with my professional duties.
I'm afraid poor Swanson is in a bad way. I took two musket-balls
out of him yesterday, and now he's been shot again."

"Swanson?" Alex questioned.

"Yes, Lieutenant Swanson of the 78th. The officer you rescued from the abandoned *doolie* . . . a very gallant young man."
The surgeon sighed. "I've given him some laudanum, but that's

all I can do. His arm ought to come off—the elbow is shattered and both bones in the forearm are broken. It's similar to the wound young Havelock sustained, but this wasn't as bad and—"

"Dear God!" Alex put in, thinking pityingly of the old General, who had endured so much in addition to the anxiety for his son. "Where is Harry Havelock, do you know? He's not out there, is he?" He gestured to the square. To his intense relief, Dr. Home shook his head.

"Two or three of the *doolies* got away, including Havelock's. The man who was with him, a private of the 78th, drove the bearers in front of him at bayonet point. There were two of them in the *doolie*, Captain Havelock and another 78th man. They were in front, with the main body of the escort . . . please God they'll all be in the Residency by this time." He found the dressing for which he had been searching and, shaking the dust from it, repeated his sigh. "I was with them and I suppose I could have gone with them. But Colonel Campbell put me in charge of all the wounded, I—I felt it was my duty to stay until help can be sent to us. Mr. Thornhill went back to warn the others—he took the wrong turning and led us into an ambush. Poor fellow, he did his best to put matters right, but then he was hit, so I sent Dr. Bradshaw and my apothecary to make sure that the rest of the *doolies* turned back. They did turn back, didn't they?" Alex nodded and the surgeon asked in a low voice, "Colonel Sheridan, help will be sent to us, will it not?"

"I am sure it will, Doctor, once our plight is known," Alex answered reassuringly, only half believing it himself. He left the surgeon to his ministrations and went across to where the second wounded officer was lying, his head pillowed on a folded tunic. He appeared to have been shot in both legs, but he opened his eyes at Alex's approach and introduced himself as Andrew

Becher, a captain in the 41st Native Infantry, serving on General Outram's staff.

"I owe my life to that brave fellow there," he pointed to a small, wiry Highlander, who had gone to the support of Fusilier McManus in the doorway, "Private Hollowell of Her Majesty's 78th. What a splendid regiment they are—Her Majesty can well be proud of them! Hollowell brought me here on his back—small though he is, he ran fifty yards with me. Had he not done so, I should have been hacked to death by those fiends of Irregular Cavalry sowars, when my *doolie*-bearers dumped me in the middle of the square and legged it for cover. But if you could assist me . . . thank you very much, sir." With Alex's aid he propped himself up against the wall behind him and went on gravely, "I imagine we may have to stay here for a while and I'd like to make myself useful, if I can. Permit me to reload your revolver for you, Colonel Sheridan, as proof of my willingness to help. I don't suppose you find it too easy with one hand . . . although I saw you charge with the Volunteer Cavalry the day before yesterday and you seemed to manage remarkably well with a saber."

"The result of years of practice," Alex told him. He handed over his Adams, and Andrew Becher dealt with it deftly. Returning it to him, the Native Infantry officer said quietly, "We're in rather a tight corner, aren't we, Colonel?"

It was a statement, rather than a question, and Alex did not attempt to deny it. "Tight enough," he admitted. "But if we can hold out here until nightfall, I'd give us a better than even chance of getting out of it.

"With—what? Five of us incapacitated?" Becher objected. "I can't walk and as for poor young Swanson—"

"We shan't leave any of you," Alex assured him.

"You may have to, Colonel. For God's sake, there's little chance of aid being sent to us before nightfall, isn't there? The rear-guard won't attempt to break out of the Moti Mahal until then, and in the Residency they'll have no means of knowing that any of us are still alive, so we can't count on earlier help from that quarter. Colonel Napier's reinforcements will go straight to the Moti Mahal—they'll almost certainly have to fight their way there. So . . ." Andrew Becher shrugged. "If it becomes a question of you or us, you must leave us to fend for ourselves, and escape with the able-bodied men. There's no sense in all of us getting killed."

He had assessed the situation accurately, Alex thought. He slid the Adams back into its holster, leaving it unfastened and smiled down at the injured staff officer. "We're surrounded, my friend," he pointed out. "Our best chance is to stay together and defend ourselves. This is a good, solid building, with only one door—the one at the back is plastered over—and I see no reason why we shouldn't do so successfully. The men have full ammunition pouches and, in any case," he jerked his head toward the square, "there are a number of wounded still alive in the abandoned *doolies* out there. So long as we stay here and our ammunition lasts, we can give them covering fire and prevent them from being butchered. If an opportunity arises, we might be able to bring some of them in here and—"

"Sir!" Fusilier McManus called urgently from the doorway. "I think they're going tae try and rush us!"

"Then let's give them a warm reception!" Alex was beside him, the Adams in his hand, searching the sunlit square with narrowed, watchful eyes. The barricade—flimsier than he would have liked—was all but completed and, without waiting for orders, two other able-bodied men flung themselves down behind it, rifles at the ready. The rest fixed bayonets and waited tensely.

The attackers came forward in a tightly packed bunch, led by a white-bearded Rissaldar of the Irregular Cavalry, a red cummerbund girded about his waist, who was armed with a curved *tulwar* and a metal-bound shield.

"Cowards! Dogs of unbelievers! Why do you not come out into the street and fight us like soldiers?" the old cavalryman challenged shrilly. "You skulk behind walls, like the curs you are!"

Fusilier McManus fixed him in the sights of his Enfield but, before he could fire, the wily old Rissaldar moved aside, taking up a position close to the wall, where he was beyond the defenders' line of vision. From comparative safety, he urged his motley band of sepoys and townsfolk to attack the accursed *feringhis.* Those who did so paid with their lives for their temerity and, when the whole mob retreated, still yelling abuse, they left seven or eight of their number lying dead in front of the door. The bodies afforded the defenders some additional protection, and one of the slightly wounded men, a Fusilier of the escort, crawled close enough to them to strip two of them of their waistcloths.

"Sandbags, sir," he said laconically, in answer to Alex's puzzled question. "There's enough dirt and dust in here to fill half a dozen." He proved his point, a few minutes later, adding his improvised sandbags to their flimsy barricade and then crawling out again to obtain another waistcloth. His action was seen by the rebels, but a second rush, aimed at removing their dead, resulted only in adding three more to the number of bodies, and even the old Rissaldar could not persuade his followers to launch a third attack. Instead, as Alex had feared they would, some of them attempted to cross the square to take vengeance on the wounded in the abandoned *doolies,* bent low in the hope of avoiding discovery. To stop them, they had to leave the shelter of the barricaded doorway and open fire from just outside it. With Hollowell and McManus, Alex leaped the barricade and, to his intense relief, a single shot from each of them sufficed to scatter the would-be butchers, who retreated with yells of fury to the loopholed buildings they had vacated and from there poured volley after volley into the walls and roof of the British-held house.

The brave McManus was hit in the left foot as he tried to reload in order to take another shot, but he limped back without assistance and returned to his post behind the pillar, insisting that his wound was no more than a scratch. The old Rissaldar, beside himself with rage, shouted taunts at his own men, reviling them as contemptuously as he had earlier reviled the British party.

"There are but three of the accursed *lal-kotes* . . . hast thou not seen how few they are with thine own eyes? Attack them, I say—kill them! *Din, din* . . . for the faith, my brothers! Art thou lacking in faith as well as courage, thou misbegotten sons of bitches?"

He was close enough for his words to be heard inside the room he was so eager to invade, and Alex replied to him in the vernacular, his tone derisive; then, turning to the men about him, he invited them to give the lie to the old man's estimate of their number. "Come on, my boys . . . let's have three rousing British cheers from you! If they think there are more than three of us, they won't be in any hurry to attack again, so make it good. Hip, hip . . ."

The response almost deafened him, wounded and all joining in and Private Hollowell observed, with a grin, "Och, that's put the wind up the sods! Now they'll be thinking we've a whole regiment here, and they'll be feared as hell tae come near us. 'Tis a gey pity we havena the pipe major wi' us, for tae mak' them believe the 78th are after their black hides!"

The cheers were succeeded by laughter. Morale was high, Alex told himself; with men of this caliber, defeat was by no means inevitable, however long the odds against them.

"Sir . . ." There was a movement behind him and he turned, recognizing the bony-faced young Blue Cap with the bandaged head, whom he had last seen when he had stopped to speak to the wounded Arnold, as the procession of *doolies* neared the Chutter Munzil.

"Your name's Ryan, isn't it?" he asked, in some surprise. "I didn't realize you were here."

The boy faced him, his expression woebegone. "I was ordered to the front of the escort, sir," he explained unhappily. "I'd promised Lieutenant Arnold that I'd stay with him and see he was all right, and then some sod of an—beg pardon, sir, meaning no disrespect—but an officer on horseback sent me forward, so I had to go—I had to leave him. And he's out there, sir, Mr. Arnold is, in one of them *doolies*. I caught a glimpse of him just now, when you went out of the door. He's alive, I seen him moving. With your permission, sir, I'd like to fetch him in here with us."

"You'll be risking your life if you try," Alex warned him. "And you won't be able to move that *doolie* by yourself."

"I don't mind risking my life for him, sir," Ryan answered without hesitation. "I can't stand by and see him cut to pieces by them bloody black bastards, not after I give him my word, sir. And I daresay one of our chaps'll volunteer to lend me a hand with the *doolie*." He glanced round expectantly and Fusilier McManus answered his appeal.

"I'll gang wi' him, sir. It's no distance and, if we tak' it at a run, we'll manage the *doolie* between us." Sensing Alex's reluctance to give his assent, he added persuasively, "It'll no' tak' us long. We'll be away and back before you've missed us, sir."

Their position was desperate enough as it was, Alex thought grimly. If they lost these two—and McManus, the champion shot in particular—it would be infinitely worse but . . . he looked into Ryan's anxious young face and knew that he could not refuse. In the entrenchment at Cawnpore, they had frequently had to take such risks and, almost always, the risk had been justified. A bold and sudden move, which took the sepoys by surprise, was usually successful. . . . He sighed.

"Can you run with that foot of yours, McManus?"

"Aye, sir. 'Tis only a scratch, it'll no' hinder me." McManus hesitated. "Can we go, sir?"

"All right," Alex agreed, still with some reluctance. "But we'll choose our moment, when they're not prepared for it or when their attention is distracted. We can't knock loopholes in that wall, it's too thick, so we'll have to shift our barricade over to the left a bit, to enable us to give you covering fire. You take over McManus's post behind the pillar, Hollowell, when he goes—and we'll need two good shots behind the barricade. What about it, my boys . . . which of you shall it be?"

Two men, who had been moving the barricade into its new position, offered their services. They were oddly alike, although of different regiments, both in their early thirties, blue-eyed and brown-bearded, quiet, steady men, who had seen service in Persia.

"Webb, sir, 64th," the shorter of the two stated.

"And Dugald Cameron, of the 78th."

"A Jock and a Geordie," the irrepressible Hollowell put in, grinning. "That's no' a bad combination, is it, sir?"

The sharp crack of McManus's rifle cut short the guffaws. In the square outside, a man who had been crawling stealthily toward the rear of the *doolies* suddenly lay very still and, with shrill cries of terror, those following his example were on their feet and dashing wildly for cover. Not to be outdone, Hollowell winged one of them and, in the momentary confusion, Alex ordered the barricade to be pulled aside.

"Off you go, you two!" he said urgently. "As fast as you know how and keep right-handed!"

Ryan needed no second bidding. Unarmed, he tore across the intervening space, and McManus, pausing only to grab his spare rifle from the loader, was after him a moment later. The unexpectedness of their appearance took the rebels completely by surprise, and they both reached the scattered *doolies* without a shot being fired at them, but as they bent together over Arnold's litter, striving to lift it, a hail of musket-balls spattered the ground about them.

From every rooftop and loophole, it seemed, men were firing on the two shirt-sleeved soldiers as they struggled with the heavy *doolie*. Hollowell, Webb, and Cameron kept up a steady answering fire, aiming at any target that presented itself, but the terrible fusillade continued, seeming to double in volume when finally— unable to lift the *doolie*—Ryan and McManus dragged Arnold out of it. The occupant of one of the other *doolies* scrambled out, both hands outheld but before he had taken two steps, he was shot down. McManus, who had gone back to meet him, took one look at his shattered body and went to rejoin Ryan. Carrying the wounded officer between them, they ran back across the square, reaching the barricaded doorway miraculously unhurt, and willing hands relieved them of their burden.

Poor Arnold was gasping with pain and shock, his face drained of every vestige of color, and he was bleeding copiously from a fresh wound in the thigh. But, when Surgeon Home staunched the flow and laid him gently in a corner of the room, he managed to thank his rescuers in a voice so faint and choked with emotion that they could barely hear it. Ryan knelt beside him, holding his own half-empty water bottle to his officer's lips, the tears coursing unashamedly down his unshaven cheeks as he relieved his pent-up feelings in a torrent of blasphemy.

"He was hit again, sir," he told Home, becoming a little calmer. "The bleeding perishers aimed at him deliberately . . . as if he hadn't had enough. Oh. Gawd, look at his legs . . . just look at them! But you'll be able to save him, won't you, Doctor? You'll try to save him?"

Dr. Home had already examined Arnold's legs. Meeting Alex's mutely questioning gaze, he gave a brief, regretful headshake but replied to Ryan's frantic questions with guarded cheerfulness and an optimism it was evident he did not feel.

"If only we could've carried him in the *doolie,*" the young Blue Cap reproached himself. "Maybe he'd have had a better chance. But we couldn't lift the sodding thing—and they aimed at him deliberately, make no mistake about that. Just as they aimed at the poor sod of a Jock who tried to run after us—he didn't get two yards before they'd put fifty balls in him, not two yards. But if we'd left Mr. Arnold in his *doolie,* he might have been all right. That's what's worrying me, sir."

"You've given him the best possible chance, lad," the surgeon said kindly. "By getting him in here, where at least he's out of the sun, poor fellow. Now leave him to me, will you? I'll do all in my power for him, I promise you."

Private Ryan rose obediently to his feet, and Alex set him to the task of repairing their barricade, in readiness to repel any renewed attack. "Were there many others left alive in the *doolies?*" he asked McManus, lowering his voice so that the others did not hear. He wanted no useless heroism, inspired by their rescue of Arnold; McManus was an intelligent man—if the full danger of their situation were explained to him, he could probably be counted on to discourage it, at all events until the right opportunity occurred. *If* it occurred . . . Alex sighed.

"Aye, there were quite a few, sir," the Fusilier answered. "Mind, I didna hae time tae count them, but at a guess I'd say most o' them are alive. One puir devil," he shuddered involuntarily, "asked me tae pit a bullet through his heid, but I couldna bring ma'sel' tae do that. I mean, sir, there's a chance that aid will be sent tae us, is there no'?"

"There's a chance," Alex said flatly. "If we can hang on until the rear-guard evacuates the Moti Mahal. I doubt if they'll attempt to do so before dark."

McManus nodded soberly. "'Twas what I was thinking, sir." He hesitated, eyes searching Alex's face, and then offered quietly, "I'll gang across tae the *doolies* again, if you wish, sir. But I doubt we'll only mak' it worse for the puir fellows if we try tae bring them in the way we brought in Ryan's Mr. Arnold. Yon *doolies* are awful cumbersome things, and they're too heavy for just twa men tae carry." Again he hesitated, as if reluctant to put his thoughts into words.

"Well?" Alex prompted.

"Well, sir," McManus said, "We canna afford tae risk mair than a couple o' our men, can we—not if we're tae have a chance of getting out of here?"

"No," Alex confirmed. "We can't. But at least we can keep the Pandies from getting near those *doolies.* So long as we're here, covering them, the wounded will be safe. See that the other men understand that, will you? It may come better from you than from me."

McManus nodded his understanding. He returned to his post and, a few minutes later, the rebels renewed their attack, urged on by the old Rissaldar in the red cummerbund, who had exchanged his shield and *tulwar* for a musket. Showing more courage than he had in the previous attacks, the old man came forward at a shambling run, to discharge his piece within a few feet of the barricade. The ball struck Webb in the right shoulder, and he rolled over, cursing, his rifle falling at his feet. Alex and Hollowell fired together, and the Rissaldar went down, his turbaned bead caught and held between two up-ended planks on top of the barricade, a slow trickle of blood staining the long white beard. Even as he died, he mouthed obscenities at them, and Private Cameron, overcome by revulsion, thrust the butt of his rifle into the contorted face and heaved the body out of sight.

The attackers withdrew, but, from the rear of the house there came the sound of splintering wood, followed by the pad of bare feet approaching the wall with the plastered-up door. The surgeon shouted a warning as several shots struck the plaster, tearing a jagged hole in the framework of the door. A spent ball struck Alex in the calf of his right leg as he moved to meet this new danger; it dropped him to his knees, but Home was up in an instant, the Colt in his hand. He fired it through the hole in the plaster, emitting a yell of triumph as the hubbub subsided and the rebels withdrew; Hollowell, coming swiftly to his side, picked off a straggler and turned, grinning, to greet Alex with the news that the rear room was once again deserted.

"There's another door at the far end, sir," he added. "This yin's nae use onymore. Maybe we should break through and set up a barricade by the far door." He tested the thin plaster with the butt of his rifle; it flaked off, revealing nothing more substantial than a crisscross screen of wooden laths. "This'll not hold them out. Will I break through, sir? The other door looks solid enough and 'twill gie us mair room."

Alex limped over to inspect the room beyond. Hollowell was right, he thought, and it would be no more difficult to hold two rooms than it had been to hold one. They would have more space to move about in, more air for the wounded and—if they had to make a run for it—an alternative to crossing the square.

The smoking revolver still in his hand, Surgeon Home peered through the hole in the plaster. "I think it would be a wise move, Colonel," he said. "It's stifling in here."

Alex nodded. "I agree, Doctor. Right, Hollowell, take your rifle to that plaster, lad. We'll go in together and make straight for the door, just in case there are any of them lying in wait for us."

"Let me go," the surgeon pleaded. "You've been hit."

Alex looked down at the congealing blood on his trouser leg and said, smiling, "In the words of our friend McManus, 'tis only a scratch. And you've got work to do, Doctor—Webb has more than a scratch, I fear. Don't worry, we'll be back before you've finished attending to him." He raised his voice, "McManus, Cameron—watch the other door. Don't let any of those swine get near the *doolies*."

Andrew Becher answered him. The staff officer had been loading rifles some distance behind the barricade but now, Alex saw, he had dragged himself up to it and was lying beside Cameron, an Enfield to his shoulder, with Ryan loading for both of them.

"Ryan's vision is troubling him, Colonel," he offered in explanation. "So I've taken his place. Have a care, won't you?"

"I will," Alex assured him. "Ready, Hollowell?"

"Aye, sir." Hollowell plied his rifle butt briskly, opening a gap large enough to admit them both. They dived through it together and reached the door side by side. It opened onto a street that appeared to be deserted but, as Alex stepped cautiously forward, he saw that it had been the scene of fierce fighting. A number of British soldiers lay dead, the nearest only a few yards from him—some Highlanders and Sikhs, killed as they had battled their way to the Residency the previous night, and one small group of five or six men of the escort who had died defending two *doolies* containing wounded. All, without exception, were headless and hideously mutilated . . . He drew in his breath sharply. The battle-hardened Hollowell, following the direction of his gaze, turned his head away, retching and then, recovering himself, gave vent to a stream of outraged invective.

"Get the door shut," Alex ordered. "It's loopholed, so we'll be able to keep them at a distance. Jump to it, lad!"

"Aye, sir." A disciplined product of a fine regiment, he did as he was told, but, when the door was slammed shut and a stout wooden bar in place behind it, he said in a shocked voice, "My God, sir—how they must hate us tae serve our dead in sic' a fashion!"

Remembering Cawnpore and the massacre of the women and children, as well as of the fighting men, Alex could only incline his head in wordless assent. But there had been no hatred, he thought bitterly, until evil men—men like the Nana, rabble-rousers like the Moulvi of Fyzabad and thousands of unknown priests and fakirs had stirred it up, so that they might turn it to their own advantage. They were playing for high stakes, all of them—the old King of Delhi, the Begum of Oudh, the Nana, who believed that a kingdom was his for the taking. They had called for a holy war, fanning the smoldering embers of both real and imagined grievances and fears until they had burst into flames—flames that now threatened to consume all of India. There had been warnings, of course, but British officialdom, grown complacent and parsimonious after a hundred years of successful and profitable rule over an alien land, had ignored the warnings or—as General Hewitt had done in Meerut five months ago— had met them with acts of provocative severity, which had served only to breed hatred and an ever-growing mistrust.

The kind of hatred that had manifested itself in the street out-side and . . . Alex's throat was suddenly tight. Dear God, the kind of hatred that would be released, to vent itself upon the unfortu-nate wounded, lying in their abandoned *doolies* in the square, and upon themselves, if they allowed the rebels to defeat them . . .

He left Hollowell to stand guard at the loopholed door and slowly, his feet dragging with the effort it was now taking him to move at all, he returned to acquaint the other defenders with the news of what they had found. There was a brief lull and, in the uncanny silence—broken only by the roar of cannonfire in the distance—they listened to what he had to say, their faces betraying varying degrees of uneasiness and anger.

"I think," Surgeon Home said practically, "that you had bet-ter allow me to dress that leg of yours, Colonel Sheridan. It's more than a scratch, judging by the way you are limping, and it will feel better if I can remove the ball before the muscles stiffen."

Alex submitted to having his leg examined. It proved to be a flesh wound, not unduly severe, but the spent bullet had lodged in his calf and, once the pain caused by its removal had subsided, it did indeed feel a good deal better. The other wounded men were considerably worse off than he was; Swanson, perhaps for-tunately, was still unconscious, the two wounded men of the escort intermittently so, and poor young Arnold, despite his valiant stoicism, was moaning with the agony of his shattered and horribly swollen legs, the cries wrung from him whenever he attempted to move. Webb squatted beside him, his injured arm secured to his body by his belt, doing what little could he done to ease his suffering, and Captain Becher, finally compelled to relinquish his place at the barricade to Ryan, was lying with his eyes closed in an attempt to recoup his strength.

The cessation of the enemy attacks came as a relief to all of them, but, with inaction came also the awareness that they were parched with thirst, exhausted, and in mortal danger. The fit men had earlier relinquished their water bottles to Surgeon Home, to be shared among the wounded, and although he had been sparing with them, only a single, half-filled canteen remained, and eyes constantly went to it with a longing that could not be assuaged and was the more poignant because none of them voiced it.

One of the men, a short, dark-haired private of Her Majesty's 84th named Roddy, who had obeyed every order he was given efficiently but without speaking to any of the others, unexpectedly broke his self-imposed silence. Sinking to his knees beside the unconscious Swanson, he crossed himself and started to pray aloud. His accent was the lilting one of Southern Ireland, his prayer simple and, perhaps on this account, oddly moving. The wounded officer, seeming to hear him from the depths of unconsciousness, roused himself to murmur a faint "Amen" and two of the others—Ryan and the slightly wounded Blue Cap who had helped to load for him—followed his example.

Sensing their mood, Alex asked quietly if they would all like to join in prayer and, receiving their assent, he led them in a

low-voiced recital of the Lord's Prayer, rising to stand between
the two rooms, so that Hollowell might add his voice to theirs.
Reminded of the torn and bloodstained prayer book he had
found outside the Bibigarh—the House of Women—in Cawnpore, in which passages from the Litany had been heavily
underlined by one of the Nana's unhappy victims, he quoted several of the passages, ending with the one that had most deeply
impressed him.

*"That it may please Thee to strengthen such as do stand; and to
comfort and help the weak-hearted; and to raise up them that fall; and
finally to beat down Satan under our feet . . . That it may please Thee
to succor, help and comfort all that are in danger, necessity, and tribula-
tion . . ."*

McManus led the response, head bowed over his rifle.

"We beseech Thee tae hear us, good Lord."

*"That it may please Thee to have mercy upon all men; to forgive
our enemies . . . and turn their hearts . . ."*

Now they all joined in, those to whom the words were unfa-
miliar echoing the responses of the others, their faces grave but
less tense and anxious than they had been a few minutes before.
The crack of Cameron's rifle brought their brief respite to an
end and there was a shout of warning from Hollowell, followed
by the ominous rumble of wheels in the street to the rear of
their refuge. Alex joined the Highlander at his loopholed vantage
point, with Roddy close on his heels.

"I fancy they're bringing up a gun, sir," Hollowell said, without looking round. "'Twill be a' up wi' us if they do and . . ." he
swore. "Hell, sir, 'tis no' a gun, 'tis a . . ." he broke off, lost for
words, and Alex, peering anxiously through one of the loopholes,
saw that some white-robed natives were engaged in pushing what

appeared to be a screen on wheels down the street toward them. Roddy, crouching behind a loophole to the left of the door, took careful aim with his Minié, but his bullet, striking the center of the wood and metal contraption, failed to penetrate its surface and Hollowell, swiftly reloading, fared no better with his two testing shots, both fired at close range.

Protected by their screen, a considerable body of rebels came forward, with the evident intention of placing the screen against the loopholed door and firing from behind it into the room so recently occupied by the defenders. They would be unable to survive such tactics for long, Alex knew, and he called urgently to Hollowell and Roddy to evacuate the room, taking with them any timber they could find, with which to repair the plastered door they had broken through earlier.

Aided by Surgeon Home and the slightly wounded Blue Cap, Murphy, they contrived to set up a second barricade, but it was hurriedly put together and by no means as bulletproof as the rebels' screen, which—before they had quite finished their task— was wheeled up to the rear door and jammed there, thus cutting off their bolt-hole. From behind it, sepoys and townsfolk armed with matchlocks poured successive volleys into the room they had vacated, screaming threats and abuse. Although the shots were ill aimed, in so confined a space they were effective and spent musket-balls penetrated the pile of planks and lumber, to rico- chet like angry hornets about the heads of the defenders.

McManus was hit in the back of the neck and had to leave his post to have the bleeding staunched; a ricocheting bullet drove a furrow across the top of Alex's scarred right cheek and Andrew Becher, attempting to drag himself to the pillar in order to load for Ryan, was struck painfully in the lower jaw and—unable to make himself heard—lay bleeding for several minutes before

Surgeon Home noticed his predicament and crawled across to his aid.

After about half an hour, the attackers unexpectedly desisted in their efforts but, almost at once, the pad of bare feet on the roof succeeded the volleys of musketry, and plaster came raining down from the ceiling as roof tiles were torn off or smashed and patches of blue sky began to appear overhead. The four men guarding the door into the square emptied their rifles in a burst of fury at any target they could glimpse through the shattered roof, but they fired too quickly and even McManus admitted to having missed the fellow he had fired at.

"The bloody swine are nae showing theirselves!" he complained wrathfully.

"Go back to your post, lad," Alex told him. "They may be trying to distract our attention, to enable them to get to the wounded in the *doolies* when we're staring up at the ceiling. Cameron, Ryan—watch to your front, my boys. Hollowell and Roddy, you keep under cover and try to pick them off if they show themselves on the roof. Dr. Home, we may have to move the wounded. Can you . . ." He broke off as, through one of the gaping holes in the roof, a bundle of lighted straw descended, propelled from a safe distance by a cavalryman's lance. It was followed by another and another and, although they managed to stamp out some of the smoking bundles, the room was soon filled with clouds of suffocating smoke and, in a far corner of the room, a pile of tinder-dry lumber swiftly caught fire and started to burn. Without water to douse the flames, they spread at alarming speed and, impeding each other in their efforts to extinguish the blaze, the men staggered drunkenly about, coughing and retching. Soon the smoke was so thick that it was impossible to see across the square to the *doolies,* and Alex, stumbling to the door, saw—or imagined he saw—several sowars, with drawn sabers, leave the shelter of the gatehouse and move stealthily toward the rear of the abandoned *doolies*.

McManus and Cameron, in response to his shout, joined him in the doorway and at the mere sight of their leveled rifles, most of the sowars retreated, screeching obscenities. Two of them had reached the *doolies,* however, and were crouching down behind them, half-hidden by the curtains and presenting a difficult target. Alex moved to his right, his vision clearing, and the Adams in his hand, but at that moment a wounded officer threw himself out of one of the *doolies,* emptied his pistol into the nearer of the crouching cavalry troopers and—seemingly unaware of the presence of his compatriots, less than twenty yards from him—made a frantic dash for the far end of the square. Instantly the rebels posted in the surrounding sheds and buildings opened up on him and the dusty ground about him was spattered with musket-balls, but somehow, miraculously, he eluded them and disappeared from sight behind a row of godowns that formed the opposite side of the square.

No shots had come from that side, Alex noticed, which suggested that the godowns were unoccupied. He turned and reentered the smoke-filled room of the house they had defended for so long, to be met by Surgeon Home, who told him urgently, "For God's sake, Colonel, we must get the wounded out of here! The fire's taken hold—they'll be burned to death or suffocated if we don't."

There was no time to reconnoiter the godowns—they would have to take a chance on their being empty. Alex gestured to them and the surgeon nodded, drawing great gulps of air into his tortured lungs.

"There's another door at the back of the room—it's much

nearer. If you'll cover us, we'll take the wounded out that way."

"Right, Doctor," Alex acknowledged. "As quickly as you can, then."

It took the combined efforts of the unwounded men to effect the evacuation. The rebels did not attempt to rush them—had they done so, they would almost certainly have succeeded in wiping out the entire party. Instead, they fired from cover, and the unfortunate Swanson was hit again in the chest, as Hollowell and Cameron dragged him painfully between them across the intervening space to the godowns. Dr. Home's discovery of the second door into the square proved providential; it, too, had been plastered over, but breaking through the plaster took only seconds and, their movements screened by the smoke and flames, the first four men got across unscathed, with Arnold and Becher. Poor Murphy, gallantly insisting that he could make his way unaided, took a musket-ball in the thigh, and Ryan was hit in the shoulder as he endeavored to go to his assistance. Alex brought him in on his back, half-carrying, half-dragging him and the poor fellow was unconscious when they gained the cover of the nearest godown.

Leaving the surgeon to do what little he could for the newly inflicted casualties, Alex made a swift reconnaissance. The godown was, in reality, an arched shed with loopholed walls and a narrow passageway at the rear which led to an open courtyard. It was considerably more spacious than their previous refuge but, being built of wood and sun-dried mud in the usual Indian style, it offered less protection and would, he realized, have to be guarded both front and rear in case the rebels launched another attack on them. A number of corpses lay scattered about the interior and in the passageway—some were sepoys, evidently killed in the first attempt to ambush the main body of the escort, and about half a dozen were *doolie*-bearers, who must have sought shelter there, only to be shot down as they entered the front of the building.

Already in the oppressive heat, the place had the stench of death, and swarms of flies added to the defenders' discomfort, but, beyond moving the bodies from their immediate vicinity, there was little they could do to make it more habitable. Poor Swanson was dying, the surgeon reported and, including himself, there were now only seven men capable of using arms, with three more wounded but capable of standing sentry.

Alex posted them as best he could and, desperately anxious as to the fate of those still lying in the abandoned *doolies* on the south side of the square, inched his way to the entrance of the godown, with Hollowell, in the hope that no harm had yet befallen the helpless occupants. It was a vain hope, he knew. In their first refuge, they had been near enough to pick off any rebels who attempted to approach the *doolies* but now, with the width of the square between them and clouds of smoke billowing across it to obscure their view, their chances of doing so were slight. He took a few paces to the side of the godown and was met by so vicious a hail of musketry that he was compelled to fling himself flat and crawl back to safety, gasping and covered with dust.

Hollowell helped him to his feet. "I doubt the swine will hae the nerve tae gang near them yet, sir," he offered consolingly.

"No, but they will, Hollowell. Devil take them, they will—it's only a question of time. And I don't see how we can stop them . . . we'd be shot to pieces if we tried to rush them from here. With only six of us, there's nothing we can do—I wish to heaven there were!"

Close to despair at the realization of their utter helplessness,

Alex found himself praying silently that the men in the abandoned *doolies* might die of their injuries rather than fall alive into the rebels' hands. Deprived of medical care and water, given time most of them probably would die but . . . It took a great effort of will to turn his back on the square and go again into the filthy, fly-infested godown, but he made the effort and, for a while at least, it seemed as if his despairing prayer had been answered.

The firing petered out and finally ceased and, although they strained their ears anxiously, they could hear nothing to indicate any fresh activity on the enemy's part. The cries and groans they had listened to with such distress earlier in the day no longer reached them, and the exhausted men in the godown thankfully took advantage of the respite. They were parched and hungry, as well as tired, their spirits at their lowest ebb. Several of the wounded moaned and screamed in delirium; the others squatted down on the littered floor to get what rest they could, the sentries leaned on their rifles to hold themselves upright, red-rimmed eyes drooping with fatigue. Alex, conscious of an almost overwhelming desire for sleep, forced himself to resist it by making a check of their ammunition. Even when the contents of the wounded men's pouches were divided among the five fit riflemen, their supply was dangerously low and he had to warn them to conserve it, firing only to ward off attack.

"We need water very badly, Colonel Sheridan," Dr. Home said, looking up from the task of reloading his Colt, "if any of the wounded are to survive. Or indeed," he added wryly, "if any of us are."

Reminded once again of Cawnpore, Alex expelled his breath in a rasping sigh. "I don't know where we're to get it from, Doctor," he answered regretfully, "But it will be dark in an hour or so and then Colonel Campbell's rear-guard will surely . . ." A terrible, high-pitched shriek of agony sent him stumbling toward the front of the godown.

By the time he reached it, pandemonium had broken out on the far side of the square, the shouts and cries of the wretched survivors in the *doolies* mingled with the crackle of flames, as burning torches were flung into their midst, setting the curtains alight. Sabers glinted in the glow of the flames; emboldened by the success of their attempt at fire raising, a mob of sepoys and sowars hurled themselves into the drifting smoke, hacking and bayoneting, their yells of triumph as they went about their butchery rising above the terrible, heart-rending screams of their dying victims.

When the ghastly slaughter was over, the hubbub faded to a savage muttering sound, as the flames rose higher and drove the mob back. A lance was raised, the dripping head of a British soldier impaled on its tip, and the muttering became a roar of exultation. Alex found himself unable to move. He stood at the front of the godown, frozen into immobility, his stomach churning and, rising in his throat, bile that he tried vainly to choke down. This was what he had feared; it was a repetition of what had been done in the Bibigarh and at the Suttee Chowra Ghat in Cawnpore and at a hundred other military stations throughout North India. Dear God in heaven, he reproached himself, conscience-stricken, he had known what to expect, he had experienced it before in all its searing horror and he had not lifted a finger to prevent it.

But *could* he have prevented it, with six exhausted men, armed only with rifles? He drew a shuddering breath, as a vision of Emmy's face floated in front of him, blotting out his present surroundings—Emmy's small, sweet face as he had seen it for the last time, gaunt from starvation and with the still pallor of death spreading over it. There had been over four hundred of them on the Ghat and only four now survived . . . Mowbray Thomson, Henry Delafosse, Private Murphy of the 84th, and himself. He would willingly have died a thousand deaths if he could have spared Emmy the slow agony of hers, but then, as now, he had been powerless to prevent the slaughter. Then, as now, they had been hopelessly outnumbered . . . Merciful heaven, was it never to end, the hatred, the barbarism, the carnage? The mobs who murdered and mutilated without pity were sepoys, their victims British officers and men, their comrades in arms, whom formerly they had trusted and even loved. But there was no trust now, no love—only fear and a mindless hatred, shared equally by both sides, which led to acts like this, crying out for some more hideous reprisals.

Alex closed his eyes, fighting for control. Beside him he heard Hollowell cursing and, opening his eyes again, saw the Highlander raise his rifle to his shoulder. But there was no clear target at which he could aim and he lowered the weapon, tears of outraged pity and frustration streaming down his cheeks. Two of the other men discharged their rifles uselessly into the melee and, recovering himself, Alex sharply bade them hold their fire and return to their posts. They obeyed him, cursing as bitterly as Hollowell had done, their faces taut with shock.

"It's over for those poor fellows, at least," Surgeon Home said, his voice choked. "God rest their souls, it's over . . . they will not have to suffer anymore." He laid a hand on Alex's shoulder, sensing his distress. "Think of that, if you are blaming yourself, Colonel Sheridan—as, I confess, I am. We all are, every one of us. But we could do nothing to save them. We should have thrown our lives away to no purpose if we had attempted to and sacrificed our own wounded in addition. You did all that any man could have done to protect them and—"

"And only prolonged their agony," Alex put in harshly. "God forgive me for that . . . and God forgive their murderers, for I cannot, I . . ." From the shadows behind him, a voice said, trembling on the edge of panic, "And now it's our turn—now them bastards will come after us and serve us the same way! Holy Mother of God, put a bullet through me, one of you! Jesus, I can't just lie here waiting for them to come, I can't. It's more than flesh and blood can stand!"

Panic was infectious. Alex turned, his own emotions swiftly hidden and, without attempting to identify or reproach the speaker, he issued brisk orders. The sentries were relieved, the less severely wounded sent to search the bodies of the dead sepoys for anything that might be of use in the way of weapons, ammunition, or food. They found some Brown Bess muskets and ammunition but neither food nor water and, returning with the muskets, reported that the courtyard at the back of the godown was deserted and flanked by a substantially built brick house.

"Could we no' break intae the yard, sir?" McManus asked. "There's just a mud wall tae be knocked doon and the house wad maybe serve us better than this midden. Indeed, sir, I've an idea we might be able tae make oor way to the Chutter Munzil through yon house. It lies in the right direction and, once it's dark, we'd hae a fair chance o' getting intae it wi'out being seen."

Concerned for their wounded, Alex glanced in mute question at Surgeon Home who, after a momentary hesitation, nodded. "Anything is better than staying here, Colonel. But before we attempt to move our poor wounded fellows again, it might be advisable to take a look around in case the house is occupied. I'll go, if you like—I've had more rest than you have."

Alex thanked him and moved wearily toward the back of the shed, but before he could examine the wall they would have to break though, Cameron called out to him that some of the enemy were on the roof. The ominous sound of splintering timber warned him that the same tactics as those that had driven them from their first refuge were once again to be employed and, shaking off his weariness, he shouted to the sentries to fire on any rebels they could see.

Roddy, on guard at the entrance, picked off one man who incautiously showed himself, and Alex emptied all six chambers of his Adams in an effort to drive off the others, but in a matter of minutes there were several gaping holes in their frail roof, through which their attackers fired down on them, driving them steadily back toward the passageway at the rear.

"Break through into the courtyard, Doctor," he requested Surgeon Home breathlessly. "It's our only hope if they set this place on fire. Hollowell, you go with the surgeon and report back to me if it's safe to move the wounded. Quick as you can, lad— we'll try and hold them off until you get back."

"Aye, sir." Hollowell went to work with the butt of his rifle, his expression grimly determined.

Cameron and Ryan, on Alex's instructions, were moving the wounded into the passageway when the man who had earlier pleaded for a bullet to end his misery broke suddenly into a torrent of weeping.

"Leave me be!" he besought them. "Give me a rifle and leave me. We're trapped, for God's sake . . . we'll never get out of here and the bloody rear-guard won't help us. How are they to know we're here? We'll have been reported missing, believed dead, if we've been reported at all."

"That poor fellow could be right, alas," Surgeon Home said.

He kept his voice low as he went on. "Facing stark facts, Colonel, they cannot possibly know that any of us are left alive, can they? Which means we can't depend on their coming to our rescue."

"In that case, my friend," Alex answered wearily, "we shall just have to dig ourselves in until we hear them coming and then either try to get word to them or break out and join them. If McManus is right, we may well be able to do so through the house across the courtyard, so the sooner we can get ourselves into it, the better." He added, a note of authority in his voice, as the mud wall yielded to Hollowell's rifle butt, "Right, Doctor, off you go. Take it carefully and keep your heads down!"

The two men clambered into the courtyard, to vanish from sight in the gathering darkness. No shots followed them, and, from the roof, the firing abruptly ceased.

CHAPTER THREE

❯❯❯ • ❮❮❮

THE FIRST intimation that disaster had befallen the convoy of wounded reached the Residency when the main body of the escort entered by the Bailey Guard gate, a little before noon.

They had fought a running battle against a large force of mutineers, meeting a vicious fire of musketry from the buildings that lined their route and of grape and canister from field guns mounted at the intersections. Having no artillery to support them, Major Simmons' Fusiliers and Sikhs had been compelled to clear each street they entered with a bayonet charge and their casualties, in consequence, were high. They had managed to bring most of them in, however, and General Havelock, waiting anxiously for news of his son Harry, was overjoyed to learn that he and a wounded private of the 78th were the occupants of the only two *doolies* from the front of the convoy to reach safety.

The little General, worn out by the strain of the previous day's fighting, had handed over his command to General Sir James Outram. With his severely wounded chief of staff, Colonel Tytler, he had accepted the generous offer of hospitality made by Martin Gubbins, the Financial Commissioner, in whose shell-scarred house he was sleeping fitfully when Harry Havelock was carried in.

The two embraced, the white-haired general unashamedly in tears, but not until his surgeon, Dr. Collinson, had dressed Harry's shattered arm and Mr. Gubbins' native cook provided him with food and drink, did Havelock permit his son to give him an account of what had happened. Harry was in considerable pain, his face like wax, but relief at finding himself miraculously safe and alive caused him to make light of the suffering he had endured and, sipping a glass of Mr. Gubbins' sherry, he glossed over the events of the previous day, making no mention of the gallantry that had led to his being shot down.

"We passed a somewhat uncomfortable night in the Moti Mahal," he admitted. "And we were all immensely pleased and relieved when Cousin Bensley arrived and Colonel Campbell informed us that all the wounded were to be evacuated to the Residency under his guidance. We had a sticky time of it until we reached the path by the river—crossing the open ground we were under heavy fire from an enemy battery on the far side and the bearers started to panic then. However, once we were under cover of the palace walls, we all imagined that the worst was over. I was even smoking a cheroot!"

The general, his hand shaking visibly, refilled his son's sherry glass. "The hospitable Mr. Gubbins tells me he has plenty of this," he said dryly. "And last night, believe it or not, my dear Harry, he regaled us on turtle soup and champagne! Hoarded especially for the occasion, he assured us, but . . . we believed that they were starving. Pray continue, my dear boy. What happened when you reached the palace? We have pickets occupying all three palaces since entering here last night—your way should have been clear."

Harry sighed. "To tell you the truth, Father," he said, "I did not see a great deal. One minute we were proceeding quite quietly along the pathway by the river—in single file, of course, because the path is narrow—and the next all hell had broken loose! We turned into a square, with an arched gateway at the far end, and we had just passed under the archway when a murderous fire was opened on us from all sides. There must have been thousands of rebels there, lying in wait for us and firing from behind loopholed sheds and houses, so that the escort hadn't a chance."

"The square in which Neill was *killed!*" General Havelock exclaimed. "Oh, dear heaven, Bensley Thornhill must have taken the wrong turning and missed his way!"

"General Neill was *killed?*" Harry questioned, in shocked surprise.

His father inclined his white head. "Yes, last night. A shot fired—at point-blank range from the arched gateway you have just described, Harry— struck him in the head. He was killed instantly. Sheridan and Spurgin brought his body in on a gun-limber."

"I cannot pretend that I shall mourn him," Harry Havelock confessed. "He was your worst enemy, Father—your cruelest, most unjust critic. All the same, it's a shock. Whatever his faults, he was a brave man, if a ruthless one. And one must allow that he saved Benares and Allahabad, which a less ruthless commander might have lost."

"God grant him peace." The general's voice held genuine compassion. "James Neill did his duty as he saw it—I trust the same may be said of me, when my time comes. He and I did not see eye to eye on many things but . . . I digress. Go on with your report, Harry."

"There's not much more to tell, sir." Harry drained his sherry glass and leaned back against the pillows. "I was in the leading *doolie,* with that most excellent fellow Private Henry Ward of the 78th looking after me. He was the one you spoke to last night,

Willie . . ." he turned to give William Hargood, his father's A.D.C., a wry grin, and Hargood—who had twice risked his life to cross from the Chutter Munzil to the Moti Mahal in order to relieve the general's anxiety by bringing him tidings of his wounded son—reddened in embarrassment and affected not to hear. The general glanced at him thoughtfully but said nothing, and Harry continued his narrative, "If it hadn't been for Ward, Father, I should not be here. There was mad panic among the *doolie*-bearers when the enemy opened on us. Half of them just dropped the poor wretches they were carrying and ran. I heard Bensley Thornhill yelling to the rear of the convoy to go back, and he and one or two of the surgeons dashed toward the rear, trying to stop them. Bensley was hit, I think, but I'm not sure. One of the walking wounded, Private Pilkington of the 78th, was hit again and he dived into my *doolie* with me.

Ward drove our bearers on at bayonet point. They tried to ditch us several times, but Ward would have none of it—he made them bring us in. If ever a man deserved a Victoria Cross, in my book that man does! He saved my life a dozen times and refused to leave me."

"I will endeavor to see that he gets a Cross," General Havelock promised. "And, for what it is worth, Private Ward has my undying gratitude, my dear Harry." He let his hand rest for a moment on Harry's sound one, unable to keep back the tears as he looked down at his son's pain-ravaged face. "If I had lost you, I . . . oh, my dearest boy, thank God you have been restored to me! I have lost so many of my brave soldiers, men who have followed me through thick and thin ever since we marched out of Allahabad, little knowing how formidable were the obstacles in our path. Over five hundred of them, Harry, in the past two days . . . it breaks my heart to think of it. And poor Fraser Tytler, one of the bravest of the brave, is lying at death's door—here in this house. Was it any wonder that I could not drink Mr. Gubbins' champagne? He is kindness itself, and I am aware that he had been saving the champagne to celebrate the relief of the garrison but I . . . merciful heaven, it would have choked me if I'd touched a drop of it when I learned what the cost had been." He straightened up, squaring his thin, bowed shoulders. "Over five hundred killed and maimed! How many more were lost in the square this morning? Not all the wounded, surely?"

He looked so frail and old and broken that Harry's heart went out to him in helpless pity. But he knew his father too well to attempt to spare his feelings by deceiving him. "No, sir, not all. The rear part of the convoy hadn't entered the square when the firing started. They would have had time to retire to the Chutter Munzil—our escort bought them time. They'll come in soon, I feel certain, by the safe route through the palaces, and Bensley with them. Poor chap, it wasn't his fault—it's easy enough to lose one's way in those palace courtyards. It's like being in a rabbit warren and—"

"I'm aware of that, Harry, and I'm not blaming young Thornhill. But how many *doolies* did enter the square, have you any idea?"

"Perhaps thirty or forty, sir. It's hard to be sure because I wasn't in a position to see much."

"And the wounded men who were abandoned when the bearers fled," the general persisted. "Is there any hope for the poor fellows or for the men who were escorting them?"

"I fear not, sir," Harry answered unhappily. "Those in my immediate vicinity were set on by a mob of sowars, armed with sabers. They were giving no quarter, and if it hadn't been for Private Ward, I should never have escaped. He held them off most gallantly."

"And the escort?"

"Well, sir, the main body of the escort were at the head of the convoy. We'd come along a narrow passage in single file, you see, and evidently Major Simmons expected an attack—if it came—to be launched against the head of the procession." Hearing his father's disapproving grunt, Harry added quickly, "Some of the officers ran back, but we were under a murderous fire, as I told you. Bensley Thornhill tried to warn the rear part of the convoy quite regardless of his own safety and so did Dr. Home and another surgeon who was with him. I saw Alex Sheridan, too—he came up from the rear with a Blue Cap and a couple of Highlanders, and they were doing what they could to protect the men in the *doolies.* They may have managed to get them back to the Chutter Munzil."

"Or they may be dead," General Havelock said bleakly. He asked Hargood for his sword-belt and started to buckle it on. "I had better go and have a word with Sir James. He's in command now, of course, so the decision will be his, but I understand he intends to send Napier with reinforcements to assist in the evacuation of the rear-guard. They were to leave at two o'clock, were they not, Willie?"

"Yes, sir," the A.D.C. confirmed. "A hundred men of the 78th, two of Captain Olpherts's guns and Captain Hardinge's Sikh cavalry of the garrison are under orders, sir."

"Campbell was having a tough battle, Father," Harry put in. "He was hit in the leg quite early on, but he insisted that he was perfectly fit for duty. One of the twenty-four-pounders Vincent

Eyre left with him had become jammed in a lane, I believe, which was causing him great concern. I doubt whether they'll be able to move before nightfall."

The general settled his cap on his head. "Then there will be time for Napier to search for the convoy of wounded if they haven't come in." He hesitated, frowning. "But you think it's unlikely that any of our men are left alive in the square where the *doolies* were abandoned, Harry?"

Harry shrugged and winced with the pain of it. "If they didn't manage to get out of the square, I doubt it, sir. God grant they did . . . and I pray you'll find that they've all got in safely by the time you find General Outram."

"Amen to that!" his father said. "Try to get some sleep, Harry, my dear boy. I shall be back as soon as I can. In the meantime, the ladies of the household will look after you."

He found Sir James Outram, with Colonel Inglis of Her Majesty's 32nd Regiment—who had succeeded to the command of the Lucknow garrison following the death of Sir Henry Lawrence—with various members of their staffs, including Colonel Napier, standing outside Dr. Fayrer's house. By happy chance, they were watching as a long line of *doolies* passed through the Bailey Guard gate and climbed the slight slope to the two-storied hospital building opposite.

Outram still had his arm in a sling, but he looked fit and rested and was moving about briskly among the survivors of the ill-fated convoy, handing out cheroots to some of the wounded and shaking hands with others. Seeing Havelock, he came over to offer his congratulations on Harry's safe arrival, his pleasure and concern very evident.

"He'd be a loss, Henry—a loss we could ill afford—that boy

of yours. I'm deeply relieved to know that he's safe and that his wound isn't too serious. You have him at Mr. Gubbins' house, I understand, with Tytler?"

Havelock nodded. After replying to inquiries as to his chief of staff's progress, he asked about the convoy of wounded and Outram's swarthy, bearded face clouded over.

"It was a bad business. I imagine Harry's told you about it. They took the wrong turning, it seems, and ran into trouble between the Hirun Khana and the outer wall of the Chutter Munzil—the place where poor James Neill was shot down last night." He went into details, most of which confirmed Harry's account of what had occurred, and added regretfully, "At least thirty officers and men, lying wounded in *doolies,* have been brutally murdered . . . devil take it, Henry, it doesn't bear thinking about. Poor unfortunate fellows! But I suppose we must be thankful that the rest got through . . . quite easily, I understand, once they were on the right path."

"I fear that my niece's husband was responsible for their taking the wrong route, Sir James," Havelock began. "Bensley Thornhill—"

"If he was responsible, he has paid very dearly for his error," Outram told him. "I was talking to the surgeon who was with the convoy, Dr. Bradshaw, a few minutes ago. He says that young Thornhill was severely wounded when he ran across, under heavy fire, to warn the rear part of the column to turn back—an action that undoubtedly saved many lives. They've taken him to hospital, but . . ." he shrugged despondently.

Poor Mary Thornhill, Havelock thought, married for so short a time . . . He sighed, as Outram went on, "Campbell's asking urgently for reinforcements, Henry, and Bob Napier will be ready to march out in half an hour. I've had to let him take a company of your Highlanders, done up though they are, and Stisted's going in command of them. I had told Olpherts to take two of his guns, but he thinks there may be a risk of losing them, and he's requested permission to take a couple of bullock teams instead, with which he's assured me he'll get that twenty-four-pounder back to us—you know they've got one of the infernal things jammed in a lane outside the Moti Mahal?"

"Yes, Harry told me they had. I take it you've agreed?"

General Outram permitted himself a brief smile. "Yes, I've agreed. If it had been anyone but Hellfire Jack, I might not have done so, but no one can accuse him of avoiding action, can they? And Bob's quite happy about it . . . besides, we want that twenty-four-pounder back and Jack Olpherts will get it back, if it's humanly possible."

"He'll certainly try," Havelock conceded. "But he may regret not taking his guns, all the same."

Outram lit a fresh cheroot from the butt of the one he had been smoking. "I shall have to watch my supply of these things," he said, inhaling smoke. "I left a couple of hundred at the Alam Bagh and I seem to have given the devil of a lot away this morning. Talking of the Alam Bagh, Henry, we shall have to try and establish communication with them as soon as we can. It might be a sound idea to send the cavalry out there—Barrow's and the irregulars and possibly Hardinge's Sikhs as well, because the garrison is short of fodder We'd have a job to feed so many horses and, in any event, the cavalry will be of more use to us in the Alam Bagh than they will be shut up here. We shall need carriage, if we're to evacuate the women and children to Cawnpore, and the cavalry will have to find it—Inglis says he has none at all."

Havelock's frown was thoughtful. "You still think that we shall be able to evacuate the women and children?"

"My God, I hope we shall! The wounded, too, if it's possible . . . but I don't know. Inglis doesn't think there's a chance of it. He estimates that the enemy have a strength of over sixty thousand and he believes the sepoys have completely terrorized the townsfolk, so that even those who might be well disposed toward us will be afraid to give us aid. You'd better talk to him yourself, Henry. He's in a better position to know than we are."

"Oh, certainly," Havelock agreed, his tone carefully expressionless.

"You consider he's being unduly pessimistic?" Outram said shrewdly.

"In certain respects, perhaps. His letters to me during the siege made me suspect that he's inclined to look on the black side. But he's had a great deal to contend with, and in the matter of the evacuation of the women and the wounded, I fear he's probably right." Havelock sighed. "It remains to be seen, of course, but—the lack of carriage apart—in my view we have not sufficient troops to hold the Residency *and* cover the evacuation to Cawnpore, Sir James."

"As you say, my dear Henry, it remains to be seen." General Outram echoed his sigh. "In the meantime, it is essential, whatever we do, that we establish a compact position here, extended to hold the whole river-face from the Iron Bridge to the Chutter Munzil and including the palaces. Aitken and his loyal sepoys of the 13th made a sortie from the Bailey Guard last night, as you know, and occupied the Terhee Kothee. A damned good thing he did or we'd never have got Maude's and Olpherts' guns in. At Inglis' suggestion, I sent 150 men of his regiment to clear the Kaptan's Bazaar area and take the Iron Bridge, first thing this morning . . ." With his gold-headed Malacca cane, he traced an outline of the position in the dust at their feet.

Havelock studied it, still frowning. "Have you had word of their progress, Sir James?"

"Yes—and they've done well. They were unable to get beyond the buildings on the near side of the bridge, unfortunately, but they took an eighteen-pounder and several light guns, and then went on, in accordance with my orders, to link up with Aitken and occupy the Furhut Baksh. As soon as Bob Napier joins up with them, they'll push on to the Chutter Munzil and open up a road for Campbell's rear-guard and, it's to be hoped, Eyre's guns." Outram's cane indicated the direction and scope of the movement. "The main thing now is to bring the rear-guard in without loss. After that, we'll extend our position along the southern face of the present defenses—here and here. But the Chutter Munzil is a veritable labyrinth of a place, and I don't think any of the garrison are really familiar with its ramifications, which is no doubt why the convoy of wounded went astray."

"You will avail yourself of Moorsom, will you not?" Havelock asked.

"Yes, indeed," Outram assured him warmly. "That young man and his maps of the city are worth their weight in gold. He has volunteered to accompany Napier and so has a civilian named Kavanagh, who is serving in the Post Office garrison as a volunteer and appears to know the city and its surroundings intimately. But . . ." he broke off, head raised, watching with critical eyes as a salvo of shells came hissing through the air from an enemy battery on the south-east side, to burst among the battered buildings eight or nine hundred yards from where he and Havelock were standing. A single gun answered the challenge and a brief artillery duel ensued, which ended as suddenly as it had begun.

"They tell me," the general went on, "that the Residency itself has had to be abandoned as a dwelling. It has been hit so often and so severely that it is now quite unsafe. Poor Sir Henry Lawrence was in his bedroom on the upper floor when he received his fatal wound . . . a shell had struck the room the previous day, and he had promised to change his quarters. But he did not, and, poor brave man, he was resting on his bed, quite done up, when a second shell entered through the window. His nephew George and his A.D.C., Captain Wilson, were with him at the time, but only Lawrence was injured. They did what they could for him, of course, and he was moved to Dr. Fayrer's, but his left thigh was fractured and amputation was impossible. It took him *forty-eight* hours to die, and he was in mortal agony, but his last words were: 'Let every man die at his post but never surrender. God help the poor women and children.' He must have been thinking of the fate of the Cawnpore garrison when he said that, I imagine."

"Yes. I expect he was," Havelock agreed sadly. He had heard the story of Henry Lawrence's last hours during dinner the night before, and there had been no pity in Martin Gubbins' voice as he had told it. Yet none of them would have survived the 88-day siege but for Lawrence's farsightedness, his careful organization of their defenses, his influence over the native troops of the garrison, and they would have starved had he not, for weeks before the outbreak of the mutiny, secretly brought in provisions, under the very noses of those who had finally betrayed him. But for the defeat at Chinhat on June 30, which had cost two hundred British lives, Lucknow could have held out for months, since there would have been sufficient troops to have garrisoned the Machhi Bhawan Fort, which had dominated the native city. As it was, Lawrence had been compelled to blow up the fortress, with its vast stock of reserve ammunition, and evacuate the garrison to swell the depleted numbers of the Residency's defenders . . .

and Chinhat had been Gubbins' doing. Havelock sighed, recalling the letter he had received at Allahabad, just after the battle.

*"I look upon our position now as ten times as bad as it was
yesterday,"* Henry Lawrence had written. *"Indeed, it is very critical
. . . unless we are relieved quickly, say in ten or fifteen days, we shall
hardly be able to maintain our position . . ."*

It had been Martin Gubbins who had goaded Lawrence to
lead out a small force to "trounce the enemy," who, his spies had
told him, numbered less than a thousand "with one wretched
gun." And it had been Gubbins who, seemingly, had suppressed a
second and accurate report, which put the enemy's strength at
six thousand, with the six-gun Fyzabad battery manned by the
finest gunners in Oudh . . . certainly it had been he who had
taunted poor Lawrence when he hesitated in an agony of indecision, "We shall be branded at the bar of history as cowards, Sir
Henry, if we fail to face our enemies," the financial commissioner
had declared, but last night, as he poured champagne for his deliv-
erers, he had made no mention of Chinhat and, in describing his
death, had denied Henry Lawrence the savior's role which,
undoubtedly, he had played.

Havelock repeated his sigh, and Outram said, uncannily as if
he had spoken his thoughts aloud, "I think that we shall have to
make Mr. Gubbins' house a hospital for officers, if you are agreeable, Henry. Dr. Fayrer has room in his house, so perhaps you
might care to make your quarters there with me—at any rate,
until other arrangements can be made?"

"Certainly, Sir James." Relieved, Havelock smiled. "I should
prefer it. My two invalids, however—"

"They must, of course, remain. They'll be well fed and cared
for—Mr. Gubbins contrives to keep a good table, I'm told, and
even has an English parlor maid to serve him!" The general's tone

was dry, his dark eyes bright with what might have been anger.

"I've seen no evidence of that," Havelock said, as always anxious to be fair. "But . . . I will have my traps moved this afternoon."

"Good!" Outram approved. He bent his head once again to study the plan he had traced in the dust. "Whether or not we are able to evacuate the women and the wounded, we must extend our perimeter without delay. And we'll divide the command. I think . . . you'll take over the outer defenses when they're secured, and Inglis the inner, with the old garrison, if that's also agreeable to you."

"It is for you to decide, Sir James," Havelock answered stiffly. "I'll serve you in any way you wish, that goes without saying."

"Thank you, my dear Henry." Sir James Outram put an affectionate arm about the bowed shoulders of the man he had now superseded. "You have achieved your goal, and all England will acclaim your feats of valor and endurance, when the news reaches London. Credit for the relief of this garrison is yours and yours alone . . . but you have worn yourself out with your endeavors. It's time you were granted respite, and sharing the responsibility for the continued defense of Lucknow with Inglis and myself will enable you to rest and recoup your strength, in readiness for the honors that will be heaped upon you. So take advantage of the opportunity, will you not?"

"Of course, I will, James," Havelock acknowledged. "I am grateful to you, as I trust you know. Indeed, I . . ."

"We'll talk of gratitude later, my friend," Outram said, cutting him short. He took a battered gold timepiece from the pocket of his stained frock coat, grunted when he saw what time it was and started to move toward the little group of staff officers patiently awaiting him. "I must see Napier on his way. Will you accompany me, or do you want to go back to Harry?"

"No," Havelock decided. "I will go to the hospital first, I think, and visit some of those poor fellows they have just brought in . . . unless you need me, of course?"

"No, you go to the hospital—they'll be better for the sight of you, Henry," Outram assured him. "I wonder, while you're there, if you'd be so good as to ascertain if there's any news of Becher—Andrew Becher of the 41st N.I.? He didn't come in with the rest, and Surgeon Bradshaw told me he saw Alex Sheridan of Barrow's Horse in the cul-de-sac when he left it . . . he was with the 90th's surgeon, Dr. Home. All three of them appear to be missing. Home was in charge of the wounded, and my poor friend Becher in one of the *doolies,* it seems. And Sheridan, gallant fellow that he is, after spending most of the night helping to bring in wounded from the Khas Bazaar area, went to the Moti Mahal with Thornhill."

"If they were left in the square with the abandoned *doolies,* I very much fear that they are lost," Havelock said. "But I will find out what I can, Sir James." They separated, and Havelock crossed the sloping roadway, acknowledging the salute of a subaltern of the 78th, whose company was marching down toward the Bailey Guard gate, led by a single piper.

The hospital, established in what had, in happier days, been the Banqueting Hall, like all the buildings within the Residency perimeter, bore the scars of the long siege. Round shot had so frequently penetrated its walls that they were honeycombed, and the upper story had recently been so severely damaged that it had had to be evacuated, leaving only the ground floor for the accommodation of both the sick and the wounded. The long, low room, with its shuttered and sandbagged windows, was dark and suffocatingly hot and, with the influx of injured men from the rear-guard convoy, it was now appallingly overcrowded and all but reduced to chaos.

Aided by orderlies and some women of the garrison, the hard-pressed surgeons did what they could for the new arrivals, but it was little enough, for the hospital no longer possessed even basic medical necessities. Every corner was now occupied, the floors could not be swept, bedding and bandages were lacking, and there were too few helpers even to respond to the constantly reiterated pleas for water, which echoed from end to end of the evil-smelling, airless ward.

General Havelock was accustomed to the hideous sights and sounds of field hospitals after battle, but even he hesitated momentarily before entering this one. The men lay on bloodstained straw palliasses or on the bare ground, some in their own excreta, the cholera and dysentery cases cheek by jowl with those who had sustained gunshot, bayonet, and saber wounds during the recent fighting. Here a poor wretch, his weight reduced to that of a child, spewed his heart out, the vomit tinged with blood; there a bearded veteran, with leeches clinging obscenely to both arms, stormed and raged in delirium, while beside him another—all too conscious of his surroundings—prayed quietly to his Maker to put an end to his torment.

Few of them had, as yet, had their wounds dressed or their makeshift bandages changed; they lay in their dusty, blood-caked uniforms, just as they had entered, and waited with varying degrees of stoicism until someone would have time to attend to their needs. A number, with fractured or shattered limbs, had been waiting since the previous night for amputation, compelled to witness the operation being performed on others at a table in the center of the ward, around which they had been grouped in

the order of their admission. They knew that, although the waiting list was long, their turn would inevitably come—unless death
came first—since amputation offered the only chance of recovery they had.

The two surgeons on duty at the operating table sweated in
the heat from the oil lanterns suspended above it. They worked
with practiced speed and dexterity, but they had already been at
the table for several hours, and, while fatigue had rendered neither less skillful, it had induced in both a shortness of temper,
which they were inclined to vent on any man who displayed
reluctance to place himself in their hands. Lucknow's supply of
chloroform—which had, initially, enabled amputations to be performed without the terrible pain normally associated with the
loss of a limb—had long since been exhausted. Laudanum was
reserved for the desperately sick, so that the man who must sub-
mit himself to the ordeal of knife and hacksaw was expected to
do so without fuss, fortified at best by a draught of rum or porter
and held down by orderlies, whom long habit had inured to the
pain of others.

The surgeons' skill lay in the speed with which they could
slice through skin and bone and muscle, and no time was wasted
in cleaning instruments or washing hands between one operation
and the next. In bloody, sweat-soaked white coats, they worked
with scarcely a pause, seeking thus to minimize the shock induced
by pain. Within a matter of minutes, a double flap of skin was
fashioned to allow for shrinkage and muscle contraction, the
injured limb was severed and discarded, ligatures applied to
control bleeding, and the flap stitched into place in such a way
as to permit the drainage of pus, still considered "laudable" by
the leading body of medical opinion.

In hospitals throughout the world, the percentage of deaths

following amputation varied between 25 and 60—in Lucknow's one-time banqueting hall only one or two had survived their terrible ordeal since the siege began. Pyemia, erysipelas, and what had come to be known as "hospital gangrene" killed even men who had been in tough fighting condition when they were admitted. Infection was rampant, and many, whose wounds required no more than probing for a bullet, had succumbed to it. The surgeons despairingly attributed their high mortality rate to congestion and tainted air, little realizing that they themselves were conveying the dreaded septic diseases from one patient to another through the medium of contaminated hands and unsterilized instruments. As yet the existence of microorganisms and the part these played in the spread of infection was unsuspected; Lister's theories and experiments in antisepsis had barely begun, while those of Semmelweis, in far-off Vienna, had been almost universally ignored or ridiculed as the ravings of a madman.

Within the boundaries of their knowledge and experience of battle casualties—much of it gained in the Crimea—the military surgeons did the best they could, but Havelock, as a fighting general, was only too well aware of the suffering his wounded men were called upon to endure and the risks they ran, even in the best-equipped hospitals. During the campaign in Oudh and after the return of his Field Force, decimated by cholera, to Cawnpore, he had deemed it his duty to pay regular visits to the hospitals. Careless of his own safety, he had spent long hours at the bedsides of sick and injured alike, his prayers often the only solace he could offer to those facing the long, slow agony of death or maimed recovery. A deeply religious man, convinced that his prayers would be heard by the God to whom they were directed, he prepared to offer them now. Picking up a pitcher of water and a ladle, he went resolutely and compassionately about his task, a small, erect, white-haired figure, whose eyes were misted with tears.

At the operating table, Surgeon Charles Scott of Her Majesty's 32nd recognized him with dismay, and, cursing under his breath, said resentfully to his assistant, "For God's sweet sake, Dickie, that's General Havelock, isn't it? Does he expect us to stop and take him on a tour of inspection, d'you suppose?"

The Hospital Sergeant of the 78th Highlanders answered his outburst, the sibilant Ross-shire voice reproachful. "He will expect nothing of the kind, Doctor. General Havelock is coming here for to visit his soldiers, and he will not be thanking you if you interrupt your work to receive him."

"Man, I stand corrected!" Surgeon Scott exclaimed wryly. "I'd no idea he was that sort of general—thank you for enlightening me, Sergeant Walker." He passed a blood-smeared hand across his streaming brow and reached for his scalpel. "Right, then, let's have the next! What is it—another leg?" To the shrinking drummer boy in the crumpled scarlet cotton tunic of the 5th Fusiliers, who was sobbing for his mother, he said with gruff reassurance, "Never fear, laddie, we'll have that leg off you before you know it. It's only hanging by a few sinews. There . . ." he sliced deftly and took a ligature from the cluster threaded through his coat lapel. "This had better be cauterized, Dickie, before we stitch it up. Let's have the pernitrate, if you please." The boy's sobs became a shriek, as the pernitrate of mercury bit into the flesh of his stump, and Sergeant Walker, struggling to hold his tortured body still, sternly bade him be silent, lest the general hear his screams. To Scott's astonishment, the boy obeyed him and, as he stitched the wound, the surgeon asked, with more than a hint of sarcasm, "Do his soldiers appreciate the general's visits, Sergeant?"

"Indeed they do, sir," the grizzled Highlander returned.

"Indeed they do." He lifted the slight body of the little drummer from the table and carried him across to where Havelock knelt with his water pitcher. "Here's a brave laddie who is deserving of your prayers, General Havelock, sir," he stated simply and laid the boy down beside him.

Havelock smiled. "Very well, Sergeant Walker," he acknowledged. "You may leave him with me." He dipped his ladle into the pitcher and, an arm round the boy's shoulders, invited him to drink. "Now, Drummer," he announced, "We will say a prayer together. Almighty God, Father of All Men, the only Giver of Peace . . ." his voice carried almost the length of the ward, and the men lying there started, in twos and threes, to join in, their responses an oddly contrasting echo to the distant thunder of the guns.

"Great Jumping Jehoshaphat!" Surgeon Scott exploded. "Now I have seen everything, damn me if I haven't!"

"With respect, sir, you have not," his next patient informed him. He braced himself, half on, half off the operating table and held out his left arm, bared to the shoulder, directing the probe for the spent bullet that was lodged there with professional exactitude. "Assistant Surgeon Bradshaw, Her Majesty's 90th," he explained, in answer to Scott's question and added, with a grin, "About our general, doctor . . . you haven't seen him fight, have you?"

"No," the garrison surgeon admitted. "But I'm beginning to believe the stories I've been hearing about him. Leads his troops from the front, they say, and every man jack is prepared to follow him anywhere?"

"To hell and back, sir," Bradshaw claimed proudly. He winced as the probe was twisted, deep in the deltoid muscle of his arm, but a moment later, it was withdrawn and Scott, with a grunt of satisfaction, displayed a flattened lump of metal on his palm.

"There's your musket-ball, my friend. You're lucky, it's done little damage. But now I'm afraid I'll have to trouble you for your shirttail if you want the arm dressed. We're out of bandages. Tell me . . ." he worked busily. "You were with the wounded from the Moti Mahal this morning, were you not? How many are missing, do you know?"

Bradshaw shook his head. "I shall try to find out, as soon as you've finished with me. General Havelock also wants to be informed. At least forty, I fear, including Dr. Home of my regiment, and possibly the general's son."

"No, he was brought in." Surgeon Scott glanced across at the kneeling figure in the faded blue frock coat and shrugged. "At least the poor old man has that to thank his God for, hasn't he?"

The light was fading when sheer exhaustion compelled General Havelock to bring his visit to an end. As he walked stiffly toward the main door, Surgeon Bradshaw caught up with him and, belatedly recalling Sir James's request, Havelock asked if Captain Becher had been among the survivors of the convoy.

"No, sir, I regret to say he hasn't been brought in," Bradshaw answered. "Lieutenant Arnold of the Madras Fusiliers is missing too, and I've been told that Colonel Sheridan of the Volunteer Cavalry was last seen with Surgeon Home, of ours, sir, in the square where we were attacked. Mr. Thornhill was with the survivors. He—"

"I have seen poor young Thornhill," Havelock put in, his tone bleak. "He was able to tell me very little, and he's sinking fast."

"I'm sorry, sir," Bradshaw responded politely. He offered a few sheets of paper torn from a notebook. "I've made out a list of the missing, sir, as well as I could from the information available. It's not complete but . . ."

Eventually it would be completed, Havelock thought sadly. Harry had said that it was of little use to hope that any of the missing would have survived, but perhaps the rear-guard, when they joined up with Napier's reinforcements and commenced their withdrawal from the Moti Mahal, perhaps they would be able to send a party to the scene of the ambush to make sure. He would have to send orders to . . . no, Outram was in command now, not himself. He would have to find Outram and request that a search be made. He took the crumpled sheets of paper from the young assistant surgeon, thanked him and continued on his way to the main door of the hospital.

"God bless you, sir!" one of the Highlanders called after him, and those who had the strength to raise their voices gave him a ragged cheer.

He had called them his "camp of heroic soldiers" at Mungalwar, he recalled, and they had more than merited that description. But now, alas, the butcher's bill had to be paid. His throat was tight and his heart heavy as he walked slowly out into the gathering darkness.

Colonel Napier's reinforcements, ably guided by the civilian clerk, Henry Kavanagh, and aided by Lieutenant Moorsom's survey maps, emerged from the Furhut Baksh Palace and onto the narrow path along the bank of the river. They met with no opposition and, joined by the small force of the 32nd and a half-company of the 78th, which, under Captain Lowe, had earlier cleared the Kaptan's Bazaar area, they advanced to Martin's House through the enclosed part of the Chutter Munzil gardens held by a detachment of the 90th. The Chutter Munzil itself was given as wide a berth as possible and, after halting until dusk behind the walls of Martin's House, Napier left a holding party there to reinforce the 5th Fusiliers and the Sikhs, and led his main body to the Moti Mahal, braving heavy cannon and musketry fire as he crossed the open ground between the two positions.

Colonel Robert Napier had joined Sir James Outram as chief of staff and military secretary, but until now—since his chief had renounced command of the Relief Force to General Havelock— his official status had been that of a volunteer, and he had chafed at the limitations of the advisory capacity in which this chivalrous action had placed him. Now, relishing his first opportunity to command a force in active opposition to the enemy, he was determined that nothing like this morning's tragic error should mar the successful evacuation of the rear-guard.

His fighting record had been a distinguished one, in both Sikh campaigns and later in fiercely contested battles against the Afridis on the Northwest Frontier, at the conclusion of each of which he had figured prominently in the official dispatches and won brevet promotion. A studious, cultured man, he was also an exceptionally able engineer and, as chief engineer of the Punjab, he had directed the construction of the great highway between Peshawar and Lahore and completed the monumental task in a little under three years. By comparison, the task facing him now was a simple one, but he set about it with characteristic forethought and efficiency.

The gallant Colonel Campbell, exhausted and in great pain from the wound in his leg, was ordered into a *doolie* and, under the escort of Captain Hardinge's Sikh cavalrymen, he and a second convoy of wounded were sent, under Kavanagh's guidance, safely back to the Residency by the river bank route. Hardinge returned, with a fresh supply of *doolies,* to report that he had seen no sign of the enemy and, by a little after midnight, all the sick and wounded had been taken in, together with the reserves of ammunition, laden onto camels.

With the fall of darkness, the bombardment had ceased, and scouts reported that, although the guns ringing the Moti Mahal were still in position, the majority of the besieging infantry appeared to have withdrawn. Only the twenty-four-pounder, still jammed—seemingly inextricably—between two walls in a narrow lane in front of the palace prevented Napier from ordering an immediate withdrawal. The heavy gun defied all efforts to remove it, and rebel marksmen, posted behind the loopholed walls of the 32nd's former mess house, kept the approaches to it under constant and accurate fire. They had its range measured to a foot and, even after dark, contrived to maintain both their vigilance and their accuracy.

Already the abortive attempts to reach it had cost several lives, including that of the Brigade Artillery officer, Major Cooper. Faced with the prospect of finding a safe alternative route for both Eyre's heavy guns—since the narrow, twisting path by the river was practicable only for *doolies* and camels in single file—Napier was tempted to order them blown up and abandoned, rather than risk incurring more casualties trying to save them.

Captain Jack Olpherts, however, accompanied by Lieutenant Crump, Eyre's second-in-command, pleaded to be allowed to make one final attempt to dislodge the jammed monster and, with a reluctance he made not the smallest pretense of hiding, Napier agreed.

"I want to get our whole force out of here while the going's good," he told them. "Young Knight of the 90th has just been brought in, shot through both legs. He says he made his escape from the ambushed *doolies* late this afternoon—the only man who did, apparently. According to him, some of our people are holding one of the houses. He doesn't know how many, but he heard them firing and thinks they may still be alive, so I must investigate . . . and be damned to your gun, gentlemen! It's cost us too much as it is." He sighed and went on, his tone one that brooked no argument, "I'll give you half an hour to get *both* guns on the road. If you can't, then they're to be blown up, is that clear? The infernal things should have been left in the Alam Bagh, as Sir James advised. It was madness to bring them with the ground in the waterlogged state it is—and without any elephants to draw them!"

The two artillery officers exchanged rueful glances, but neither offered any comment. It had been General Havelock who had insisted on bringing Eyre's twenty-four-pounders, and yesterday, when they had made their final advance on the Residency, those guns had proved their worth. The battery commander, Major Vincent Eyre, had been taken to the Residency, suffering from an attack of fever and his young second-in-command said indignantly, when they were out of earshot, "Bloody staff, always knowing best, as usual! Over my dead body will Napier abandon those guns to the blasted Pandies. I tell you, Jack, I gave my word they'd be brought in and—"

"Don't you worry, old son," Jack Olpherts retorted. "We've got half an hour, haven't we, and our plan of action worked out? Duffy's so small, the Pandies won't spot him—so come on, let's see if we've done our sums right." His jaw obstinately set, he stalked over to his patiently waiting bullock teams, and the man who had volunteered to assist him, a stocky little private of the Madras Fusiliers named Duffy, picked up the length of rope he had been working on and said breathlessly, "I'm ready, sorr, when you are."

"Get your breath, man—you'll need it," Olpherts chided him. He subjected the chain that had been lashed to the end of the rope to a careful inspection and nodded, satisfied. "Right, you know what to do. Crawl out slowly and keep in the shadow of the wall. Above all, don't rush—if they fire on you, freeze, and remember they can't see you, they're firing blind. We will try to draw their fire, in any case, and Mr. Crump will cover you. When you get to the gun, use it as cover, and take your time . . . understand?"

"To be sure I do, sorr." Duffy grinned, his smoke-blackened, unshaven face aglow with excitement. "And when I have the rope secured, I'm to leg it back to you with the end and—"

"You're to crawl back slowly," Olpherts corrected. "Right, off you go and good luck, lad!"

Duffy obediently set off, bent low, with Crump after him, armed with an Enfield. He adhered to his instructions until he reached the wall he had to climb; then, vaulting nimbly over it, he ran, and Crump was hard put to keep up with him. Shots spattered the ground all about them, but in the dim light, the two crouching, shadowy figures presented an elusive target, and the riflemen Olpherts had mustered to answer the rebels' fire effectively distracted their attention. Duffy flung his small body flat beneath the gun and, under its massive cover, took his time attaching his rope, in strict accordance with Olpherts's orders, Crump lying behind him to make sure that he did.

"'Tis done, sorr," he announced, breathing hard. "'Tis through the trail."

"Good lad!" Crump said. "Right, then—back with you to Captain Olpherts."

Duffy needed no urging. He was off, the end of the rope secured to his belt, wriggling and squirming his way back to where Olpherts waited. The battery commander took the rope from him, pulled in the slack and, as the heavy chain rattled into place, he made it fast to the limber, and Crump, dashing back to join him, yelled to the drivers to get their bullock teams in motion. The animals heaved and strained, men on either side urging them on with yells and curses, while others put their shoulders to the wheels of the limber and pushed. It was a laborious task, even with two teams of bullocks yoked to the limber, but the great gun, at long last, started to move. It came free with a crash of shattered masonry, as part of the retaining wall collapsed, permitting its huge, iron-shod wheels to turn. A fusillade of shots came from the mess house sharpshooters, and Crump, who had gone forward to free the chain from an obstacle, went down with a strangled cry.

He was dead when Duffy got to him, but the gun, ponderously, reluctantly it seemed, was moving out of the lane now, and, well within Colonel Napier's stipulated thirty minutes, it was safe and under cover in the outer courtyard of the Moti Mahal Palace.

At 3 A.M. the night became overcast, the moon was obscured, and rain started to fall in a steady torrent. With no sign of enemy activity between the Moti Mahal and Martin's House, Napier gave the order for the evacuation of the rear-guard to begin. The picket he had dispatched to investigate Lieutenant Knight's report had been driven back by a large force of the enemy, but they, too, had reported firing from a house in the square in which the *doolies* had been ambushed and a sergeant asserted that he had heard the sound of British voices, cheering them on.

"We'll get those infernal guns parked, under guard, in the Chutter Munzil garden enclosure," Napier told Colonel Stisted of the 78th, as they passed Martin's House, and its weary defenders thankfully prepared to form up in their rear. "And then Moorsom says he can guide us through the palace and close enough to the square where the *doolies* were abandoned to make a reconnaissance in strength. If any of our fellows *are* still holding out there, I'd like to get them out if I can."

"You can count on my support, of course," the Highlanders' commander assured him. "But do you really think we can get them out?"

"We can have a damned good try. There's just one thing that worries me though . . ." Napier hesitated, peering anxiously into the rain-wet darkness to where, ahead of them, Captain Hardinge and his sowars were spread out, scouting the river bank and the open ground they were about to cross.

"What's worrying you?" Stisted asked. "The absence of opposition?"

"Yes," Napier admitted. "What the devil d'you suppose they're playing at? I mean to say, we're not exactly moving silently, are we? Those blasted guns are enough to give us away . . . damn it, the Pandies must know we're on the move. After attacking us all day, are they just going to let us walk into the Residency?"

"It's to be hoped they will," Stisted returned wryly. "I've had enough fighting to do me for a while. But . . ." he shrugged. "The possibility of an ambush has to be considered, and the Chutter Munzil would seem to me to be the most likely place for them to lie in wait for us. Unless, of course, they're expecting us to follow the route we took yesterday—through the square where the wounded were massacred."

Napier turned in his saddle to look at him in surprise. "Why the devil should they expect us to do that?"

"They'll know we can't bring the guns in by the river path. And they miscalculated yesterday—they expected us to take the direct route, along the Cawnpore road from the Char Bagh. Our detour took them completely by surprise."

"True," Napier conceded. "I think, Stisted, that we shall have to try to outwit them. Link up with the detachments in the Furhut Baksh and McCabe's party in the Terhee Kothee and flush 'em out of the Chutter Munzil, if they're there. It will delay us a little, but if we don't do it, it won't be safe to park those guns. And I intend to park 'em. The general is going to occupy all the palaces tomorrow and include them within the Residency perimeter, so the guns can be brought to where they're needed then. I'll have a word with Moorsom and . . ." he was interrupted by the crackle of musketry, coming from the Chutter Munzil enclosure and growing in volume. "What the devil!" He flung a crisp order to his galloper and, as Stisted swiftly deployed the 78th, set spurs to his horse and rode forward to join the advancing line of skirmishers as they approached the enclosure in open order and with bayonets fixed.

"Pandies, Colonel—several hundred of them!" Colonel Purnell, who was in command of the detachment of the 90th, informed him, when he reached the enclosure. "They're in a walled garden behind this one, on the city side of the river. They must have been skulking there for some time. Captain McCabe discovered them when he came through from the Furhut Baksh. My men are ready to go in, and I've sent word to McCabe . . . we'll catch them in a cross-fire and then go in with the bayonet —subject to your approval, of course."

"You have my approval and my blessing," Napier assured him. "I want to park my guns and wagons here for the night, so let us get the whole area cleared while we're about it. In you go and good luck to you! I'll support you with the 78th if necessary."

"Thank you, sir," Purnell acknowledged and drew his sword.

CHAPTER FOUR

➳➳➳ • ⬅⬅⬅

IN THE SHED on the north side of the square a strange, menacing silence reigned. There had been no attempt on the part of the rebels to set the refuge on fire, to Alex's relief, but the stealthy pad of feet on the roof warned him to take no chances. He posted Webb and Roddy at one end of the shed, Cameron and McManus at the other and, assisted by Ryan—who had staggered to his feet like a sleepwalker, on hearing his name called—he completed the removal of the wounded into the passageway, ready for their anticipated flight.

Lieutenant Swanson was unconscious and made no sound, Murphy screamed in delirium, and poor Andrew Becher, holding his shattered jaw between his hands, maintained his enforced silence, although, he all too evidently, was fully conscious. Lieutenant Arnold, who had lain motionless and stoically uncomplaining for most of the day, talking in occasional whispers to Becher and the men who tended him, asked them to sit him up, and it was evident that he, too, was fully aware of the perils of their situation when he offered to hold off pursuit with a revolver.

"Leave me and make your escape, Colonel Sheridan, with the fit men," he pleaded. With infinite effort, the sweat pouring down his haggard cheeks, he took his Colt from the waistband of his trousers and held it up with courageous steadiness. "I can still use this, I promise you—and I'll see they don't follow you. Don't worry," he added, as Alex started to shake his head. "I heard what happened to those other poor devils in the *doolies*. I shall keep the last shot for myself."

Becher painfully grunted his approval of this suggestion and Ryan, who had listened to it with dismay, dropped to his knees beside the Blue Cap officer. Looking up at Alex, he said quietly, "I'll stay with Mr. Arnold, sir. We could hold them bastards off between us—long enough for you to get across to that house with the others, anyway. I can't leave him behind, sir. He's my officer and it wouldn't be right."

Arnold let the Colt fall and his hand closed about the young Blue Cap's. "Good man, Ryan," he whispered. "And God bless you! But you've got a chance and you've got to take it. I'm finished in any case . . . for God's sake, look at my legs! You go with Colonel Sheridan and the others."

"We're not leaving anyone," Alex told them firmly. He forced his dry lips into a smile. "Good Lord, we're not beaten yet! We've held our own all day, and the rear-guard will start to move out soon—it's practically dark. We shan't have to wait much longer. When Hollowell and the doctor get back, we'll move into a more substantial building, which will be less malodorous and a darned sight easier to defend than this hovel. Cut along and watch out for them, will you, Ryan?" Ryan rose and went obediently to the hole in the wall behind them and, when he was out of earshot, Arnold said, a note of strain in his voice, "Colonel Sheridan, I really do think you should leave Captain Becher, Swanson, and myself here. Without us, you could fight your way to the rear-guard and—"

"I told you, we're not leaving anyone. We—"

"With respect, sir," Lieutenant Arnold interrupted. "We shall all be killed if we just stay here, depending on the rear-guard to come to our rescue. For pity's sake, they probably imagine we're dead already. The doctor as good as said so, didn't he?"

He was right, Alex thought dully. Colonel Campbell would have no means of knowing of their continued presence in the square; the firing would not be heard above the roar of the cannon outside the Moti Mahal and, whatever reports he might have received, they would be unlikely to include any mention of a small party of men, cut off in the city. In any event, Campbell had problems of his own. The evacuation of the rear-guard and whatever reinforcements had been sent to him would have to be his first consideration. He . . .

"Look at us," Arnold went on. "Swanson's dying, if he's not dead already, Captain Becher's had half his face shot away, and as for myself . . ." he gestured to his legs. "In God's name, sir, if you bring me in, it will only be for the sawbones to take my legs off. A good clean bullet from this," he tapped his Colt, "is infinitely to be preferred. And they wouldn't take us alive, I'll guarantee that."

Alex sighed. His logic was irrefutable but . . . Ryan's low-voiced warning saved him from the necessity for a reply.

"They're coming, sir—the doctor and Hollowell! And they're carrying something . . . a water *chatti,* I think, sir."

A few shots from the rebels on top of the roof shattered the silence, but their vigilance left as much to be desired as their marksmanship and Home and Hollowell clambered unhurt through the gap in the wall, breathless but triumphant as they exhibited their prize. The *chatti* was barely three-quarters full of lukewarm water, but it tasted like nectar to the parched and weary men, even Becher contriving somehow to swallow his share in slow, agonized sips through the clumsy bandage wound about his mouth and lower jaw. Flagging spirits were revived when Surgeon Home described the house across the courtyard.

"It might have been made by Providence for our defense," Home said. "The walls are thick, the doorways few, and there is a spacious courtyard on the far side, overlooking a walled garden, about sixty or seventy yards beyond. Hollowell thinks the garden is part of the Chutter Munzil Bagh, but I'm not sure. It could be, but we didn't really get a very good look at it. It was crawling with rebels, and we didn't dare show ourselves."

"And the house?" Alex questioned. "Was it unoccupied?"

"As far as we could make out it was, yes. I thought—" the Doctor hesitated.

"Well?" Alex prompted, sensing his uneasiness.

"Well, Colonel, although as I said, it's a very much better defensive position than this one, I fear we may have some difficulty in transferring ourselves to it. They have men posted on the roof, as you know—perhaps if we wait until it's completely dark, we might manage to get our wounded men across without their seeing us and opening fire. But if they do . . ." Home spread his hands despairingly. "They might well bring the mob we saw in the walled garden down on us before we could enter the house."

"Then you think we should remain here until it's dark?"

"Or until we hear the rear-guard coming in and then make a run for it."

"I see."

Alex turned to Hollowell, and the Highlander, forestalling his question, said with conviction, "Aye, sir, the doctor's right. The walled garden is the south side o' the Chutter Munzil enclosure, I'm pretty sure, and I'd say there were at the verra least five hundred Pandies there. We canna risk attracting their attention."

"The fit men could get into the house, sir," Arnold began. "If you'd—"

"No." Alex shook his head, his mind made up. "We'll sink or swim together, my friend. If Hollowell's right about the position of the Chutter Munzil garden, we're near enough to the route the rear-guard will take to be reasonably sure of hearing them, so we'll get what rest we can, while we can. Two fit men will act as sentries for the first hour, then they'll be relieved by two others . . ." he arranged a roster, putting himself on for the first hour with Roddy.

There were no alarms; except for the occasional footfall overhead, the rebels appeared content to leave them in peace. Probably because they were preparing to attack the rear-guard when it left the Moti Mahal, he thought wryly, but Colonel Campbell or whoever was in command would be expecting an attack and certainly would not leave the Moti Mahal unless and until he had been substantially reinforced. Campbell had said that Colonel Napier, of Sir James Outram's staff, was expected but had not yet arrived and . . . Alex's tired brain could not be cudgeled into remembering. It all seemed a very long time ago, as he paced slowly up and down in front of the hole in the wall in an effort to keep himself awake. He ought, he knew, to make a personal inspection of the house across the courtyard, but he was too exhausted to do so now, and he decided to wait until he had snatched an hour's sleep, at least. They were all exhausted; it was essential that they rest before attempting to move from their present quarters, for they would need all the strength and reserves of energy they could muster, in case they had to fight their way through to join the rear-guard, hampered by four severely wounded men. Whatever poor Arnold said, whatever sacrifices he was willing to offer, the wounded could not be left . . . Alex peered through the broken wall into the courtyard, listening intently, and then wearily resumed his pacing.

He wakened Cameron and McManus at the end of the allotted hour and, after instructing them to call him at once if anything untoward occurred, lay down on the mud floor and fell instantly asleep.

A sudden burst of firing and the rush of feet overhead roused them all. Alex, from the habit learned so painfully in the Cawnpore entrenchment, wakened as instantly as he had fallen asleep, alert and in possession of all his faculties, and it was he who first realized that the firing was not one-sided . . . some of it, at least, was coming from British Enfields.

"Cheer, my lads, cheer for all you're worth!" he bade them. "Those are our fellows—let's make sure they know we're here!"

The men, wild with excitement, responded with a will, the sound of their voices rising above the crackle of musketry.

"Europeans!" the surgeon yelled. "We're Europeans!" "Charge them, boys—charge them!" Ryan urged and Hollowell, keeping his wits about him, shouted out directions.

"Keep to your right, lads! They're holding the square!"

They raised a concerted cheer; McManus and Cameron fired their rifles through the broken wall, and they waited tensely for some sight or sound that would tell them that relief was on its way and their ordeal over. It did not come. Abruptly the firing ceased, and they looked at each other in shocked dismay, unable at first to take it in.

"They were so near," Ryan said brokenly. "So near . . . sod them, they must have heard us. Oh, sod them, sod them!"

"They were beaten back, lad," Hollowell told him. "They couldna get tae us. But wasna for want o' trying—there were too few o' them, that's a'."

"Probably a small picket," Alex added, again thankful for the veteran Highlander's calm common sense. "Scouting the route for the rear-guard. But they must have heard us and, if they did, they'll report our presence, which gives us a chance." He was anxious to keep up their spirits, determined not to let them yield to despair but, as he talked on, he sensed their bitter disappointment and was hard put not to reveal his own.

Surgeon Home came valiantly to his support. "Could we not move into the house, Colonel?" he suggested. "It would be worth the risk, surely, because we'd be that much nearer the rear-guard when they come."

"Or maybe we could get tae the Residency through the square," McManus offered thoughtfully. "While the Pandies are concerning themselves wi' the rear-guard. Will I gang tae look, sir?"

Roddy answered him, his voice flat, "Sure and I looked, sorr, when our chaps were firin' . . . they've not gone, there are more of them than ever. Meself, I'd say they're waiting i0 n the hope of serving the rear-guard the way they served us this morning. They're expecting them to come this way, that's for certain."

McManus swore. He limped across to the door of the shed, which Roddy had been guarding, and Alex followed him, ducking behind a pillar for a better view of the square. "They've lighted a fire, sir," the Fusilier said disgustedly. "Bloody bastards. they're burning what's left o' our men in the *doolies,* and there are hundreds o' the swine . . . in the houses and outside them. Roddy's right—they *are* expecting the rear-guard tae come this way!"

It was unlikely in the extreme that Colonel Campbell would repeat this morning's tragic mistake, Alex thought—the rear-guard would use the river path, linking up with the detachments in the Terhee Kothee and the Furhut Baksh Palaces and perhaps clearing the Chutter Munzil, if they had sufficient strength to do so, and if they had brought the heavy guns out with them. The rebels had miscalculated . . . he returned to the passageway and, in a few crisp words, explained his deductions and saw the faces about him, white and strained in the moonlight filtering through from the courtyard outside, relax and lose some of their tension.

"You're sure the rear-guard will not come through the square, as we did?" Surgeon Home asked.

"As sure as I can be. Our coming was a mistake—our guide took the wrong turning, and that fact will be known to the rear-guard commander by this time. Colonel Napier was to lead the reinforcements, and he'll have Lieutenant Moorsom to advise and guide him. Moorsom knows Lucknow like the back of his hand . . ." Alex paused, letting his words sink in.

"Then 'tis the house for us, sir, is it?" Hollowell suggested shrewdly. "We canna gang through the square, so 'tis either the house or we maun bide where we are?"

"That's about the size of it, Hollowell." Alex cut short Arnold's attempt to interrupt him. The Blue Cap lieutenant was much weaker than he had been even a couple of hours before; it was doubtful now whether he could, for all his courage, manage to use his revolver and, recognizing this, he did not argue, and Alex went on, his tone decisive, "I'll go and make sure that the house is still unoccupied. If it is, I'll come back and we'll decide whether to move across right away or wait until we hear the rear-guard coming. We'd be nearer their route if we move, but . . ." he frowned, remembering what Arnold had said earlier. If the fit men could fight their way through to the rear-guard, a single fit man would stand a better than even chance of getting through—even past enemy pickets, if he spoke the language and . . . he looked down at his uniform. Stained and crumpled, his loose fitting white cotton tunic and breeches resembled native cavalry undress and, if he removed his pith helmet and retained only the *pugree* that was wound about it, he could almost certainly pass himself off as a sowar. Had he not done so before, had he not ridden from Sheorajpore to Batinda in similar guise, without arousing suspicion or provoking a single challenge? He started to unwind his *pugree*.

"What are you doing?" Surgeon Home asked, with weary curiosity.

Alex told him. "If I see an opportunity to make contact with any of our pickets, I shall take it and bring help as soon as I can. Be so good as to hold the end of this *pugree* for me . . . thanks, that's fine." He straightened up, the cloth now firmly wound about his head, and taking the Adams from his belt, checked its six chambers and asked, smiling, "Do I pass muster?"

Home raised an answering smile. "Indeed you do—so well that you will have to take care our own people don't fire on you."

"Right, then I'll be on my way. I'll signal my intention by giving you a whistle. Like this," he demonstrated, "which will mean that the house is unoccupied and I've gone. In that case, Doctor, you can either come across or stay where you are. For the sake of the wounded men, it might be better if you stay, but it will be up to you to decide. Rest assured that if I'm able to make contact with the rear-guard, I'll send help to you immediately."

The surgeon nodded his understanding. "But if you find the enemy in occupation of the house, Colonel, what then? You'll come back, won't you?"

Alex shrugged. "Yes—unless there's a chance that I can get past them without being seen. If there is, I'll take it . . . but you will get no signal."

Hollowell, who had been listening intently to their conversation, checked the contents of his cartridge pouch and picked up his rifle. "I'll come wi' you, sir," he offered. "If yon house is occupied, we'll stand a better chance if there's twa of us. There's an eight-foot wall tae climb if you're wantin' in tae the enclosure on the far side—you'll no' manage that by yoursel'. I can help ye over it and then come back tae report. can I no'?"

It was a sensible suggestion and Alex accepted it gratefully. "Right—come on, then. We'll take it slowly and carefully— we don't want those swine on the roof loosing off at us if we can help it. How many rounds do you have left?"

"Four, sir. But I've this." Hollowell grinned, indicating his long bayonet.

"It's dark enough, anyway," Surgeon Home said. "Good luck!"

Outside in the courtyard it was, indeed, darker than Alex had expected, the moon no longer visible and rain starting to fall heavily. Either this had driven the watchers on the roof to seek shelter or else they had fallen asleep, for no one moved and no shots were fired as he and Hollowell climbed through the sagging wall of the shed and made their way cautiously to the house. It was in darkness and Alex, making a stealthy inspection of the rear, could detect no sign of any occupants. He pushed open a heavy, iron-bound door, which creaked alarmingly on rusty hinges; waited, pistol in hand and, when nothing happened, he turned left, following Hollowell's whispered directions, to find himself in a long, low room with shuttered windows, of which he could make out little, save that it was empty.

"There's not a soul here, sir," Hollowell reported, after investigating the room beyond. "And hasna been for a gey long while." He sniffed disparagingly. "The smell puts me in mind o' ma grannie's auld house in the Broomielaw when I was a wee laddie . . . musty and damp, wi' open sewers! But 'tis cleaner than yon shed, there's that tae be said for it. Will we hoe a look in the courtyard now, sir—the one that backs on tae the walled garden?"

Alex nodded. He asked, as they returned less cautiously to the rear of the house, "If you're a Glasgow man, Hollowell, what are you doing in a Highland regiment?"

Hollowell gave vent to a low chuckle. "I fancied ma'sel' in the kilt, sir! And I've nae regrets—nae serious regrets—after fifteen years wi' the regiment. To your right here, sir."

The wall into the further courtyard was, as he had warned, a good eight feet high, the arched gateway into it locked and barred. "Up on my shoulders, sir," the Highlander invited, when they had waited, listening intently for some moments, without hearing anything to arouse their suspicions. "The walled garden is away over tae the left," he added. "It wasn' dark when I was here before wi' the surgeon, so we were able tae see into it frae the top o' this wall. And as I said, sir, the whole garden was swarming wi' Pandies, so have a care."

Alex clambered onto the wall. He located the walled enclosure but, in the rain-wet darkness, could discern no movement to suggest the presence of several hundred rebel troops. If they were there, they were keeping pretty quiet; the only sound was a spasmodic crackle of musketry, coming from the direction of the Moti Mahal, a sound that, intermingled with the thunder of heavy guns, had been going on for most of the day.

"Can ye see anything, sir?" Hollowell asked anxiously. "Are the Pandies still there?"

Alex eased the Adams into his belt, ready to hand. "No," he began, "no, I . . ." and stiffened as, from the walled enclosure below, a man coughed and—almost as if it were a signal—a number of others followed suit. The coughing came from different sides of the enclosure and he knew that, although he could not see them, men were there, probably as many as Hollowell had estimated earlier. They were there and they were waiting . . . He moved to an angle in the wall and stood up, trying to orient himself and locate their exact position.

The Chutter Munzil was ahead of him and to his left, Martin's House and the Moti Mahal perhaps half a mile away and to his right—musketry fire was still coming from that direction, which meant that the rear-guard was holding both positions and had not yet attempted to evacuate them. He could not see the river—even if the darkness had not blotted it out, the intervening bulk of the Chutter Munzil would have done so—but he knew where it was in relation to the enclosure and his own position and remembered suddenly that, this morning, when he and Bensley Thornhill had passed through it on the river side, a British detachment had been holding part of the walled garden enclosure. Part but not all . . . the rebels had seized an adjoining enclosure on the south side, between the Hirun Khana—the Deer Park—and the river and were probably in the Hirun Khana in considerable numbers as well.

Private Roddy had been right—more right than he knew—the rebels were not only expecting the rear-guard to take this route to the Residency, they were gambling all they had in the conviction that no other route was possible, although why was anybody's guess. Unless . . . Alex drew in his breath sharply, conscious of a sudden chill about his heart. Surely they were not gambling on his small, exhausted party to bait a trap for the rearguard? Even if they were, Colonel Campbell was too experienced a soldier to be drawn by such a bait—Napier, too, of course, if he had superseded Campbell in command. Neither would risk his command for the sake of a handful of men, holed up in the heart of the city, who might at any time be overcome when their ammunition ran out. A handful of men who could have been overcome several hours ago, if the enemy had pressed home their attack. For God's sake, there were hundreds of them in the square—one determined rush would have done it! But there had been no rush, no second attempt to burn them out, no more firing, even, through the flimsy roof of the shed. The rebels had held off, almost certainly because they had been ordered to hold off, and he and Hollowell had been permitted to cross the courtyard unmolested . . . Hollowell, in his all too conspicuous scarlet jacket and kilt! Which could add up to only one conclusion . . . he swore under his breath and Hollowell, hearing him, asked anxiously if there was anything wrong.

"I'm afraid there may be," Alex admitted. He slid down from the wall and, in a few whispered words, explained his doubts and fears. "I may be wrong—it's possible that they're counting on the heavy guns to force the rear-guard to take the route through the square. But we daren't take a chance on that, Hollowell."

"No, sir," Hollowell agreed, with bleak resignation. "So what are we tae do, sir?"

"We must evacuate that shed at once, get the wounded across to the house," Alex told him. "We're on our own, lad—we can't ask for help . . . we'll be leading our own people into an ambush if we do, in all probability. Go back and tell Dr. Home and the others, will you? Tell them it will be safer here—the house can be defended—but if the worst comes to the worst, we may have to hang on until daylight, so they'd better bring the Brown Bess muskets and ammunition with them, as well as their rifles."

"Aye, sir," Hollowell acknowledged. He hesitated. "You'll no' be trying tae mak' contact wi' the rear-guard now, will you, sir?"

Alex shook his head. "Not yet, no. I'll see you safely across and then watch the front of the house until you and the others get here." He felt for the Adams. "Right—off you go!"

Hollowell vanished into the murky darkness. Alex waited, giving him time to reach the shed, and then made his way to the rear door of the house, wary this time of its rusty hinges. It opened, under his cautious pressure, with scarcely a sound. He entered the low back room hearing, as he did so, a faint scuttling noise that appeared to be coming from the room beyond. Rats, he wondered, instantly on his guard—rats or humans? He had to make sure before the wounded were brought across and, with so many rebels close by, he dared not take a chance . . . moving as silently as he could, he crossed to the shuttered window and peered out through a crack in the wood. The window looked out on the walled courtyard, and he could see little or nothing save a pool of rainwater gathering beneath the dripping eaves of the house, his first reaction to which was a feeling of thankfulness, since it promised a readily available supply of water for the wounded.

The scuttling sound continued, louder now, only to cease when, approaching the room from which it had been coming, he blundered into some object—a stool or the end of a *charpoy,* unseen in the darkness—which sent him crashing to his knees, the Adams jerked out of his hand. Cursing his own clumsiness, he groped along the floor for the weapon, found it and crouched there, straining his ears, instinctively uneasy, yet hearing nothing to cause him the slightest alarm. His first guess had probably been correct, he told himself. The scuttling sound had been made by rats or lizards; there was no one in the room. He got to his feet and strode into the room, making no attempt at concealment, only to halt in dismay when he realized that the door leading into the street was open. Through it, he could see the gleam of lights in the house opposite, shining through a curtain of rain. But . . . Hollowell had inspected this room, he had reported it empty and had made no mention of an open door, which could mean only that someone had come, in the interim, and unbarred the door. Someone who could not be permitted to return, if the wounded were to use this house as a refuge . . . Alex moved forward, intending to shut the door when suddenly, without warning, the darkness erupted into menacing life.

There was a rush of feet; several bodies hurtled into him, bringing him down, a man's arm closed about his chest and shoulders from behind, while a second grabbed his wrist, seeking to wrench the Adams from him. There were more men, entering through the door into the street, silent men, who gave no indication of who they were, but the pungent odor of sweat and breath heavy with the spicy, faintly acrid scent of betel nut, which emanated from those who were holding him, told him that his assailants were natives.

Intent on warning Surgeon Home and the rest of the British party rather than on attempting to defend himself, Alex got off four shots before his pistol was wrested from him, and he felt the sharp, cold prick of steel, as a knife was pressed against his throat.

A voice said, in English, "Do not move and do not call out to the other *feringhis* or I shall slit your throat!" He remained still, spent and breathless from the struggle, and heard, without comprehending its significance, a fusillade of shots coming from the courtyard. But the high-pitched whine of Enfield and Minié rifles mingled with the crackle of Brown Bess muskets suggested that his party—if it had been fired on—was replying to the rebels' fire, and a moment or two later, to his intense relief, he heard an excited shout from the rear of the house.

"They have returned to the shed. Subedar Sahib!"

His captor grunted. "All of them?" the subedar demanded, in his own tongue.

"*Ji-han,* all. The dogs of matchlock men drove them back."

"Misbegotten curs!" the subedar grumbled. "Bring a lamp in here, one of you, and let us see what manner of prize we have taken."

The knife remained, the point of its blade pressed against his throat, and Alex said, in English, "Let me sit up. I am disarmed—I will not struggle."

The subedar, evidently an old regular, responded to the note of authority in his voice. "Give me your word, Sahib," he requested.

"You have my word. I will not struggle."

The knife was removed, and Alex dragged himself into a sitting position, as a sepoy, in correct scarlet-jacketed uniform, came in bearing two small oil lamps. Taking one of them, the subedar held it above his head, looking down with narrowed eyes at his prisoner. He was an old man, Alex saw, his uniform impeccable and the ribbons of the Sutlej and Punjab campaigns pinned to his tunic, the medals gleaming in the lamplight. His own uniform, being that of a Volunteer Cavalry officer, bore neither medals nor badges of rank. and he saw the old subedar's look of bewilderment as he subjected it to a careful inspection.

"Your name, Sahib?" he asked, his tone—almost from habit, it seemed—respectful. One of the sepoys, quicker-witted then he, gestured to Alex's empty sleeve.

"This is the sahib who has lost his sword-arm!" the man exclaimed. "He is Sheridan Sahib, for whom the Moulvi has offered a reward of a thousand rupees."

"Dead or alive?" another man demanded. He hawked up spittle, directing it, with insolent deliberation. at Alex's face. "We waste time, Subedar-ji. Let us take his head to the Moulvi—that will be all the proof we need to earn us the reward."

The subedar studied Alex's scarred face bravely and memory stirred. *"Nahin!"* he said forcefully. "This is no matter for us to decide. Let the Moulvi Sahib put him to death, if that is his wish, but we shall take him alive. There is a Colonel Sheridan of the Cavalry who escaped from Cawnpore . . . if this is he, then he is a prize of more worth than a paltry thousand rupees."

"Ask him, Subedar Sahib," the sepoy who had brought the lamps suggested. The subedar started to do so in English, but the man who had spat in Alex's face said derisively, "He speaks our tongue—canst thou not see, in his eyes, that he understands? Let him speak it!"

The subedar struck him a stinging blow across the mouth, which sent him reeling. "Keep thy place, Gupta Ram," he ordered angrily. "I am in command, not thou. In our *paltan,* there is discipline and officers are treated with respect." To Alex he said, again in English, "Are you Colonel Sheridan, Sahib?"

"I am, Subedar Sahib."

"And the Moulvi of Fyzabad, Ahmad Ullah, is well known to you?"

"He is well known to me," Alex confirmed.

"Then we shall take you to him. If you will give me your

word that you will not attempt to escape, you will be conducted respectfully, as befits your rank, Sahib."

Alex hesitated. His chances of escape were, in the circumstances, remote and he gave his promise. "While I am in your custody, Subedar Sahib, I shall make no attempt to escape."

"So be it." The subedar stood back and Alex got to his feet. He was still wearing his saber, but none of the men made any move to take it from him. Two of them formed up on either side of him and, in a disciplined column, they marched down the dark, rain-wet street, muskets shouldered and booted feet in step. They had turned right on leaving the house—away from the river and the Chutter Munzil enclosure—and Alex strained his ears in an effort to hear, above the tramping footsteps of his escort, some sound that would indicate the movements and possible intentions of the rebels gathered within the enclosure. But there was none and he could only suppose that they were waiting until the British rear-guard began its withdrawal from the Moti Mahal.

"Where are you taking me, Subedar Sahib?" he asked, scarcely expecting a reply, but again speaking in English in the hope that, since his men probably would not understand, the old man might answer him. The subedar, however, was not to be drawn.

"To the Moulvi of Fyzabad, Sahib, as you already know."

"True, I know that. But where is the Moulvi?"

"You will see, Colonel Sahib." The old native officer barked an order to his men, and they took a second right turning, into a narrow lane, flanked on either side by tall buildings. The one on the left had a high, loopholed curtain wall, from which the long barrels of flintlocks protruded at intervals, and Alex identified it as the outer wall of the Hirun Khana. The column turned left at the next corner, the subedar answered a challenge from a sentry and then marched them down a dank, evil-smelling alley for some fifty or sixty yards, which brought them to a wide main road, with trenches dug across it and two field-guns mounted so as to cover the intersection. Guns and trenches were manned as if in expectation of an attack, and the subedar had to answer a number of other challenges from vigilant sentries before leading his small column across the road and then through a strongly guarded, arched gateway.

He halted them in a flagged courtyard, lined with trees, while he went to make inquiries of the guard commander. Alex, peering about him in the dim light, did not need to see the gilded domes and cupolas that crowned it in order to recognize the Kaiser Bagh—the king's palace—a vast edifice, screened by high walls and surrounded by gardens, which the last King of Oudh, Wajid Ali, had built to house the tomb of his most famous ancestor, Sa'adat Ali Khan, founder of the royal dynasty a century before. It had never been intended to serve as a fortress, but now, in addition to their wrought-iron gratings, the windows, he saw, had been bricked up and loopholed and the verandahs sandbagged, so that it closely resembled one. In place of the fountains that had played there in the old king's heyday, two huge twenty-four-pounder cannon and a squat, bell-mouthed howitzer were parked beneath a canopy, their *golandazes* squatting beside them, wrapped in sodden cloaks, the fire they had lighted to cook their evening meal flickering to extinction under the assault of the dripping rain.

These were the guns that had caused so many casualties the previous day, when General Havelock's column had been held up between the Moti Mahal and the king's stables and, recalling how gallantly the 78th Highlanders had attacked and endeavored to put them out of action, Alex looked at them with searching interest. But before he could ascertain whether or not they had been permanently damaged, the subedar returned and one of his escort thrust a rifle butt into the small of his back and harshly bade him, "*A-jao-jeldi,* Colonel Sahib!"

They marched across the courtyard, passed under another arched gateway and then ascended a flight of steep stone steps, terminating in a heavy, iron-bound door, which was guarded by a smartly uniformed havildar and two sentries, one of whom held a lantern aloft as they approached. The two native officers greeted each other by name and, on the subedar stating his business, he was saluted and given permission to proceed, all three guards regarding Alex with avid and unconcealed curiosity. He was conscious of their eyes following him, as his escort mounted a finely proportioned stone staircase, above which—reminiscent of the old king's former splendor—hung a crystal chandelier, ablaze with hundreds of flickering candles.

The staircase opened on to a balustraded gallery, hung with tapestry and Persian rugs, and the subedar, with some hesitation, approached a curtained archway. where he halted and motioned the escorting sepoys to wait. Turning to Alex, he whispered, "I have your word, Sahib—you will enter with me and remain here, by the archway, while I seek audience with the Moulvi?"

It was thanks to this old soldier of the Company that he was still alive, Alex reflected wryly. Had he been captured by townsfolk or by Oudh Irregulars, they would undoubtedly have shot him . . . he inclined his head. "I gave my word that I would not try to escape from your custody, Subedar Sahib. Rest assured—I shall not break that promise."

The native officer looked up at him and, for an unguarded instant, there was regret in the dark eyes. "These are not happy times, Colonel Sahib," he said softly. "I am sorry that I must deliver you to the Moulvi as a prisoner. But it is my duty—believe me, I am not doing it for the reward alone, although I am a poor man." He thrust the curtain aside and signed to Alex to follow him.

The room they entered was ablaze with light, as the entrance hall and staircase had been. It was a vast room, running half the length of the building at least and furnished in the oddly incongruous mixture of Oriental and Western styles so beloved of native rulers since the coming of John Company. Shabby leather armchairs, of the type popular in military clubs in London, were scattered among exquisitely carved examples of native craftsmanship; a billiard table, denuded of its cloth, occupied one corner and was piled high with silver goblets and tankards—some bearing British regimental crests—while priceless Persian rugs were scattered piecemeal over the inlaid marble floor and the remnants of a meal lay, scarcely touched, on a dining table in the center of the room, the lamplight striking reflections from the gold plate on which it had been served.

The appearance of the room occasioned Alex little surprise; during his service as a political officer, he had seen and been entertained in many others that resembled it. The occupants—of whom there were about fifty or sixty—were a different matter, however, and he drew in his breath sharply as he looked about him, seeing a number of former trusted British allies, *talukdars* and petty rajahs, whose loyalty had earned them pensions and grants of land at various times prior to the mutiny. They were here now in fighting garb, and he was shocked to recognize, standing a little apart, the Brahmin Rajah Man Singh of Shahgunje, to whom, during the past few perilous months, countless British fugitives owed their lives. Man Singh had protected them, dealing kindly and hospitably with their womenfolk and children; not one had applied to him in vain for refuge and all had been escorted from his domain to safety in defiance of the Nana's threats and pressure from the rebellious *zamindars* of Oudh. Yet he was here and he had, seemingly, thrown in his lot with the Mohammedan Court of Oudh although, for the moment, even in their midst, he was holding himself apart, standing in silence with his *vakeel,* while the others gathered in chattering groups, old feuds and grievances in abeyance—if not, perhaps, forgotten.

At an open window on the far side of the room, the Moulvi of Fyzabad also stood aloof, a bevy of staff officers keeping a respectful distance between him and the resplendently clad Oudh nobles. Scorning the costly magnificence with which the rest had bedecked themselves, he still dressed as he always had, in a long white robe, the green turban of a follower of the Prophet framing his dark, hawk-like face. The *tulwar* hanging from his waist was a workmanlike weapon, its scabbard silver but innocent of jewels; he had a pistol thrust into his cummerbund and a pair of cavalryman's leather gauntlets, which he had evidently just discarded, lay on a small table at his elbow, together with a telescope and a heavy, rain-wet cloak, which suggested that he had only recently joined the gathering from outside.

Isolated and unnoticed by the curtained doorway, Alex watched him. The Moulvi was staring intently out the window, as if listening for some expected sound, his beetling dark brows gathered in a frown, and the fingers of one hand beating a restless tattoo against the frame of the window. The old subedar, who had made his way hesitantly through the chattering groups toward him, reached his side at last, only to be accosted by one of the staff officers, who drew him away, a hand firmly gripping his arm. He pointed to the window, and the subedar obediently waited, and Alex saw that he, too, was listening. Except for a few spasmodic shots, there was little to be heard, save the murmur of voices from within the room and the clink of glasses as some of the officers helped themselves from the *chatties* on the disordered dining table. Among those who did so was a thin, frail-looking old man, in the gold-laced *chapkan* of the old king's army, scarlet slashed with yellow, his plumed turban and the jewel-encrusted gold chain of office around his neck proclaiming him an officer of high rank.

Alex stared at him for a moment in bewilderment before recognizing him as Mirza Guffur Khan, one-time general of artillery in Wajid Ali's service. In the days when he had been commissioner of Adjodhabad, he had known Mirza Guffur as a plump, slothful but immensely likable old aristocrat, living in opulent retirement, whose hunting parties he had attended several times and whose hospitality—despite his adherence to the Moslem faith—had called for a strong head on the part of his European guests. Now, stripped of the corpulent cheerfulness that had characterized him, he looked ill and unhappy and, as he filled his glass with a perceptibly unsteady hand, he glanced apprehensively in the Moulvi's direction as if expecting to be called to task for his indulgence.

The Moulvi, however, had no eyes for his artillery commander or, indeed, for anyone else. The subedar, who was clearly growing anxious concerning the prisoner he had left unguarded, signed agitatedly to Alex to withdraw from the room to where his escort was waiting, but his efforts earned him a reprimand from the staff officer who had first accosted him, and Alex, affecting not to understand what he wanted, remained where he was, the door curtain providing him with at least partial concealment. No one else gave him a second glance; the Moulvi did not turn away from the window, the old subedar resigned himself to waiting for a chance to gain his attention, and the voices of the *talukdars* became louder and more slurred, as more of them followed Mirza Guffur's example and replenished their glasses from the bottles and *chatties* on the table.

Then with startling suddenness, the sound of volley after volley of musketry echoed throughout the room and the Moulvi raised a hand for silence. The hum of conversation died to a whisper and he turned, his hand still upraised, to face his followers.

"You hear?" His deep voice was exultant. "They are on the move at last and the jaws of the trap are wide open! Allah guide the *feringhi* dogs into our hands, my brothers, that this night may see the first of many victories, when we embark on the reconquest of all Hind!"

There was subdued murmur of approval, which grew in volume to a savage roar. Alex, alone in the curtained doorway, knew a moment of paralyzing fear, the fear not for himself but for the men he had been compelled to leave behind him and for those who might even now, be risking their own lives to go to their aid. The sounds of battle were too far away for him to be able to pinpoint the scene of action precisely but the firing appeared to be coming from the general direction of the river and the Chutter Munzil, and he guessed that the sepoys he had glimpsed in the walled enclosure, half an hour before, had come from concealment to attack the rear-guard. Distorted by distance, cries and shouts could be heard, mingled with the beat of drums and the trumpeting of native horns, which suggested that some of the *rajwana*—irregulars and matchlockmen of the *zamindari* forces—were preparing to join battle in support of the sepoys.

He craned forward anxiously, hearing the Moulvi's voice but

unable to make out more than a word or two of what he was saying, his stomach churning as he visualized the all too familiar scene and then, as suddenly as it had started, the shooting ceased. The lull, which lasted perhaps four or five minutes, was followed by the unmistakable sound of British cheers and Alex's heart lifted. They had done it, he thought, praise be to God, against all the odds, the rear-guard had done it!

Forgetful of caution, he advanced into the room to find himself virtually alone, since the Moulvi's guests had gathered about him at the window, all of them now staring out of it as intently as he. The rain had stopped and when a pale moon appeared, to cast a faint, watery radiance across the night sky, the Moulvi raised his voice to give thanks to Allah.

"Our sepoys have done as I commanded them, my brothers!" he asserted. "Now they and the *rajwana* will retreat in seeming panic into the city and the British—who must, in any case, take their heavy guns by road to the Residency—will follow them, confident of victory."

"Canst thou be sure," Mirza Guffur asked querulously, "that they will follow, Moulvi Sahib?" He belched loudly, but the drink he had consumed had evidently loosened his tongue and, ignoring the Moulvi's baleful look, he went on, "This is not war as *I* know it . . . and the British are not fools, to walk blindly into thy trap. What are two guns to them? They have guns and to spare in the Residency!"

"It is a matter of honor to British soldiers. They will save their guns at any price," the Moulvi retorted angrily. "And their wounded also, if it is possible. They have survivors from this morning's ambush to rescue . . . or so they imagine. I tell thee, the trap has been well baited and its jaws are open. They will follow and it will close. When word is brought to me that all is in readiness, we will go and witness the slaughter, which few of them will escape . . ." he talked on boastfully, apparently in no doubt that his carefully planned strategy would be successful, and the *talukdars,* impressed by his eloquence, applauded him noisily.

Only Rajah Man Singh remained silent, still keeping his own counsel and, when the Moulvi focused on him and charged him with lack of enthusiasm, the Brahmin answered quietly that he would reserve judgment until the final outcome was known.

"Where learned you the art of war, Ahmad Ullah?" he questioned cynically. "Not, surely, in action against the British, of whose character you profess to have such profound knowledge and understanding? Like the General Sahib, I do not consider them foolish when they make war—the reverse, in fact. Foolish they may be in other matters, but in war I do not underestimate them."

"Perhaps, *Huzoor Bahadur,* you underestimate *me!*" the Moulvi countered, his tone cold. "Certainly you place too much reliance on the drunken babblings of an old man, whose excesses offend against the teaching of his Faith." He gestured contemptuously to Mirza Guffur, but, before Wajid Ali's old general could reply to the insult, there was a shout from the doorway and Alex made a swift retreat into the shadows. Man Singh saw his sudden movement and glanced across at him with a puzzled frown, but he said nothing, and the attention of everyone in the room became centered on the two mud-spattered native officers who came hurrying in, calling urgently for the Moulvi.

One was stout and gray-haired, wearing the uniform of the Company's Native Infantry and the rank badges of a colonel; his companion was younger and similarly attired—presumably his adjutant or aide—and the shocked, unhappy expressions on both their faces gave warning that the news they brought was anything but good.

Seeing the man he sought by the window, the colonel stumbled over to him, breathing hard. He did not salute or come to attention but stood, his head bowed, to blurt out, with a bitterness he made no attempt to conceal, "My *paltan* has been wiped out, Moulvi Sahib!"

"Wiped out, Behari Lal? What do you mean, wiped out? In the name of Allah, what are you telling me?" The Moulvi's voice cut like a whiplash, and the native officer retreated a pace, quailing before the fury in his eyes.

"We waited, well hidden in the enclosure, as you bade us, Moulvi Sahib," he answered sullenly. "But we were discovered before the *rajwana* came to support us. The British were in much greater strength than we had been led to expect. They are in occupation of all the palaces, and they attacked us from two sides, catching us in a terrible crossfire—and then they came in with the bayonet. We were overwhelmed . . . there were hundreds of them and we had no chance. The cowardly dogs of the *rajwana* fled across the river, ignoring our cries for aid. We—"

"Across the river?" the Moulvi flung at him. "Not, as I had commanded, to the Khas Bazaar?"

"There was nowhere else to go, Moulvi Sahib," the stout little colonel defended. "Ram Chand and I . . . we are the only ones to reach here and we came, at the risk of our lives, to bring you word. The rest—the few that are left of my *paltan*—fled in the only direction they could. Many were drowned, cut off by more of the *lal-kotes,* who issued from the Furhut Baksh and the Terhee Kothee to prevent them from reaching the iron bridge. The power of their Enfields is terrible. I tell you truly—we had no chance and—"

The Moulvi cursed him as if he were a low-caste menial.

"And Gomundi Singh, who was posted with two regiments in the Hirun Khana—did you not send to him for support?"

"There was no time—the attack came without warning. I—"

"You are a cowardly incompetent," the Moulvi accused. "One cannot fight when yellow-livered curs of your caliber run at the mere sight of a *feringhi* bayonet. You are not fit to hold command of your *paltan*, Behari Lal—you are relieved. You—"

"I have no *paltan*, Moulvi Sahib." Behari Lal was trembling, his plump face ashen. "Did I not tell you, my *paltan* was wiped out and—"

The Moulvi brushed his protests aside. "What of the guns?" he demanded harshly. "Do the British rear-guard take them to the Residency?"

"No, they do not!" Behari Lal answered, sounding as if the dashing of the Moulvi's hopes gave him pleasure. "They have left them in the enclosure beside the river, and they guard them from the Chutter Munzil, which they now occupy, in addition to the other palaces . . ." he explained the new British depositions, and Alex was conscious of an unholy joy as he listened. His spirits rose still further when he heard Behari Lal describe, in graphic detail, how a small party—taking advantage of the confusion caused by his regiment's flight—had made a dash through the enclosure from which they had been driven and from there, guided, he could only suppose, by Moorsom, had brought out Surgeon Home and the others without suffering a single casualty.

It was a miracle, he thought, thankful beyond measure to learn that his companions in misfortune had been saved. His own situation, he was well aware, remained fraught with danger—even if the scene he had just witnessed had driven all thought of danger from his mind, it would behoove him to remember it now. The Moulvi, beside himself with rage at the failure of his much-vaunted plan to ambush the British rear-guard, would show him no mercy when his presence was revealed, as inevitably it must be . . . unless he broke his word to the subedar and attempted to make his escape. The old man was still standing, awkward and ill at ease, on the edge of the group by the window, elbowed aside by some of them but still patiently awaiting an opportunity to hand over his prisoner and claim his reward. It was only a question of time before the Moulvi noticed him and demanded to know his business and then . . . Alex's throat tightened.

When that moment came, he decided, the only course open to him would be to sell his life as dearly as he could, taking as many of them with him as circumstances would allow. He had faced death too often to fear it now, but, when it came, as a soldier, he wanted to go out fighting—not to suffer some fiendish torture such as the Moulvi might devise if he yielded himself up as a prisoner. He remembered the Suttee Chowra Ghat at Cawnpore and the ghastly shambles in the Bibigarh and shivered involuntarily; he remembered, too, the terrible death the Nana had inflicted on poor young Saunders, of the 84th, who had attacked him when he had been dragged from one of the blazing boats on the evening of the massacre—a death even the Nana's followers had deplored for its calculated cruelty. And he remembered Emmy, as he loosened his saber in its scabbard . . . dear God, what terrors could death hold for him, if he forced them to kill him quickly and cleanly, for would not Emmy be waiting for him on the other side?

He moved a pace or two forward, calculating the distance between himself and Ahmad Ullah, the Moulvi of Fyzabad, who was engaged in a low-voiced conversation with a tall man in

Sikh cavalry dress, to whom he appeared to be listening with more respect than he had shown to any of the others. The Sikh's face was in shadow, and Alex could not place him, but at least he was holding the Moulvi's attention, which would be to his advantage. If, Alex thought, he approached the group by the window with sufficient confidence and behaved as if he were one of them, no one, probably, would notice or challenge him. There might even be some among them—the humiliated Behari Lal, for one—who would stand by and watch him attack the Moulvi without raising a hand to stop him . . . at all events until the deed was successfully done. The Moulvi, it was evident had done little to endear himself to those now serving under his command; as at Cawnpore and in his own domain of Fyzabad, he had inspired fear but no trust or liking, particularly among the Brahmins.

Alex started to move toward the window, pausing to help himself from one of the *chatties* on the table and, as the *talukdars* had done, he drank a generous measure of *arak* slowly, as if savoring its contents, while keeping a wary eye on the Moulvi. He saw that the old subedar was watching him in open-mouthed amazement but apparently without suspecting his intentions, and he held his ground, venturing a smile in his direction, in the hope of allaying any doubts he might be harboring. The old man hesitated uncertainly but, instead of crossing the room to take him again into custody, he went over to where Behari Lal was standing and attempted to speak to him. The stout colonel, sunk in sullen and uncommunicative misery, looked at him blankly and then waved him away and the subedar, after another prolonged hesitation, resumed his original position and once more sought to gain the Moulvi's ear.

"Moulvi Sahib . . ." the old voice was quavering and diffident "I beg you to hear me."

The Moulvi glanced at him without interest. "Who are you gray-beard?"

"I am Subedar Kedar Nath of the Muttees-ki-Paltan, *Hoozor.* For thirty-two years I have served in the Company's Army and I—"

The Moulvi impatiently cut him short. "I have no time to listen to your record of service. What is your business, Kedar Nath?"

"I have a prisoner, Moulvi Sahib. A *feringhi* whom I—"

"A prisoner . . . and you bother me with such trifles? Shoot him, hack him to pieces with your *tulwar*—what matters it, so long as he dies? We take no prisoners. All *feringhis* taken in battle are to be put to death."

"But *this* prisoner . . ." the subedar began, only to be silenced by the Moulvi's imperiously raised hand.

"Allah give me patience! Is our army officered by brainless dolts? I have given you an order—obey it, Old One, and get out of my sight!" He turned away, shrugging off the interruption, and Alex, who had been listening with every nerve stretched almost to breaking point, felt some of the tension drain out of him. He set down his glass, feeling the better for the heady spirit he had consumed, and let his hand slide down to grasp the hilt of his saber.

A mere thirty paces separated him from the Moulvi's unguarded back, and he had nothing to lose. He had been condemned to death with as little thought as if he had been a pariah dog and Subedar Kedar Nath would, without much doubt, consider it his duty to carry out the sentence. He was a native officer of the old school, not overgifted with brains and too set in his ways to disregard an order and although it was possible that he might regret having to obey this one, he would still do so without questioning its justice. Under cover of the table, Alex started to draw his saber, but a hand came out to close over his and, from behind him. a voice said, very softly, in English, "Wait, my friend. The time is not yet ripe and besides, you would be torn limb from limb if you were to attempt anything of the kind."

"I shall have no other time," Alex objected. He turned to look at the owner of the hand and saw, to his astonishment, that it was the tall Sikh cavalryman to whom the Moulvi had been talking so earnestly a few minutes before. In the dim light, his skin appeared to be a dusky, golden brown, but when he moved to interpose his powerful body between the table and those who surrounded the Moulvi, it was revealed in the brighter glow of the chandelier overhead as the tanned skin of a European. His features, too, were European, and his beard, for all its Sikh luxuriance, was not the henna red hue to which some inhabitants of the Punjab dyed their facial hair, but a rich natural auburn, faintly flecked with gray.

"I have been watching you since you first entered the room," the stranger stated. He bent closer and added, his mouth against Alex's ear, "While, in this particular case, I can understand your desire to play the assassin, it would be a pity were you to throw your life away unnecessarily, would it not?"

"What alternative is left to me?" Alex demanded wryly. "You heard my sentence."

"I can offer you an alternative, Colonel Sheridan," the tall cavalryman assured him. "But we risk discovery if we remain here. Take up your glass and follow me . . . without haste. The gods have watched over you thus far, but you and I will both be in danger if that old imbecile of a subedar comes in search of you." He filled two glasses from the *chatti,* gave one to Alex and, a restraining hand on his arm, guided him to an anteroom to the left of the main doorway. There was a window at the far end, opening onto a balcony that, Alex saw when his companion drew back the shutters, overlooked a dark and apparently deserted courtyard some thirty or forty feet below.

The room was lit by a single oil lamp and the stranger, leaving him on the balcony, strode across and swiftly extinguished it. He returned, moving as silently as a cat, and there was a six-chambered revolver in his hand, which he offered, holding it by the barrel.

"This will be of more use to you than a saber, I think—for whatever purpose you may wish to put it to, Colonel Sheridan. And now, if you will wait here, I have certain essential arrangements to make for your safety, but I shall be back as soon as they are made." He started to close the shutters, but Alex prevented him.

"How do you know my name?" he asked. "And for God's sake, man . . . who are you?"

His rescuer permitted himself a brief smile. "I am indebted to Rajah Man Singh for your name, Colonel. And I am known here as Kaur Singh, newly appointed to the same rank as yourself in the Begum's army. But we cannot talk now . . . I have to intercept that subedar—what is his name? Kedar Nath of the 48th. He seeks a reward, I imagine, for your capture? And you gave him your parole when he brought you here?"

Alex nodded. "The Moulvi offered a reward of a thousand rupees, it seems, for my head. I regret that I haven't even a hundred to offer him but—"

"The promise of it will probably satisfy him, if Man Singh guarantees it. Has he any sepoys with him?"

"Yes—half a dozen, outside in the gallery."

"Then give me what money you have to buy them off."

Colonel Kaur Singh was busy with the shutters. He took the coins Alex offered him without counting them and started to push the shutters into place. "I shall bar these. If you have to make a run for it, lower yourself into the courtyard and I will look for you there. I trust, however, that you will be undisturbed." He did not wait for a reply. The bar slid into its sockets with a faint click, and he was gone.

Left alone, Alex made a brief inspection of the balcony and peered down into the courtyard, without seeing or hearing anything calculated to alarm him. The courtyard was devoid of life, the balcony strongly built of stone, with an ornamental wrought-iron balustrade. He removed his sword-sling and belt and secured them to the balustrade, as a precaution; they did not, of course, reach anywhere near the ground but would at least serve to break his fall if he were compelled to seek safety in the courtyard. This done, he settled down to wait, conscious of a lingering regret because his attempt on the Moulvi's life had been prevented. The chance he had thrown away this evening would probably never again be given to him, he thought bitterly, and he had let it slip through his hands on the word of a glib-tongued, renegade European, about whose motives he knew nothing . . . save that he was involved in some way with Man Singh.

Man Singh himself was of doubtful loyalty. True, he had sheltered and protected a number of British fugitives from out-stations during the past few months; he had treated them well and had them escorted safely to Allahabad. He had also reported—and reported accurately—on the Nana's movements in Oudh, both to General Havelock and to the financial commissioner, Martin Gubbins, during the siege of Lucknow . . . yet here he was, in the rebel camp, admitted to their leaders' inner council and seemingly accepted as one of them, even by the Moulvi. He commanded a considerable army of *rajwana* troops and had almost certainly brought them with him to Lucknow with the Begum's full knowledge and approval but . . . to whom was he loyal? Was he, perhaps, playing a waiting game—as Havelock had suspected— keeping a foot in both camps so as to ensure that, whichever side was eventually victorious, he would range himself with the victors? If so, it was a dangerous game, and the Moulvi, should he suspect his new ally of double-dealing, could prove an extremely dangerous enemy.

Small wonder, then, that Man Singh might want the Moulvi dead . . . but did he? Had it not been he who, through the medium of Colonel Kaur Singh, had prevented his own desperate plan from being put into action a short while ago? Alex sighed. There was no fathoming the Oriental mind, he told himself wearily; no understanding the torturous depths to which treachery could sink, but one thing, at least, he could be sure of—Man Singh had an ulterior motive in bringing about his rescue. It might be that he was to be held as a hostage—a witness, perhaps, to the Hindu chief's good intentions should Sir Colin Campbell succeed in recapturing the city of Lucknow and raising the siege of the Residency.

On the other hand, Kaur Singh had spoken of offering him an alternative to playing the role of assassin . . . He shivered in the warm darkness and felt for the revolver in the waistband of his overalls, finding a measure of reassurance in its touch. Kaur Singh had also said that the time was not yet ripe for the Moulvi to die, which could well mean that a time had been chosen and his role—when that time came—would be unchanged.

It was a possibility he had to accept but . . . Alex got to his feet and started restlessly to pace the narrow balcony. He was letting his imagination run away with him, he chided himself. The *arak,* potent devil's brew that it was, had gone to his head . . . for God's sake, he had eaten nothing for 24 hours and had scarcely slept for two days and nights! He was confused, not thinking clearly. Had not Man Singh shown himself a loyal friend—not once but a hundred times—when British fortunes were at their lowest ebb and the tide of victory was flowing always the rebels' way?

The Nana had won Cawnpore, massacred its garrison and gathered the *talukdars* and *ryots* of Oudh to his banner . . . yet Man Singh had continued to shelter British refugees, aware that they might never be able to repay the debt they owed him. And Kaur Singh—whatever he might call himself—was a European, or appeared to be. At worst, he was of mixed blood, and he was well educated and civilized brought up, in all probability, in the high tradition of the Sikh warrior class. Between them, he and Rajah Man Singh had saved his life and he had to trust them. He . . . Fingers scraped against the barred shutters behind him and Alex spun round, the revolver in his hand, as the bar was removed and the shutters were cautiously drawn back.

"Colonel Sahib . . ." The voice was the familiar, diffident voice of Subedar Kedar Nath, and he tensed, the revolver leveled at the native officer's bemedalled chest. "Have no fear, Sahib," the old man exhorted him. "I come by the order of the Lord Man Singh to escort you to his camp."

"Come you alone?" Alex demanded, his suspicions only partially allayed.

"*Ji-han,* Sahib. My men are dismissed, well satisfied with the reward the Rajah Sahib has paid them . . . as am I. The Colonel Bahadur, Kaur Singh, has gone with the Moulvi, but I am to tell you that horses await us below and an escort of the Rajah Sahib's horsemen." Kedar Nath smiled and pulled the shutters wide, to reveal that the lamp was burning again in the room at his back.

"Take my word, Sahib," he added, with a dignity that Alex found oddly moving. "As I took yours."

"I will take it, Subedar-ji. And I am ready . . . which way do we go?"

"By the way we entered, Sahib. All are gone, save the sepoys quartered here and they will not question me—they are of my *paltan*."

He had spoken the truth, Alex realized, as together they descended to the entrance hall and walked out, unchallenged, to the main courtyard, where the *golandazes* now slept beside their guns and the promised horsemen were waiting. The *vakeel* who had been with Man Singh earlier in the evening was in command of them; he saluted, one of his men led out horses for himself, and Kedar Nath assisted Alex to mount, and they were on their way at a steady canter, across open country toward the river. Skirting the observatory and the Koorshid Munzil—the one-time mess house of the officers of Her Majesty's 32nd—they headed, as dawn was breaking, for the river, crossed by a bridge of boats and then turned westward, to reach a tented camp pitched among the trees and gardens a quarter of a mile beyond the Badshah Bagh.

The *vakeel*, who had spoken little during their hour-long ride, conducted Alex to a tent, furnished in some luxury with a *charpoy*, tables and chairs, and a carpeted floor, and told him that food would be brought, together with bath water and fresh clothes.

"My master asks for your parole, Colonel Sahib," he added, his tone almost apologetic.

"And if I do not give it, *Vakeel* Sahib? What then?"

"A guard will be posted and you will not be permitted to leave your tent. I would advise you to give it. Sahib. Provided you do, you may go anywhere you wish in the camp, attended only by the subedar, who has volunteered to serve you."

He was a prisoner, Alex thought resignedly; but a privileged one, with such quarters as these . . . and he would have fared a great deal worse at the Moulvi's hands. "Very well, you have my parole, *Vakeel-ji*. It will hold good until I have had audience with your master."

The *vakeel* bowed. "So be it, Colonel Sahib. I will leave you to break your fast and rest. If there is anything that you need, you have only to inform the subedar."

Alex thanked him and, within a few minutes of his departure, a small procession of servants entered, bringing with them a hip-bath, hot water, and tea, served on a silver tray. He drank the tea, savoring every delicious mouthful, and then soaked his aching body in the almost forgotten luxury of a bath, which had been liberally sprinkled with a pleasantly pungent oil. A barber shaved him, with silent efficiency, and then dressed the slight wound on his leg; another servant brought him a freshly laundered *chapkan* and cotton, ankle-length trousers, and assisted him to don them, while two more served a meal of curry and rice, which he consumed to the last grain, his appetite sharpened by his long fast.

Finally the servants left, and he stretched himself out on the *charpoy*, to fall into an exhausted sleep.

He was awakened by the sound of someone tiptoeing into his tent and, sitting up, startled, he realized that it was dark, and the moon, seen through the half-open flap of the tent, newly risen. He had lain down to sleep leaving his revolver on the table beside him and he felt for it now before challenging the intruder. "*Koi hai*—who is there?"

"Oh, please do not shoot," a soft voice besought him nervously, in English. "I . . . I heard that they had brought an English officer here and I . . . it is so long since I have seen or spoken to one of my countrymen that I came in search of you. I did not realize that you were asleep or I should not have ventured into your tent. I waited until dark in case they saw me and tried to stop me, but I . . . oh, please forgive me, I will go. I . . . that is, I will wait outside until you have dressed and . . ."

The voice was a woman's, Alex recognized dazedly—an Englishwoman's. He got to his feet, seeing her in silhouette against the moonlit aperture of the tent flap as a slim, ghostly figure that might, at any moment, vanish from his sight . . . unless somehow he could persuade her to remain.

"Don't go," he begged her. "Please! I lay down fully dressed, intending only to close my eyes briefly, but I was tired and— good heavens, I must have slept the clock round! Believe me," he said as she still hesitated, "I am respectably clothed and delighted to receive a visitor who is also a countrywoman. There's a lamp here somewhere. I'll light it." He found the lamp and a box of matches and, after some fumbling, managed to light it. By its soft glow he saw that his visitor was a tall, thin young woman of perhaps twenty-five, wearing a native sari, which became her unexpectedly well. Her face was burned brown by the sun, her hair dark, and she could have passed for a native, except for the fact that her eyes were blue. They stared at each other, and the girl was the first to cry out in glad recognition.

"Colonel Sheridan . . . it *is* Colonel Sheridan, is it not? I mean, I'm not mistaken—you are the Colonel Sheridan who was in my father's garrison at Cawnpore?"

Her father's garrison . . . then that made her one of General Wheeler's two daughters. Alex eyed her incredulously. He had known Amelia, the general's elder daughter, quite well and would have known her again, no matter what sufferings she had endured.

The younger, who had been only eighteen, he had seen once or twice but had never spoken to . . . surely this could not possibly be she? He searched his memory for her name, and she said, with conscious bitterness, "You don't remember me, do you? I'm Lettice—Letty—Wheeler. The others—Amelia and my brother Godfrey—used to call me Pet."

Sick with pity, Alex reached for her hand. "Miss Wheeler, I'm thankful to see you—more pleased than I can begin to tell you, I . . . I had believed you dead, with your whole family. Your father—"

"They killed my poor dear father," Letty told him. "Before my mother's eyes, when we reached the ghat. They hacked him to death with their sabers, as we watched. We were on the Nana's elephant, Amelia and I. The *mahout* made it kneel and one of them shot my mother. Amelia and I were dragged down and . . ." her voice broke on a sob.

"Don't speak of it, don't distress yourself," Alex beseeched her. He led her to a chair and dropped to his knees beside her, still retaining his clasp of her hand. "It's enough that you are alive."

She shook her head, bravely biting back her tears. "No, I must tell you," she insisted. "So that you will know what I am, what I've become. Your wife was killed, wasn't she? They told me she was."

"Yes," Alex confirmed flatly. "They shot her and she died before the first boat left the ghat."

"She was fortunate, Colonel Sheridan," the girl said in a shamed whisper. "I wish that they had shot me. But they did not. Two of the troopers took us, my sister and me. Amelia was brave, much braver than I, and my father had given her his pistol. I wasn't there, I did not see it, but they told me what she did, how she killed the sowar who took her and then turned the pistol on herself . . . but I . . . I had no pistol and I was so terribly afraid."

In broken words and in tears, General Wheeler's daughter told the story of her enforced conversion to the Muslim faith, which had enabled a sowar of the Light Cavalry—one of her father's murderers—to take her as his wife. He had brought her to Lucknow, but, there, suspicion that she was an unwilling convert had put her in danger of her life and finally her husband had handed her over to Man Singh, with the plea that he protect her. He was among the rebel troops, Letty said, but she had not seen him for over a week.

"His name is Mohammed Khan Aziz and he is a *daffadar* in the Second Light Cavalry," she added. "And, after his fashion, Colonel Sheridan, he has been good to me. But I am a general's daughter and a Christian . . . I cannot dishonor my father or forsake my faith, I . . ." she was suddenly overcome, and burst into a torrent of weeping.

Alex held her to him, vainly seeking for words with which to comfort her, but she was still sobbing, her face pressed against his shoulder, when the *vakeel* came to summon him to Man Singh's presence.

CHAPTER FIVE

⇶ • ⇷

The rear-guard and Colonel Napier's reinforcements marched into the Residency as dawn was breaking on the morning of September 27, and both General Outram and General Havelock were waiting to receive them. Napier reported, with some satisfaction, that in addition to the Terhee Kothee and the Furhut Baksh, the greater part of the Chutter Munzil Palace had now been occupied.

"Colonel Purnell, with a company of the 90th, and Captain McCabe with a strong party from the old garrison, discovered a large force of the enemy in occupation of part of the Chutter Munzil enclosure, Sir James," he said. "They were there, I suspect, with the intention of catching us in an ambush, but Purnell and McCabe, assisted by Lieutenant Aitken and his Bailey Guard sepoys, annihilated them. Eyre's guns are safe—they can be brought in through the palaces whenever you wish . . ." he gave details of how the guns had been gotten out, praising Olpherts' courage and ingenuity, and then added, with a tired smile, "And a party, under Lieutenant Moorsom, succeeded in breaking through to the square where our wounded were massacred yesterday. They rescued Surgeon Home of the 90th and ten survivors, of whom four are unwounded. One of the wounded officers— poor young Swanson of the 78th—died as we were bringing him in, and I regret to have to tell you that Colonel Sheridan, of the Volunteer Cavalry, who went out to seek aid for the party, is missing and must be presumed dead."

"Sheridan was a most gallant officer," Outram said. "And you say Crump has also been killed . . . dear God, we can ill sustain the loss of such men! What of Andrew Becher, Bob? Did you bring him in?"

Napier inclined his head. "He's badly wounded, sir. I had him taken to the hospital, and young Arnold of the Blue Caps with him. But I'm afraid . . ." he did not complete his sentence and instead asked anxiously, "Are we to go or stay, Sir James?"

Sir James Outram exchanged a wry glance with General Havelock. "That question is still under discussion . . . and may well be decided for us by expediency. Up to the present, both General Havelock and I incline to the feeling that—provided we can secure the essential carriage for the wounded and the women and children—the old garrison should be evacuated to Cawnpore as soon as possible. Our relief force would then continue to defend the Residency."

"And Colonel Inglis doubts that the carriage can be secured," Havelock put in wearily. "He also doubts whether we can feed our combined forces—least of all the cavalry horses—until the commander-in-chief gets here. So it would seem to be a choice between two evils, Colonel Napier. The gun-cattle we have brought with us will suffice to provide fresh meat for a limited period, of course, and if Barrow and Hardinge can break through with their cavalry to the Alam Bagh, all may be well. In the meantime, Sir James intends to extend our defensive perimeter . . . is that not so, Sir James?"

Outram nodded vigorously. "Whatever fate decides for us, we are all agreed that a compact and extended perimeter is essential. You've secured our river frontage, Bob, my dear fellow, and you have acquitted yourself magnificently. But," he laid an affectionate hand on his chief of staff's shoulder, "you are done up and, I am sure, in need of food and a change of clothing. We'll call a conference for noon—that will permit you time for a short rest. In the interim, I shall consult with the engineers and the commissariat officers . . . a decision has to be made and made very soon. In all humanity, I should like to get the women and the wounded away—conditions in the hospital are appalling and, if starvation is to be added to the perils they face, the risks inseparable from evacuation may well prove the lesser of the two. But . . ." again he glanced at Havelock. "As General Havelock says, it's a choice between two evils, but I shall not be happy until we have driven the enemy back from our south and south-eastern fronts and put their batteries out of action. We can do it by a series of sorties, I believe. However, the precise nature and order of these must wait to be decided at our conference."

"Then with your permission, sir," Napier said, "I'll go and clean up and break my fast."

"Of course, my dear fellow," the General assented warmly. "We'll see you at Dr. Fayrer's house at noon." Watching his departing back, he observed thoughtfully to Havelock, "Bob Napier is a fine soldier, you know, Henry. He'll go a long way . . . if he survives this."

Havelock expelled his breath in a long-drawn sigh. "I wonder," he said, his voice low and strained, "how many of us *will* survive if the commander-in-chief does not reach us soon. Government gave us too little, Sir James, and expected too much of the handful of men they sent us. The odds have been stacked against us right from the outset."

"But we succeeded," Outram reminded him. "Against all the odds, Henry, we are in Lucknow."

"Because we commanded a force of heroes, in which each man gave his all and because this is a heroic garrison. But how

how much more can flesh and blood stand? I would say this to no one but you, of course, I . . ." Havelock looked up, meeting his companion's gaze squarely. "Sir James, we both know that we are trapped here, do we not? We both know, as experienced soldiers, that our losses have been too great to permit a division of our force, and therefore evacuation will not be possible, even for the women and children. Should we not admit it?"

"You are worn out, Henry, my friend," Outram countered. His tone, however, was uncritical and even sympathetic as he urged Havelock to rest. "You take too much out of yourself. Up till now, you have born the responsibility—but that is over, since I bear it now and shall continue to bear it until Sir Colin Campbell relieves me." He smiled. "Did you not say to Harry: 'If the worst comes to the worst, we can but die with our swords in our hands?'"

"Yes," Havelock admitted. "I did . . . before we left Cawnpore at the end of July and I began to realize the enormity of the task I was expected to perform."

"It still holds good, Henry. The worst has not yet come to the worst but, if it should, I think we shall both know how to die."

"I pray God we shall, James. At least as well as those of our brave company who have gone before us."

"Amen to that," Outram said. "Unlike yourself, I am not a religious man, but that shall be my prayer nightly, from now on." He added, with a flash of wry humor, "I shall also pray that it will not be necessary! Now get some rest, Henry, I beg you, before the staff conference, because I want to get our plan of operation mapped out today. With, in all probability, no more than seven or eight hundred men available for sorties, it will behoove us to plan carefully and I shall need your expert advice. How are your invalids? Have you seen them this morning?"

Havelock shook his head. "The surgeons assure me they are progressing reasonably well. Poor Fraser Tytler is in a good deal of pain, but Harry, they say, is quite cheerful, and Vincent Eyre's fever is down. I intend to visit them now, but I must first see those poor fellows of Dr. Home's in the hospital. From what I have so far heard, their courageous and stubborn defense was something of a minor epic—one, indeed, that you might consider worthy of a Cross, perhaps."

"I shall certainly consider making a recommendation," Outram agreed, "when I've studied Home's report. I'm saddened by the loss of Alex Sheridan, greatly saddened, for he, I understand, inspired their defense." He sighed and, after another concerned glance at Havelock's lined and weary face, took out his pocket watch. "I shall have time to visit the hospital, Henry . . . you go straight to your invalids, my dear fellow, and give them my warmest regards. Rest a little in Harry's company and we will meet at Dr. Fayrer's at noon."

"Thank you," Havelock acknowledged. They separated, and Outram, attended by his aide, Lieutenant Chamier, made for the hospital.

Inside, among those awaiting the attention of the surgeons, they found Becher and Arnold lying side by side. Poor Becher could not speak and Outram dropped to his knees, tears filling his eyes as he looked into the ravaged face of the staff officer who had been closer to him than a son.

"We'll have you moved, Andrew," he promised. "As soon as the surgeons have dressed that face of yours. Mr. Gubbins' house is to become the hospital for officers . . . you'll have every comfort there, my dearest boy. General Havelock tells me that Gubbins contrives somehow to keep a very good table, although I fear it may be a little while before you are able to take advantage of it.

I . . ." he broke off, unable to say more and aware that Andrew Becher was not deceived by his forced cheerfulness. Wordlessly, he clasped the injured man's hand; then, his eyes still misted, he turned to Arnold. "I promised General Neill I would see to it personally that you were recommended for a Victoria Cross for your gallantry at the Char Bagh bridge the day before yesterday, Mr. Arnold . . . and now, it would seem, you have earned a second recommendation. Rest assured that I shall keep my promise most gladly."

Arnold managed a smile. "The man who earned it is standing over there, sir," he corrected. "Private Ryan of my regiment. I should be greatly obliged, sir, if you would recommend him in my place."

General Outram seemed scarcely to have heard him. He moved on, Chamier at his elbow, to speak to Colonel Campbell, who had suffered the amputation of his right leg after being sent in from the Moti Mahal some hours earlier, and Ryan and Webb, both with their arms in makeshift slings, stood respectfully at attention when the A.D.C. pointed them out.

Surgeon Scott wiped the sweat from his brow with a blood-caked arm and made a wry grimace as he watched the general cross the ward. But he said nothing, simply gestured to his assistants and they lifted Arnold onto the operating table; Sergeant Walker, after a cursory glance, reached for one of the pannikins of rum left in readiness at his back and waited expectantly. Scott's examination was hardly less cursory.

"I'm sorry, laddie," he told Arnold gruffly. "I shall need to take both your legs off for you."

"Both of them?" Arnold pleaded. "Could you not save me one?"

Scott shook his head. "You'll not feel the second," he promised. "And the first will be off before you know it"

Sergeant Walker held out his pannikin, but Ryan stepped forward and, with a mumbled, "Let me give it to him, Sergeant," took it from him and held it to Arnold's lips.

The operation was mercifully swift. Arnold made no sound and when it was over, Ryan went with him, to pillow his unconscious head on his knees. He was still there, stiff and motionless, when Scott, coming to check the dressings, told him, with brusque pity, that his officer was dead.

"You'll get his Cross, lad." he said, motioning the young Fusilier to his feet. "Be proud of it—he wanted you to have it, you know. I heard him tell the general so."

Ryan nodded and walked blindly away.

The first sortie was made that afternoon, when 120 men of the Madras Fusiliers, under the command of Major Stephenson, launched an attack on the enemy's Garden Battery from the Bailey Guard gate. It met with limited success; the battery was gallantly stormed and the guns spiked, but the Fusiliers came under a galling fire from light field guns and musketeers posted in the surrounding buildings and were compelled to retire, after suffering a number of casualties. Next morning, however, a party of only fifty men of the 5th Fusiliers and the 90th advanced through the Chutter Munzil Palace, drove a large enemy force from buildings between the palace and the Khas Bazaar and established a picket that commanded both the Khas and Cheena Bazaars.

General Outram, determined to secure the bridge across the river as a means of opening communication with the city, ordered a second attempt to be made to take it on September 29. His plan of action, worked out in a day-long conference with Havelock and Inglis and their staffs, was to launch three simultaneous sorties against rebel gun batteries, with two columns attacking from the south of the perimeter and one from the north, employing the total seven hundred available troops.

At dawn, the attacks were launched. The column from Innes' Post and the Redan, on the north-west, unhappily failed to reach the Iron Bridge, which was its main objective but in some desperate fighting, two mortars and four light guns were taken and, compelled to withdraw after suffering very severe casualties, the column took and blew up a twenty-four-pounder cannon that had done immense damage during the first part of the siege. The two columns that emerged from the Brigade Mess and Sikh Square positions, on the south side of the Residency defenses, met with more success. The object of the first was to capture an enemy eighteen-pounder gun on the left front of the Brigade Mess and another in front of the Cawnpore Battery with, if this should prove possible, the guns to the left of the Cawnpore road, known to the defenders as Phillips' Garden Battery. To take the latter, which was strongly defended, the two columns were to link up in a combined assault.

Initially all went according to plan. The guns, including the eighteen-pounder on the left front, were taken and blown up, and the 78th Highlanders under Captain Lockhart, forming the main body of 140 men, once again distinguished themselves. Covered by the fire of a small party of the 32nd from the roof of Martin Gubbins' house, they charged the second 18-pounder about which the rebels had rallied and the gallant, red-bearded Sergeant James Young, dashing ahead of the line, seized it at bayonet point before the gunners could reload. He went down, badly wounded by a *tulwar* slash on the head, and Lockhart fell beside him, but the gun was put out of action and broken by the artillery officers who had charged with them.

The second column, having gained its objectives, linked with the first and a party of two hundred men, led by Captain McCabe of the 32nd, advanced in file, over the debris of a house that had been destroyed during the siege, in the direction of the Cawn-pore road. They came under artillery fire but scaled the breastwork and took the two guns that had been firing at them, only to find themselves again under heavy fire from a building to their left. McCabe was mortally wounded when leading a party to clear the lower story; his place was taken by Major Simmons of the 5th Fusiliers, who led the party along a narrow lane running toward the Garden Battery and the road. They were within sight of the leading gun of the battery when Simmons was killed by a musket shot. The Garrison Engineer, Lieutenant Anderson, sent for the column's reserves and reported the position to Outram, who ordered them to retire. They did so, after demolishing three large houses that had provided shelter for enemy musketeers and blowing up the guns they had taken. The two columns returned to the entrenchment at nine o'clock, having cleared a range of some 300 yards in front of the Brigade Mess position and lost 18 men killed, with a number of others wounded, including the Garrison Engineer.

That evening, Colonel Napier brought in Vincent Eyre's heavy guns from the Chutter Munzil and, during the hours of dark-ness, Lousada Barrow and the commander of the Sikh Irregulars, Captain Hardinge—faced with the prospect of near-starvation for their horses if they remained—made an attempt to break out with the entire force of cavalry, in the hope of reaching the Alam Bagh. They were barely 200 strong and they found the investment of the Residency so close and strong that all their efforts failed, and at dawn they were compelled to return with the loss of five of their number but with the heartening intelligence that Major McIntyre appeared to be safely ensconced with his small holding force behind the strong walls of the Alam Bagh.

On the afternoon of October 1, Outram ordered a final sortie to secure possession of Phillips' Garden Battery and control of the Cawnpore road. It was brilliantly planned and commanded by Napier, the assault force consisting of detachments from every regiment in the combined garrison and amounting to a total of 568 men of all arms. Just after midday, the column formed up on the road leading to the Paen Bagh and it advanced through the buildings near the jail, occupying the main houses on the left and front of the garden. Those in front were barricaded and strongly defended and, leaving a detachment to engage the rebel defenders' fire, Napier led his main body to the right, to find that the battery was separated from them only by a narrow lane, some fifteen feet below the garden. The garden, however, was surrounded by a deep mud wall, with strong points at intervals, and the face of the battery, being scarped, was quite inaccessible without scaling ladders. A heavy fire was kept up from the face of the battery and a patrol reported that the lane was blocked by a loopholed barricade. As, by this time, it was dark and a direct attack would be certain to cost many lives, Napier decided to postpone his assault until daylight. The force occupied adjacent buildings to snatch what sleep they could and, at first light, with the artillery opening fire from the Residency in their support, the column reformed and began to advance under a withering deluge of grape and canister and musket balls.

A company of the Madras Fusiliers, under Lieutenant Creagh, succeeded in turning the position by the Cawnpore road, and the rest of the column doubled through the lane, fought a way through the stockade and drove the rebels from it. Phillips' House was occupied without opposition and, leaving a picket to hold it, Napier ordered a charge to take the guns, which had been withdrawn to the end of the garden. The charge was successful, despite a spirited defense with musketry and grape and, with a company of the 5th in the lead, the guns were seized, dragged back into the garden, and burst. A party of engineers, under Lieutenant Innes, placed explosives in Phillips' House and blew it up, while the column returned to the buildings they had occupied the previous night, having suffered fewer than thirty casualties.

The next four days were spent in blowing up houses on the Cawnpore road and clearing the whole area of rebels. On October 6, a permanent position was set up in front of Phillips' Garden and held by the Highlanders; Brayser's Sikhs entrenched themselves between the Paen Bagh and the Khas Bazaar, and the Fusiliers and the 90th occupied the Chutter Munzil and its two walled enclosures at the river's edge, with the 64th in the Furhut Baksh, and a detachment of the 84th in the jail. The work of extending the defensive perimeter was, unhappily, not done without loss and, when Napier returned to report his task complete, the name of Neill's successor to command of the Blue Caps, Major Stephenson, and that of Major Haliburton of the 78th were added to the growing list of killed and wounded. In the new Officers' Hospital in the financial commissioner's house, Colonel Campbell of the 90th and Andrew Becher died of their wounds, and Surgeon Home, appointed to serve there, confessed to considerable anxiety over the condition of the gallant Fraser Tytler, who was in great pain and barely holding his own.

Sir James Outram, still anxious to render possible the evacuation of the women, children, and wounded, ordered stretchers to be constructed, which would be light enough for two men to carry and considered a new plan, put forward by Brigadier Inglis, for the capture of the Iron Bridge. He had informed Inglis and Havelock that he had virtually made up his mind to leave the 90th Regiment, with the old garrison, to hold the Residency and to fight his way to the Alam Bagh with the rest of the force and the 470 women and children who had survived the siege, and Havelock—somewhat against his better judgment—had agreed. An inspection of the Commissariat Stores, however, revealed that a large supply of grain had been laid in by Sir Henry Lawrence, when he had provisioned the Residency for the anticipated siege, which—owing to Lawrence's premature and sudden death—had not been included in the inventory. Part of this stock, buried in a dried-out swimming pool, had not as yet been touched.

The discovery that, far from being in imminent danger of starvation, the garrison had sufficient provisions to sustain it at full strength for six to eight weeks—or even longer, if supplies were strictly rationed—caused Outram to revise his plan of action. The urgent, underlying reason for evacuation had now been removed and, it being evident that even a limited removal to the Alam Bagh would be fraught with peril for the women and children, he decided, instead, to remain in Lucknow with his entire force until Sir Colin Campbell could advance to his relief.

Communication with the Alam Bagh was established by means of a wooden semaphore and *cossids* were sent through the enemy lines to Cawnpore to advise the commander-in-chief of this decision. Outram wrote on October 7: *"It will be impossible to carry off the sick, wounded, women and children amounting to 1,500 souls. Want of carriage alone . . . renders the transport through five miles of despoiled suburb an impossibility."*

He added: *"The force at Lucknow is now besieged by the enemy, but we have grain and gun-bullocks and horses upon which we can subsist for another month . . . although we have no hospital comforts and little medicine . . . Our losses in killed, wounded and missing since the force crossed the Ganges has been very heavy—256 killed and 700 wounded and 16 officers missing."*

This message, written partly in Greek characters, was addressed to Captain Bruce at Cawnpore, for transmission to Sir Colin Campbell by telegraph and, in a separate note to Bruce, Outram urgently requested that reinforcements and supplies should be sent to the Alam Bagh. *"A wing of European infantry and two guns at Busseratgunj and Bunni would secure the whole road for the safe convoy of provisions to Alam Bagh,"* he suggested and then, with the threat to Cawnpore itself in mind, he warned Bruce to obtain more guns if he could and to send out spies to report on the movements of the Nana and Tantia Topi, with the Gwalior troops.

He had done all he could; now he must concentrate on the defense of the Residency. A strong system of earthworks, barricaded houses, and gun batteries, linked to smaller outposts, formed an inner and an outer ring of defense. Havelock was given command of the outer ring, defended by regiments of the force he had commanded in Oudh, and Inglis, promoted to acting Brigadier General, retained command of the original Residency entrenchment and his old garrison, which was strengthened by Barrow's Volunteer Cavalry and detachments of the Artillery, Madras Fusiliers and the 78th Highlanders.

Inglis' command included the north-west face, from the Redan and the post known as Innes', the Sheep and Slaughter Houses and Gubbins' House on the west, and terminated at Anderson's Post, which was immediately to the rear of the Cawnpore Battery and the now barricaded Cawnpore road on the south-eastern side. Of the two, Havelock's was by far the more demanding, since all his posts were bordering those of the enemy and under constant attack by artillery and infantry, with mines and saps dug beneath them. He was responsible for the three riverside palaces— the Terhee Kothee, Furhut Baksh, and Chutter Munzil—and eastward as far as the advanced Garden Post held by the 90th and, in addition, for the new post set up by the 78th Highlanders on the south front, which was known as Lockhart's, after its commander.

From his new residence in Ommaney's House, an inspection of all the posts in the palaces entailed a walk of over two miles, but Havelock made it daily, leaving the house at daybreak with his surviving staff and conscientiously visiting every post before reporting to Outram and breaking his fast. The palaces provided ample accommodation for his troops and for the native camp followers, but much had still to be done to fortify and strengthen the occupied buildings. The indefatigable Captain Crommelin, chief engineer to the Oudh Field Force, was disabled by a wound, and Havelock, who had for so long depended on Crommelin's skilled services and advice, missed him sorely, for he had never been more greatly needed. Heavy losses had been inflicted on the rebels and their gun positions driven back over 1,000 yards by the various sorties made by the garrison, but during the early part of October, they concentrated on waging subterranean warfare, directing their efforts mainly against the 78th's new post, where they exploded a number of mines. The Highlanders, under the guidance of Crommelin's successor, Lieutenant Hutchinson, were compelled to countermine, sinking their first 500-foot-long shaft while still engaged in barricading their post. Brayser's Sikhs, who were holding the area between the Paen Bagh and the Khas Bazaar, also came under this form of attack, and both they and the Highlanders soon became expert at the laborious task of digging galleries in order to intercept and destroy those of the enemy, rivaling in skill the more experienced men of the old garrison.

Gun batteries from across the river pounded the newly fortified defensive positions and in the rabbit-warren buildings of the Chutter Munzil there was constant danger from exploding mines, but Havelock refused to let this deter him from his duty, and his small, erect figure, plodding resolutely over the rubble of damaged buildings, became a familiar and welcome sight to the men under his command. His soldiers, as devoted to him as ever, nevertheless began to notice a change in their courageous little general—a lack, not of physical effort or resolution, but rather of heart. He had been greatly saddened by the losses his Field Force had sustained and, in particular, by the death of his nephew, Bensley Thornhill—who had survived the massacre of the wounded by only three days. He was anxious concerning his son Harry and the other wounded members of his personal staff, and his health—for so long strained by the rigors of the campaign in Oudh—was beginning to fail. He tired easily and lost weight and, apart from his conscientious round of his command, spent most of his time reading books on military history. Now it was Outram who was the leader, he who inspired the men's cheers when he made his tours of inspection and he who—even more regularly than Havelock—visited the hospital, accompanied by the old garrison's heroic chaplain, the Rev. James Harris.

There was increasing reason for optimism. Communication with both the Alam Bagh and Cawnpore was established on a more or less regular basis and, on October 9, he received confirmation of the fall of Delhi and news of the dispatch from there of a small but well-equipped force under Brigadier Greathead, whose ultimate destination was Lucknow. Regiments of defeated sepoys from Delhi were also reported to be making for Oudh, but no intelligence was received of any threatening move toward Cawnpore by the Gwalior Contingent, although Colonel Wilson, commanding the Cawnpore garrison, warned that the Nana had returned to Bithur to gather troops. On October 18, Wilson attacked and dispersed this gathering and the Nana again fled into Oudh. In response to Outram's request, Major McIntyre was reinforced at the Alam Bagh, two companies of infantry, fifty cavalrymen and two guns being sent on from Cawnpore, together with the supplies for which the isolated garrison commander had asked.

In Lucknow itself, rationing was strict; tea, coffee, milk, and tobacco unknown luxuries, but the defenders remained cheerful and uncomplaining, even when their rations once again had to be reduced. Outram made strenuous efforts to open up communications with the surrounding country, in the hope of obtaining supplies of fresh meat and vegetables, but the blockade was vigilantly maintained and all attempts to negotiate with merchants in the city met with failure. Inevitably, the general health of the garrison suffered; while none starved, almost all suffered from boils and ulcers, many were debilitated and, with *chapattis*—small cakes, made of unleavened flour—constituting their staple diet, outbreaks of diarrhea and dysentery became increasingly common.

In one of his reports, Outram wrote: *"Never could there have been a force more free from grumblers, more cheerful, more willing. Among the sick and wounded, this glorious spirit is, if possible, still more conspicuous than among those fit for duty. But . . . it is a painful sight to see so many poor fellows maimed and suffering and denied those comforts of which they stand so much in need. Yet it . . . makes me proud of my countrymen to observe the heroic fortitude and hearty cheerfulness with which it is borne."*

Yet, for all their fortitude, the wounded suffered and died in ever increasing numbers. In addition to the top floor of Martin Gubbins' shell-scarred white mansion, a large room in the Begum's Kothee was appropriated for the accommodation of wounded officers, but they gained little from the change, although the women billeted there nursed them with the most devoted care. No amputation cases survived for more than a few days; gangrene invariably appeared, the wounds did not heal, and even the loss of a finger could lead to death from infection. Some of the private soldiers moved to the hot but open sheds in Horse Square, or placed in tents pitched near the main hospital, recovered better than those kept within its tainted walls, where cholera and dysentery took heavy toll, even of the unwounded. Ironically supplies of arrowroot, sago, and the tobacco, which might have mitigated much of the suffering, were at the Alam Bagh, four miles distant . . . as remote from the Residency garrison as if they had been four hundred miles away.

Yet news from the outside world, as it filtered through, kept morale high. The garrison learned that the King of Delhi and his Begum had surrendered themselves as prisoners and that the treacherous princes had been executed. A letter, received by Outram, described Delhi as a city of the dead. *"Our road . . . lay through the Lahore Gate and passing along the Chandni Chouk not a sound was heard, save the deep rumble of our gun-wheels or the hoarse challenge of a sentry on the ramparts. Here might be seen a house gutted of its contents, there a jackal feeding on the half-demolished body of a sepoy; arms, carts, shot, dead bodies lay about in the wildest manner. Outstretched and exposed to the public gaze lay the bodies of the two sons and the grandson of the wretched King; they had been captured and executed the day before near Hymayoun's tomb . . ."*

Of even greater importance to the Lucknow defenders was

the report of Greathead's victory over the rebels at Bulandshahr and speculation as to when his column might reach Lucknow became increasingly optimistic . . . until it was learned that appeals from Agra had caused him to abandon his initial plan and make a forced march to the relief of the garrison there. Hopes were dashed but rose again when a *cossid* from Agra brought word of a second decisive victory and a promise that the Movable Column—now commanded by Colonel Hope Grant of the 9th Lancers—would resume the march southward through the Doab within a day or two. They had marched 66 miles and fought two actions in the space of forty hours; nine miles of the route had been covered at a trot by cavalry and artillery, through high crops and plowed fields, and men and horses were exhausted. Nevertheless, after a 48-hour rest, their ammunition replenished from the Fort, on October 14 the column left Agra, made up by reinforcements to almost its original strength of 930 European and 1,860 native troops.

Lady Outram had taken refuge in the Fort at Agra, and the general was greatly relieved to learn that she was safe; he was still more elated when the messenger he had dispatched to find the column en route returned to Lucknow to inform him that Hope Grant—after clearing Mynpuri of rebels on the nineteenth—had been at Bewar, the junction of the Agra, Fategarh, and Cawnpore roads, on the twenty-first. He replied to Outram's message, assuring him that he would continue his advance with all possible speed and that he expected to join forces with the commander-in-chief at Cawnpore during the first week of November.

Outram, aided by his two brigadiers, prepared detailed plans for the relief of the Residency and sent these, by native messengers, to the Alam Bagh for dispatch to Sir Colin Campbell. Morale among both British and loyal native defenders was now higher than it had ever been, and Outram ordered a parade of the loyal sepoys, at which he thanked them publicly for their services. Of the 765 who had remained with the original garrison, 133 had been killed and 230 had deserted during the early part of the siege. The survivors were rewarded by promotion and the promise of pensions; Ungud, the brave messenger, who had maintained contact with Havelock's Field Force in Oudh at the risk of his life, received a subedar's pension and the assurance that the payment promised him by Brigadier Inglis would be met in full. The Bengal Army pensioners, who had answered Sir Henry Lawrence's appeal to return to the Colors and serve in Lucknow's defense, were told that their pensions would be doubled, and to their venerable leader, Subedar Runjeet Singh, the general gave a personal assurance that he would receive the Company's Order of Merit.

The sepoys cheered him and only a few of the 32nd—wearily loading and firing their borrowed Enfield rifles with home-made bullets from the mold fashioned by a staff officer named North—grumbled at the notice taken of the natives. "Bloody black bastards!" a corporal complained, coughing earth from his lungs as he emerged from a mining tunnel deep beneath the Chutter Munzil. "There the sods go, as usual, petted and rewarded, while the likes of us get nothing! Not even a smoke or a chew of plug . . ."

On the whole, however, the rewards were approved of even by the European private soldiers, and those who bore resentment swiftly forgot it when the latest news of Hope Grant's gallant column spread like wildfire throughout the old and new garrisons. The women, crouched in their *tyekhanas* and behind bullet-scarred barricades or toiling in the hospitals, gathered to pray for deliverance and wept for the children who had not lived to see it.

"They are coming!" they told each other joyfully. "Soon it will be over—soon we shall be safe!"

On October 26, the relief column had entered Cawnpore, after fighting a running battle with isolated enemy forces endeavoring to flee across the Ganges to escape retribution . . . and the Nana's troops were said to be among them, although one report suggested that he was making for Kalpi, with the object of joining forces with Tantia Topi and the Gwalior Contingent. Hope Grant's column consisted of Her Majesty's 9th Lancers and the 8th and 75th Foot—battle-hardened veterans of the siege and recapture of Delhi—two troops of the Bengal Horse Artillery, Blunt's and Remington's, Bourchier's Field Battery, and detachments of Punjab cavalry and infantry, the former with squadrons commanded by Watson, Probyn, and Younghusband, and a squadron of Hodson's Horse, of which Hugh Gough—late of the 3rd Light Cavalry from Meerut—was in command.

By October 30, four companies of the 93rd Highlanders and some other infantry detachments had arrived to reinforce them— pushed up-country ahead of him by the commander-in-chief— and Hope Grant crossed the river into Oudh. He reached Bunni Bridge on the 31st and, while there, was informed that Sir Colin Campbell was at Cawnpore. On November 2, the Movable Column advanced to Buntera, a village only six miles from the Alam Bagh, and won its first victory against the besiegers of Lucknow. On the 6th, an advance party was sent to the Alam Bagh. It brought away the sick and wounded and dispatched them, under strong escort, to Cawnpore.

Then, on instructions from Sir Colin Campbell, Hope Grant

halted at Buntera to await his coming with, it was confidently expected, wings of various infantry regiments and a siege train manned by the two hundred–strong Naval Brigade under the command of Captain William Peel, Royal Navy, captain of H.M.S. *Shannon*.

Sir Colin Campbell, reviewing the situation on the morning of November 3, found himself facing a dilemma. Reliable intelligence gathered for him by Captain Bruce revealed the position of Cawnpore as one of extreme danger. The Gwalior Contingent, numbering five thousand men, with sixteen guns of heavy caliber and twenty-four field guns, was at Kalpi only forty miles distant, on the other side of the Jumna. The Nana, with his own followers and remnants of sepoy regiments from Delhi—amounting in all to a further five thousand—was on his way to Kalpi and the commander-in-chief was aware that, as soon as he advanced to the relief of Lucknow, an attack on his base at Cawnpore was virtually certain. With 60,000 rebel troops surrounding Lucknow, he could not divide his force—the most he could afford to leave as a holding force in Cawnpore were 500 British and 550 Madras infantry and gunners.

Sound military strategy demanded that he secure his base before attempting to reach Lucknow, but this could only be done by meeting and defeating the Gwalior Contingent and, since all the boats he would require if he were to cross the Jumna were in the hands of the rebels, the Nana and Tantia Topi could avoid coming to action for as long as seemed to them desirable. In the meantime, Lucknow might fall from lack of food . . .

Outram, it was true, learning of his dilemma, had written: *"We can manage to screw on till near the end of November, on further reduced rations, since it is obviously to the advantage of the State that the Gwalior rebels should be first effectually destroyed . . . our relief must be a secondary consideration."* To Colin Campbell, however, the relief of the Residency's heroic garrison was all important and he, who had often in the past been criticized for overcaution, decided to take a desperate gamble. During the six days he remained in Cawnpore, he provided for every contingency he could. General Windham was left in command of the entrenchment that Neill had constructed and held while Havelock was fighting in Oudh, and his orders were *"to show the best front possible but not to move out to the attack unless compelled to do so by the threat of bombardment."* The commander-in-chief added that, should he be severely threatened, Windham was at once to inform him.

On November 10, having sent on Peel's *Shannon* Brigade with its formidable siege guns and arranged for the dispatch of ordnance and engineer parks, commissariat and medical stores, Sir Colin Campbell left Cawnpore with a small escort of cavalry, prepared to take the greatest gamble of his long and distinguished career. In a letter to the Duke of Cambridge, he wrote: *"I intend to trust to the valor of my small but devoted band, make a dash for Lucknow, rescue the garrison and return—swiftly enough, I hope—to save Windham from any danger that may threaten him."*

CHAPTER SIX

➤➤➤ • ◄◄◄

FOR ALEX SHERIDAN, the weeks he spent as a prisoner behind the rebel lines were among the most frustrating he had ever been called upon to endure.

He was well, even generously treated. With servants to wait on him, food, drink and tobacco freely provided, his life might have been envied by many poor souls in the Residency garrison, and his health benefited greatly from the more than adequate diet and the enforced rest. The slight wound he had sustained in his left leg was dressed daily by a native physician, a skillful old man, who took a great interest in him and insisted on treating his scarred face with herbs and lotions, which wrought a remarkable improvement in the puckered scar tissue on cheek and brow.

Rajah Man Singh, at their first interview, made it clear to him that there was an ulterior motive behind the decision to preserve his life, but the tone of their conversation suggested to Alex that he was required rather as a living proof of the Hindu chief's continued loyalty to the British Raj than for any more sinister purpose. Initially he made no mention of Lettice Wheeler's presence in his camp; instead he explained, at considerable length, the reason for his own presence in Lucknow.

"Understand, Sheridan Sahib," he said earnestly, "that ever since the sepoy regiments broke out in mutiny, I have done all in my power to give aid and sanctuary to those British officers and their families who were driven as fugitives from the stations. I turned none away. Despite threats from those who, like the

Nana of Bithur, have joined in the rebellion, I fed and clothed your countrymen and, when it was possible, I sent them under escort to Allahabad or Benares." He gave names and dates, and Alex, who had met some of the refugees he mentioned and been told of others, had no reason to doubt his claim. "Also," Man Singh went on, "I have sent reports concerning the movement of the Nana's troops and, of late, those of the Begum, to Gubbins Sahib in the Residency, as well as to the General Sahib, Sir James Outram."

"But you are here with your own troops, Rajah Sahib," Alex reminded him. "Ranging them with the ranks of mutinous sepoys, who hold the Residency under siege."

"My troops are here only for my protection," Man Singh corrected. His round, golden brown face was innocent of guile and his tone indignant. "I came here for the sole purpose of effecting the rescue of my aunt, the widow of Rajah Buktwar Singh, whose person was unlawfully seized by the rebels. The brother of Gubbins Sahib, Commissioner in Benares, was aware of my desire to ensure the Rani's safety, since I informed him of it before coming here. I demanded her release and my demands were complied with, but the Begum insists on keeping me here, seeking to persuade me to join her cause. If I attempt to withdraw my troops, as was my intention, twenty *koss* from Lucknow, the rebel sepoys will be incited to attack me . . . and my men are lightly armed, without guns." He spread his hands in a gesture of resignation. "I wait only for the opportunity—perhaps when the British send more soldiers to relieve the garrison—and then I shall withdraw my troops. I have no connection with the rebels, Sheridan Sahib . . . save of necessity. And assuredly I have no quarrel with the British—I have not and will not take up arms against my friends, nor will I betray any of your people. Am I not protecting you? I recognized you the night you came to the Kaiser Bagh . . . if I were a traitor, would I not have delivered you to the Moulvi?"

"True, Rajah Sahib," Alex conceded. "And I am grateful. You gave me my life and I am in your debt." He hesitated, searching the inscrutable face opposite him and then, unable to learn anything from it, asked bluntly, "How may I repay you?"

"I ask no repayment or reward," Man Singh answered, smiling. "If, when the opportunity occurs, I am able to deliver you to Cawnpore or even to aid you to return to the Residency, all I shall ask is that you will inform General Outram and Mr. Gubbins of my continued friendship and loyalty."

"That, of course I shall do," Alex promised.

"Then it is enough," Man Singh assured him. He rose to signify that the interview was at an end, and added, "You have the freedom of my encampment, Sheridan Sahib—go where you will within its confines but, for your own safety, do not go beyond and keep always with you the escort I shall provide. Do not attempt to return to the Residency without my help for, if you do, the rebels will kill you."

The escort, obviously, would be under orders to prevent any attempt at escape, Alex thought and, after a momentary pause, he inclined his head in assent. There was more, a great deal more that he wanted to know, but he sensed that this was not the time to question his rescuer concerning Kaur Singh or the other *taluk-dars* . . . first he must persuade Man Singh to trust him. Letty Wheeler was, however, a different and more urgent matter, and he said, his tone deliberately casual, "Rajah Sahib, it has been brought to my knowledge that you have also the daughter of General Wheeler under your protection."

"That is so," the Rajah admitted. "I had much admiration for

General Wheeler. When his daughter sought my help, I gave it."

"Do you intend to release her, when I am released?"

"You speak as if I imprison you! That is not the case, Colonel Sheridan—did I not make it clear that you are not a prisoner?"

"My words were ill chosen," Alex apologized, swiftly on his guard.

"Then, in reply to your question . . . the general's daughter is free to go with you, when I restore you to your own people, or to remain, as she herself chooses. But here in my encampment, it would be better if you did not associate with her, save when others are present. I am aware," Man Singh raised a hand, as Alex started to speak, "I am aware that the *mem* sought you out, contrary to my instructions, which, like my advice to you, Sheridan Sahib, I gave only to ensure both your safety and hers."

"She will come to no harm in my company, Rajah Sahib," Alex began. "Her father was also my friend and my commander, I—"

"You are man of honor, Sheridan Sahib," Man Singh put in smoothly. "Of that I have no doubt but—"

"Then trust in my honor, if you please. The *mem* is young, scarcely more than a child, and she has suffered much. She was in the entrenchment at Cawnpore, she witnessed her father's murder, and it is natural that she should seek the company of one of her own countrymen."

There was a flicker of uneasiness in Man Singh's dark, intelligent eyes. "You may see and converse with her, Colonel Sahib," he agreed. "But not alone—that would be misunderstood by my people. And by her husband, who is of the Moslem faith. He—"

"Her marriage, like her conversion to the Moslem faith, was forced upon her," Alex protested indignantly.

"True," the Rajah conceded. "Nevertheless, both marriage and conversion took place and must be recognized here. I myself have to tread warily, for I am among many enemies. I cannot afford to offend the followers of the Prophet. But," he shrugged, "matters can be arranged. A woman of my household shall be appointed to accompany General Wheeler's daughter, one who has no knowledge of your language, so that you may speak freely in her presence. Will that suffice?"

"It will suffice, Rajah Sahib," Alex answered, controlling his impatience. "And I thank you." He accepted his dismissal and returned to his own tent under the respectful but nonetheless vigilant escort of Subedar Kedar Nath and the Rajah's *vakeel,* Ananta Ram.

Despite the Rajah's promise, however, he did not see Letty Wheeler for over a week and, when he was finally permitted to do so, she was heavily veiled and accompanied by a pock-marked old crone, whose presence inhibited conversation. Her voice muffled and her face hidden by the all-enveloping *boorkha,* Letty assured him that she was in good health and being well treated and then the crone hurried her back to the women's tents, clucking over her charge like an agitated mother hen. Alex sensed that all was not well. But, unable to question her, he could only guess at the cause until, that evening, when he left his tent to take such exercise as he was permitted, he found his escort augmented by a *daffadar* of the 2nd Light Cavalry—a tall, light-skinned man, who subjected him to a lengthy scrutiny and then fell in behind him without a word. He walked to the eastern side of the camp, as he always did, and stood there staring into the gathering darkness, in an attempt to deduce—from the direction of the distant firing—what progress the Residency defenders had made and, a trifle to his surprise, the *daffadar* volunteered the information that Phillips' House had been taken after a desperate battle and the gun battery put out of action.

Questioned, he gave details of the attack, his tone openly contemptuous as he described how the covering infantry had fled when the battle seemed to be going against them, leaving the *golandazes* to be cut to pieces beside their guns and the whole battery to fall into the hands of a vastly inferior force of British soldiers. Rebuked by the old subedar, the tall cavalryman was unrepentant.

"I tell only of what I saw with my own eyes, Subedar Sahib," he returned sullenly. "My troop was called upon to aid in taking away the ammunition tumbrils, but they called upon us too late. Yet there were but a handful of *feringhis* and our sepoys were behind a stockade, with a strong building to their rear, loopholed for musket fire, which they could have held easily against so few. They did not even attempt to hold it—as soon as they saw the *lal-kotes* fix bayonets and prepare to charge them, the dogs took to their heels, abandoning the *golandazes* to their fate. Now all the buildings overlooking the Cawnpore road are blown up and the guns likewise."

"Your brave sowars did nothing to prevent it," the subedar accused.

"How could we, when our horses were harnessed to tumbrils?" the *daffadar* defended hotly. "As I said, they called upon us when it was too late. We saved the ammunition but, alas, to no purpose, since the guns from which it should have been fired were destroyed by the *feringhis* . . . thanks to your dogs of sepoys!"

They continued to argue, forgetful of his presence as the argument grew more heated and Alex remained silent, listening and inwardly rejoicing as the scraps of information they let drop revealed that the defenders of the Residency were more than holding their own. Later, when he returned to his tent, he made an opportunity to talk in private to the *daffadar* and found him unexpectedly communicative and, at times, savagely critical of the manner in which the siege was being conducted. He gave his name as Mohammed Khan Aziz but did not, at first, mention his marriage to Letty Wheeler, and Alex, taking his cue from this omission, made no mention of it either, content to bide his time until the man should see fit to confide in him.

Mohammed Khan was an intelligent and experienced soldier, and, on his own admission, he had been one of the leaders of the mutiny in his regiment, believing the Moulvi's impassioned claim that all Muslim India was about to rise in order to restore the Mogul emperor to his throne . . . and the deposed Wajid Ali to the throne of Oudh. Now, while not admitting that he regretted having joined the revolt, he made no secret of his disillusionment at the turn events had taken or of his dissatisfaction with his present circumstances, which he attributed mainly to the rebels' divided and inept command, and to the religious differences and jealousies by which they were beset.

"I had thought to march to Delhi, with my *paltan,* to pledge my sword and my life to the service of the Shah Bahadur," he confessed. "But instead, Teeka Singh—our Rissaldar Major—gave ear to the false promises of the Nana of Bithur. He allowed himself to be bribed, to be named as general of Cavalry and throughout the siege of General Wheeler Sahib's entrenchment, he thought of nothing save how to enrich himself with plunder. I had wished the General Sahib no harm—he was a good man and a valiant soldier—yet we were all compelled to take up arms against him and, in the end, to betray him and his garrison. You were there, Sheridan Sahib, you know what befell them."

"Yes," Alex confirmed, his voice without expression. "I was there and I know, Mohammed Khan."

The *daffadar* talked on, seeming almost glad to relieve his conscience as he spoke of the massacre of the Cawnpore garrison. "I rode down to the Suttee Chowra Ghat with Vibart Sahib and his Memsahib. I had one of the Sahib's children on my saddlebow . . . a golden-haired little girl, and we were laughing and making jokes with the Sahib, as if we, too, were children. We—"

"Knew you not what was planned?" Alex interrupted harshly, unable to contain himself as memory stirred.

"*Nahin*, Sahib, I knew not." Mohammed Khan's denial was unhappy and it had the ring of truth. "Some knew, it is true . . . our Rissaldar among them. But not I. That I swear to you. When the bugle sounded and the guns were unmasked, I was taken by surprise. The Rissaldar was not. He rode into the water, striking at the *mems* in the water with his *tulwar* and urging us to do likewise. Then one of the sahibs shot him down and—"

"I was that sahib," Alex told him. "I killed your Rissaldar, Mohammed Khan."

The *daffadar* eyed him somberly. "You were fighting for your own life, Sheridan Sahib, and for the *mems* and the *baba-log*." He shrugged and, after a momentary hesitation, continued his narrative. "I rode back toward the bridge. I wanted no part in what was being done. I am a soldier and I have seen many men die . . . but not like that. The garrison had fought well, they had accepted honorable surrender, and the Nana Sahib had promised them safe conduct. Yet he ordered them to be massacred—all of them, the *mems* and the *baba-log*. He is a Mahratta, an accursed Hindu. I am of the Faith and I do not break my word or make war on women." Again he hesitated and Alex asked, without anger, "Is that why you took the General Sahib's daughter?"

Mohammed Khan inclined his turbaned head. "*Ji-han*, Sahib. I had not reached the bridge when I saw the old general. He had been wounded, he could scarcely walk, but they put his *doolie* down and bade him rise to his feet. He tried and they let him stagger a few paces, mocking him, and then they set upon him and hacked him to pieces. One of them, a dog of a Hindu, cut his head from the body and held it up. His *mem* was watching, with his two daughters. I could not stand by and do nothing. I took the girl, lifted her onto my horse and rode with her back to the city. I did not harm her, I thought only to save her, to protect her. She is young, hardly more than a child. I took her honorably, Sheridan Sahib—I arranged for her to receive instruction in the Faith and then I took her as my wife, after her conversion. In the eyes of Allah, she is my woman."

He spoke with such evident sincerity that Alex did not doubt that he was telling the truth. Letty, he thought, had been more fortunate than her elder sister on the face of it, but . . . "Have you other women in your *zenana?*" he questioned sternly. "Other wives to the number permitted by your Faith?"

Mohammed Khan shook his head. "*Nahin,* Sahib . . . and I shall take no others. The General Sahib's daughter now bears my name and the name she was given on her conversion to the Faith —Auliah. She is my woman—I shall not yield her to any man. If you would take her, you must first kill me, Sheridan Sahib. Be that understood."

"I seek only to restore her to her own people, Mohammed Khan," Alex told him. "If that were her wish, if she were to plead with you to allow her to go, would you still refuse?"

"Even then," the *daffadar* answered, stone-faced. He added defiantly, "She does not wish to go . . . nor will she. She is my wife, she will bear my child. It is said that you are a man of honor, Sheridan Sahib. Do not seek to take Auliah from me. But for me, she would be dead. She is in the camp of Man Singh—

as you are—for her own safety." He launched into a harrowing
account of the perils they had both faced from other rebel
soldiers, who had doubted the truth of Letty's conversion.
"The men of my *paltan* do not forget how her elder sister
served the sowar who, as I did, saved her from the massacre
at the Suttee Chowra Ghat. They taunt me constantly and
threaten Auliah's life. It was for this reason that I brought her
here, that she might escape from her enemies. I had not thought
to find you—a *feringhi*—among them, Sheridan Sahib."

He saluted and took his leave abruptly, as if afraid that
he might have said too much, but he came to the camp
whenever he was off duty and frequently relieved the old
subedar of his escort, so that Alex, by dint of judicious questioning, was able to build up a fairly accurate picture of the state
of affairs among the rebel host in Lucknow. As before,
Mohammed Khan was critical of their leadership and of the
fighting qualities of the Hindu sepoys and, assured of a sympathetic hearing, he talked freely of both. His allegiance had been
given, he explained, to the young Birjis Quadr—recently
enthroned as Nawab of Oudh and, through him, to his mother,
the Begum Hazrat Mahal, but, to Alex's surprise, he confessed to
mistrust of the Moulvi.

"First, Sheridan Sahib, he sought a kingdom for the Nana,
but now, it would seem, he seeks one for himself. Already he
claims to be the *Khalifat-Ullah*—the vice-regent of Allah—no
less!" The *daffadar* spat his disgust. "He pays lip service to the
Begum, and she reposes absolute trust in him, but the young
Nawab is kept hidden from his people—in Fyzabad, it is said—
and appointments to high command go always to men of the
Moulvi Sahib's choosing. Many are Hindus, and it is known that

the Moulvi is in communication still with the Nana, whom he urges to march with the forces he commands on Cawnpore."

"*On Cawnpore?*" Alex echoed, every sense alert.

"*Ji-han,* Sahib," Mohammed Khan asserted. "Tantia Topi has taken command of the Gwalior Contingent, it is said, and is awaiting the Nana at Kalpi. Together they will attack Cawnpore . . . instead of marching against Agra or to the aid of the Shah Bahadur in Delhi." He sighed in frustration. "The Moulvi told us that we must wage *jihad*—a holy war—for the Faith. He told us that we must overthrow the Company's Raj since, if we did not, we should be compelled to adopt the Christian religion. That was the Company's policy, he said. First we were to be tricked into breaking our Faith by using the accursed cartridges greased with pig fat and then, when our spiritual purity was lost, we should have no choice but to become Christian outcasts." He broke off, to eye Alex anxiously. "Was that the truth, Sheridan Sahib?"

Alex, his own anxiety centered on Cawnpore, forced himself to meet the *daffadar*'s gaze squarely. "No," he answered quietly. "It was not the truth." He gave chapter and verse and then asked again about the proposed attack on Cawnpore but, beyond the fact that this was planned to take place after Sir Colin Campbell's relief force began to march to Lucknow, could glean no more, since the *daffadar*'s knowledge was based on camp gossip.

"I would not have betrayed my salt save in defense of the Faith, Sahib," Mohammed Khan told him earnestly. "I had pride in my regiment and in the Company's service, as most of us had. But when the Moulvi called upon us to rise and fight for our beliefs, we heeded his words. We followed him blindly, little thinking that we were to be called upon to fight and die in the cause of an accursed Mahratta!" Again he hesitated, eyes now on his booted feet as if undecided, and then, evidently coming to a decision, he looked up. "Sahib, we hear rumors that Delhi has fallen and the Shah Bahadur is a prisoner . . . but these are denied. Do *you* know if it is so? Tell me truly, Sahib, I beg you!"

"Yes, it is so, *Daffadar-ji,*" Alex confirmed. "General Outram received word before we left the Alam Bagh. The forces of the Government assaulted and recaptured the city of Delhi and the Red Fort, and the king yielded himself as a prisoner to them. The mutiny there is over."

Daffadar Mohammed Khan was silent for a long, tense moment, his eyes searching Alex's face. "We should have gone to Delhi!" he exclaimed with bitterness. "We and the Gwalior troops also. We should not have permitted the Moulvi to turn us from our purpose. This," he waved an arm despairingly toward the domes and minarets of the city of Lucknow, etched in graceful silhouette against the glow of the sunset, "this is no holy war, Sahib! It is not being waged for the Faith but by evil men with political ambitions, who seek power and wealth for themselves. I did not betray my salt that they might achieve their desires, nor did I watch the brave old General Wheeler die that the Nana might place a crown on his head. Auliah tells me that I dishonor myself by—nay, I . . ." he bit back whatever he had intended to say, unhappy color rising to burn in his dark cheeks, but Alex seized upon the smothered admission. The general's daughter, he thought in relief, was not the only one to have undergone a form of conversion . . .

"Mohammed Khan," he demanded sternly, "do you now regret that you did not remain true to your salt?"

The *daffadar* expelled his breath in a long-drawn sigh. It was evident that he was fighting an inward, emotional battle with himself, but finally he bowed his head.

"I regret many things, Sheridan Sahib," he conceded. "I stay here only because four months' pay is owed to me. When I receive that, I shall depart for my village and take my wife with me."

"Would you not be willing to return to the Company's service?" Alex persisted.

Mohammed Khan stared at him in disbelief. "I, a mutineer? Sahib, you jest with me cruelly! If I were to return, should I not be blown from a cannon or hanged and my body defiled and burned? It is known to us that General Neill served the men of my *paltan* thus, if they fell into his hands and—"

Alex cut him short. "Not if you returned with me to the Residency, *Daffadar-ji,* having aided me to escape. And if you brought the daughter of General Wheeler with you, a full pardon would be certain and probably a pension also."

"And she would be taken from me!" Mohammed Khan flung at him accusingly. "That is what you want, Sahib, is it not—to restore Auliah to your people?"

"Only if that is her wish, Mohammed Khan."

"She is not wholly white, Sahib. Her mother was of Hind. She—"

"Then it will be for her to choose, will it not?"

"You know how much choice your people would permit her, were I to bring her to the Residency, Sheridan Sahib."

"Speak to her of it, at least," Alex pleaded.

"She is my wife. She must obey me and leave such decisions to me. But," the *daffadar* eyed him sadly, "I will mention the matter to her. And as to aiding you to return to the Residency—why, Sahib, are you not free to go? I had understood that the Rajah Man Singh does not hold you as a prisoner."

"Do I appear to be free?" Alex challenged wryly. "Are you not guarding me?"

"For your own protection, Sahib. Your life would be at great risk were you to venture beyond this encampment."

"Not in your company, dressed as one of your sowars—"

"The risk is too great, Sahib," Mohammed Khan said with conviction. "If you take it, that is not my affair, but I cannot aid you without the Rajah's knowledge and consent."

"And if the Rajah gave his consent?"

Mohammed Khan smiled. "Then I would aid you," he promised. "And, if assured of a pardon, I would return to the Company's service. But I would come alone."

With this, Alex had to be satisfied, and he did not press the point, although, with each day that passed, his anxiety to rejoin the defenders of the Residency became more acute. Kaur Singh did not, as he had hoped and expected, make any attempt to contact him, and requests for an audience with the Rajah were met with bland excuses.

"You are not comfortable, Sahib?" Ananta Ram, the *vakeel,* asked reproachfully. "You are being well treated, surely? If there is anything that you lack, you have only to make your wishes known to me. A woman, perhaps, to beguile these hours of enforced leisure?"

"I would speak with the Rajah Sahib," Alex retorted, "concerning my return to the Residency or to Cawnpore. I am a soldier and my people are at war, Ananta Ram. It ill befits a soldier to beguile himself with women at such a time."

"True," the *vakeel* agreed. "But my master is at present unwell. He can see no one until he has recovered his strength. Have patience, Sheridan Sahib, I beg you. Your release will be arranged when it is possible to escort you safely to rejoin your people."

It was almost a week before Alex's demands were finally complied with, but Man Singh, at their second interview, was evasive, although, as always, courteous and friendly. He spoke of the advance of Hope Grant's force and of their successful engagement at Agra and confidently predicted the arrival of substantial reinforcements in Cawnpore, even naming the regiments that had arrived or were on their way there. He had sent his *vakeel* to deliver a letter to Captain Bruce—commanding the newly raised native police in Cawnpore—with the request that it be forwarded to General Outram, he added, smiling. The letter made his own position clear; his ties with the British were too strong to be broken and he had assured both Bruce and the general of his continued loyalty and good intentions.

"Of this you, Sheridan Sahib, will be able to bear witness, will you not?" he concluded, still smiling.

"I shall be happy to do so, Rajah Sahib," Alex assured him. "In person and at once, if you can arrange for me to return to the Residency . . . or even to follow your *vakeel* to Cawnpore."

"It shall be arranged," the Rajah promised. "At the first possible opportunity. At present, however, the road to Cawnpore is too dangerous, and for you to attempt to regain the Residency would be to run the risk of falling into the hands of the mutineers."

"I am prepared to take that risk—" Alex began, but Man Singh shook his head. "I cannot permit you to do so, Sheridan Sahib," he stated firmly. "Be patient, if you please. You will be sent on your way as soon as it is safe . . . safe for us both, you understand. I run a considerable risk in giving you shelter."

This was true, of course, Alex was forced to concede, and, aware that argument was useless, he thanked his host stiffly and took his leave, to spend the rest of the day planning how best to make his escape. With *Daffadar* Mohammed Khan's help, he might manage to reach the Residency—or, failing the Residency, the

Alam Bagh—but alone, he knew, he would stand a very slim chance of avoiding detection, since the river banks and all approaches to the city were heavily guarded. He was waiting with impatience for the *daffadar* to report for escort duty that evening when, to his surprise, Letty Wheeler appeared at the tent-flap to ask, with a humility he found oddly hurtful, if she might speak with him.

She was veiled, as before, and the crone was with her, but, when she entered the tent, she firmly bade the old woman wait outside and, disregarding her protests, pulled the tent-flap shut behind her. Seating herself, cross-legged in the native fashion, she said in an urgent whisper, "Colonel Sheridan, I dare not stay more than a few minutes, but I had to see you."

"Of course," Alex acknowledged, recovering from his surprise. He remained standing, his body interposed between her and the tent-flap. "How may I serve you?"

"Those days are past," she answered bitterly. "Men do not serve me, I . . ." she broke off, her eyes behind the thin slits in her veil filled with tears. Then, her tone apologetic, she went on, "I think of myself now not as the daughter of General Sir Hugh Wheeler but as the wife of Mohammed Khan. I shall grow accustomed to my role and . . . I am not unhappy. My husband is good to me, insofar as custom and his religion permit. He is a good man and an honorable one and I owe him my life."

"But, Letty, my dear child," Alex began. "If you make your escape to the Residency with me, you—"

Letty Wheeler cut him short. "My husband has spoken to me of that, Colonel Sheridan. He says he is willing to aid you and to return to the Company's service with you, on the promise of a pardon. He"—there was a catch in her voice—"he told me that if I truly wanted it, he would take me back also. But we both know what the outcome would be, do we not? He would be pensioned and sent away, while I . . . oh, Colonel Sheridan, surely you know what *my* fate would be?"

He knew, of course, Alex thought wryly. British society would never accept her; no matter what excuses were made, there would be smug British matrons ready to point the finger of scorn at her, ready to condemn her because—even if it had been the means of saving her life—she had been married to a native and was, in any case, the child of a mixed marriage. Her mother had been a high-caste woman of impeccable family but . . . she had still been an Indian. Recalling the comparison Letty had made between herself and her elder sister, on the occasion of her first visit to his tent, Alex's heart went out to her. He laid his hand gently on her shoulder.

"Then," he asked pityingly, "what have you decided to do?"

She looked up to meet his gaze, her own unflinching. "To remain the wife of Mohammed Khan. I am to bear his child, but I . . . for my father's sake, Colonel Sheridan, the reason I have come here now is to beg that you will not tell of our meeting. Let my father's people believe me dead—murdered at the Suttee Chowra Ghat with all the rest. It will be better so, believe me."

"If that is what you wish," Alex sighed. "If it is truly what you wish."

"It is," Letty assured him. She rose to her feet and stood facing him, a small yet oddly dignified figure in the shapeless *purdah* robe. "I am to go to my husband's village, to the house of his father, who is the headman, there to await the birth of my child. Mohammed Khan has sent for one of his brothers to take me there, and he will ask leave to escort me through the rebel lines.

The journey will take only 24 hours—he will return and place himself at your service, trusting in your word that, if he aids your escape from here, you will obtain a pardon for him. You will keep your word, will you not, Colonel Sheridan?"

Deeply moved, Alex inclined his head. "Yes, I'll keep it, Letty."

"And my . . . my secret also?"

"That, too, my dear child."

"Thank you," Letty Wheeler said softly. "It would not be fitting for a general's daughter to be the wife of a mutineer, but, if Mohammed Khan returns to the Company's service, then I shall be content." She hesitated, hearing the old woman's querulous voice from outside the tent. "My chaperone grows impatient. I must go, for it is she who will suffer if I am discovered here. But . . . I have spoken only of myself and there are rumors being bandied about that may be of some concern to you, if you have not heard them . . ." she broke off, seeking to silence the crone with the promise, delivered sharply in Hindustani, that she was about to take her leave.

"What rumors?" Alex prompted, as she turned to face him.

"First that Rajah Man Singh is not entirely to be trusted," Letty warned him gravely. "It is said that he will not release you— that he intends to keep you as a hostage until he is certain that the relief of the Lucknow garrison can be successfully accomplished and the rebels defeated."

"That was what I suspected," Alex confessed ruefully. "Man Singh is trying to run with the hare and hunt with the hounds, I'm afraid. He is not in sympathy with the rebels and, if left to himself, would give us his support. Unhappily, as he pointed out to me quite recently, he's in a precarious position here. His levies don't amount to much and he has no guns, whereas the Begum and the Moulvi have vastly superior forces at their command."

"I have also heard it said that there is bad blood between Man Singh and the Moulvi, Colonel Sheridan, and that each plots the overthrow of the other. My husband and many of his comrades believe that in spite of their religious differences, the Moulvi still supports the cause of the unspeakable Nana Sahib and that they are in league together for their own ends. Did he—did Mohammed Khan tell you of this?"

"Yes," Alex answered. "He did, in general terms. He—"

"Did he tell you that the Nana is expected here?"

"Expected *here?* No, he didn't mention that possibility. But . . ." Mohammed Khan had said that the Nana was about to join Tantia Topi and the Gwalior troops at Kalpi, with the intention of launching an attack on Cawnpore, Alex recalled. He stared down at Letty Wheeler, in some bewilderment, his brain racing as he considered the implication of her words. "When is he expected, Letty, do you know?"

She shook her head. "It will be soon, that is all I know. I . . ." she bit back a sob and her voice was choked with emotion as she went on, "that cruel, treacherous man! He betrayed my father's friendship and his trust, he . . . oh, Colonel, it is wrong to hate, I know, but I pray the Nana may meet the end he deserves—I pray that someone will take revenge on him for what he did to us at Cawnpore! He . . ." the old woman called to her from outside, more urgently this time, but Letty ignored her plea. "Those poor, poor people from Sitapur . . . they were brought in at the Nana's instigation, in fetters, and they had been so cruelly mistreated that they were barely alive, my husband said. He saw them with his own eyes and was moved by their plight. Colonel Sheridan, when you return to the Residency—as I hope and pray you soon will—you'll tell Sir James Outram about them, won't you?"

"Yes, of course I will, Letty," Alex promised, puzzled. "Do you know where they are being held and who they are?"

"They were taken to the Kaiser Bagh but . . ." the tent-flap parted and the old woman's dark face appeared in the aperture, mouthing reproaches. She was so insistent and so clearly frightened that Alex grasped her by the shoulder and drew her into the tent, looking about him for something with which to buy her silence. His cheroot case lay on the table in front of him; it was silver, with his initials engraved on it, and Emmy had given it to him to mark their wedding anniversary, but . . . it was about the only thing of value he now possessed. He thrust it into the gnarled old hand and said harshly, in Hindustani, "Wait . . . the *mem* will only be a few more minutes," and the crone sank grumbling onto her haunches, clutching her unexpected prize to her bosom and still looking more alarmed than pleased.

Letty smothered a sigh. "I don't know their names," she said. "Only that they are from Sitapur and that there are three officers and a lady with a child—or there may be two ladies, one with a child. They had escaped from the mutiny of the native regiments and taken refuge at Mithowlee, with the Rajah Lonee Singh. He treated them most cruelly and finally betrayed them to the Nana, who ordered them to be brought here. My husband said that they were starving and barely able to walk, poor souls, and, as I told you, they were fettered. One of the men, he said, had gone quite out of his mind."

"A middle-aged man?" Alex questioned. George Christian had been commissioner at Sitapur, he remembered; a kindly, charming man in his late forties, with a young wife and one—

no, two small children. His assistant, Sir Mountstuart Jackson, was a youthful baronet, whose two sisters had come out to make their home with him, following the death of their parents.

Letty shook her head helplessly. "I don't know, Colonel Sheridan. My husband said that one of the gentlemen was white-haired and he thought the ladies were young—there must have been two, because he spoke of them as *mems*. He said they were in rags and barefooted, poor creatures, and that the child was whimpering all the time, as if it were ill. My heart bleeds for them, I . . . you will do what you can for them, won't you? When you return to the Residency, I mean—there is nothing, alas, that you can do for them while you are held prisoner here."

He might, perhaps, put Man Singh's loyalty to the test by requesting his aid for the fugitives, Alex thought wryly. Beyond that . . . dear God, he must delay his own escape no longer. If the Nana was, in fact, coming to Lucknow, it was on the cards that he would demand the execution of the unfortunates from Sitapur and . . . the old woman, clinging to his cheroot case as if it were a talisman, was on her feet, again begging Letty to hasten her departure and warning her of the consequences if she did not.

"I will stay here no longer," she chided. "If the *daffadar* should discover where you have been, little one, he will slit my throat and doubtless yours also! And the Rajah Sahib will be angry—" The girl cut her short.

"All right, I am coming." She looked up at Alex, hesitated, and then held out her hand. "We shall not see each other again, Colonel Sheridan, but I shall think of you and pray for you."

"And I for you, Letty," Alex assured her. He took her hand in his and, disregarding the old woman's outraged protests, bore it to his lips. *"Khuda hafiz,"* he added, using the old Muslim bless-ing. "Go with God, Auliah!"

"I do not know any longer with which God," Letty answered wretchedly. "But perhaps it does not matter. There is no God but God, I have been taught, and I shall try to believe that."

She slipped from the tent in the wake of her anxious atten-dant, and Alex was conscious of an overwhelming sadness as he watched the darkness swallow her up. In the circumstances, she had, he knew, made the only possible decision, but all the same it had been a heartbreaking one, both for her and for himself.

Next morning, Subedar Kedar Nath told him that Mohammed Khan had departed at dawn with his wife; significantly, it was the first time the old man had referred to Letty as such—always pre-viously he had called her "the daughter of General Wheeler." Alex asked him about the newly arrived prisoners in the Kaiser Bagh, but he denied all knowledge of them and, to the request that an interview be arranged with Man Singh, he returned a blank, uncomprehending stare and then claimed unconvincingly that the Rajah had left the camp. Some hours later, however, the *vakeel,* Ananta Ram—who had evidently just returned from his mission to Cawnpore—presented himself in Alex's tent and, after some politely meaningless inquiries as to his health and well-being, volunteered the information that his master had interceded on behalf of the British fugitives.

"Are they to be brought here?" Alex asked eagerly, but the *vakeel* shook his head.

"That will not be possible, Sheridan Sahib. My master endeav-ored, of course, to persuade the Begum to allow them to be placed under his protection, but the Moulvi raised strenuous objections . . . and the Begum alas, listens to no one else." Ananta

Ram shrugged his plump shoulders. "Nevertheless," he qualified, sensing Alex's dismayed reaction to this news, "they have been placed in the custody of Daroga Wajid Ali, who is a kindly, well-intentioned man and indebted to my master for many favors in the past. He will see to it that the *sahib-log* are not abused and that they are given food and water and changes of raiment. They are still held in the Kaiser Bagh, guarded by the Moulvi's soldiers, but already Wajid Ali has caused their fetters to be removed and he has summoned a physician to attend them."

"Are they ill, Ananta Ram—or wounded?"

"Regrettably it seems that all are sick, Sahib," Ananta Ram admitted. "Lonee Singh is a cruel and treacherous man, who let them wander in the jungle and starve, after they fled from Sitapur to seek his protection—and it was he who betrayed them, being paid in gold by the Nana for his betrayal. My master intends to inform General Outram of this, so that just punishment may be meted out to Lonee Singh when the British Raj is restored."

"And to the Nana also," Alex reminded him.

"Most assuredly, Sahib," the *vakeel* agreed hastily. He made no mention of the Nana's impending visit and was, as usual, evasive when Alex brought up the subject of his own return to the Residency, but he seemed anxious to speak of his journey to Cawnpore, describing in enthusiastic detail the number of troops now gathered there in expectation of the arrival of the commander-in-chief. If he had learned nothing else during his enforced sojourn in Man Singh's camp, he had at least learned patience, Alex thought ruefully; he hid his own anxiety and let the man talk, hearing much that was calculated to raise his spirits. Hope Grant's column, it seemed, was continuing to carry all before it, and his cavalry had engaged and defeated a strong force of the Nana's Irregulars, driving them once more across the river into Oudh.

He listened for the most part in silence, only now and then interposing a question but had to suppress an exclamation of incredulity when the *vakeel* described the entry into Cawnpore of what appeared to be a naval advance party, with a battery of twenty-four-pounder guns, drawn by elephants, which he claimed had come up from Allahabad.

"And they are saying that more sailors with heavy guns will come up by river, Sahib," Ananta Ram confided, a broad grin curving his lips. "Bruce Sahib told me also that Delhi is again in British hands—he had received definite confirmation of this and I heard it, too, from sepoys I met on the road, who had themselves fled from there. The tide is turning at last—soon, surely, Lucknow will be liberated!"

"Very soon, Ananta Ram," Alex retorted crisply. "It would therefore be a wise move on your master's part if he were to insist on the Sitapur prisoners' release from the Kaiser Bagh. If they are brought here, they will be safe, and they can then return with me to the Residency as added proof of the Rajah Sahib's loyalty and goodwill."

"My master has used his best endeavors, I assure you, Sheridan Sahib, but without success. The Moulvi will not let them go. As I told you, they are sick—too sick to be moved and—"

"Have you seen them?" Alex interrupted.

The plump Brahmin shook his head. "No, Sahib, it was not permitted. I am only just back from Cawnpore, but I went with all haste and—"

"But Daroga Wajid Ali is in your master's debt! Surely *he* will permit you to see them?"

"I shall try a second time, Sheridan Sahib."

"Soon?" Alex persisted.

"This evening, if it is possible," Ananta Ram promised "Have you some message you wish me to deliver to them?"

Alex pondered the question, frowning. A written message might be dangerous, both for himself and for the recipient, he knew, but a verbal one, offering encouragement to the fugitives, could do no harm. It was as much as Ananta Ram's life was worth to disclose his presence in the Rajah's camp to the Moulvi, so that obviously the *vakeel* would take every care in its delivery.

"Yes," he said. "I will send a message. Do you know who the prisoners are? Have you heard their names?"

"Alas, I know little, Sheridan Sahib. But there are eight of them—four sahibs and two *mems,* with two small girl-children, I was told." Ananta Ram hesitated, licking his lips uncertainly. "One name I did hear, Sahib . . . it was, I think, Jackson."

Mountstuart Jackson, Alex thought . . . eight of them, including the children. Oh, merciful heaven, were they the only survivors of the outbreak in Sitapur? He cast his mind back, having to make an effort to remember. Jackson's two pretty young sisters —Madeline and . . . what had been the elder girl's name? Mary . . . Margaret? He could not remember very much about them, except that they had stayed for a time in Lucknow with their uncle, Coverly Jackson—at that time chief commissioner of Oudh and, ironically, the man responsible for the abrupt termination of his own civil appointment in Adjodhabad. Well connected, young and fresh from England, both girls had been popular and very much part of the social scene in Lucknow—he had a vague recollection of having met them at a ball or dinner at the Residency, which he had attended when Emmy . . . he drew in his breath sharply. When Emmy had been alive . . .

"I will find out the names for you, Sahib," Ananta Ram offered.

"Then you can compose the message I am to deliver to them."

He was as good as his word and, just after sunset, returned with the names of the Kaiser Bagh captives. "The sahibs are Assistant Commissioner Mountstuart Jackson, Lieutenant Burns, Adjutant of the Tenth Oudh Irregular Infantry, and Sergeant Major Morton of the same regiment—who is an old man, Sheridan Sahib, and like to die from the sickness that possesses him. The fourth sahib is from Mohumdi, Captain Orr, with his *mem-sahib* and girl-child, and the other *mem* is the sister of Jackson Sahib. In addition, there is another small child, whose parents are dead—Sophie Christian."

So the kindly George Christian was dead and his wife with him, Alex thought bitterly—they and God knew how many more unfortunates, who had remained at their isolated stations without regard for their own safety, in the vain hope that, by their continued presence, they might stem the tide of revolt. Although always outnumbered by the sepoys and native police they commanded, the officers had stayed and most of their womenfolk also, aware that no help could reach them if their regiments mutinied, yet trusting in their loyalty until the last and paying with their lives when that trust was betrayed . . . all of them, for the women and children had not been spared.

Young Mountstuart Jackson was without one of his sisters, Burns without his wife; the Orrs, seemingly, had contrived to keep together and somehow, between them, they had saved the Christians' little daughter . . . Alex's mouth tightened into a grim, hard line. Patrick Orr was from Mohumdi, where he had been assistant to the commissioner, John Thomason, he remembered. His brother Alexander, who had held a similar political appointment in Fyzabad, had also barely escaped with his life when the 17th Native Infantry had mutinied. He had joined Sir James Outram in Dinapore and—if he had survived the battle to enter Lucknow—was now in the Residency with the rest of the relief force. He . . .

"Sahib . . ." Ananta Ram's voice broke into his thoughts. "They sent a letter. I have it here."

"A letter? Then—you saw them?"

"*Ji-han*, Sahib." The *vakeel* produced two crumpled sheets of native-made paper from the concealment of his tightly wound cummerbund. "It is addressed to General Outram, but Orr Sahib said that any in the Rajah Sahib's camp might read it if they wished. I shall prepare a translation for my master when he returns and later, no doubt, the letter will be delivered to the General Sahib by one of our most trusted *cossids*."

Alex spread out the crumpled sheets on the table in front of him and read the scrawled words in shocked and angry silence. Orr described the outbreak of mutiny at Shahjehanpur, listing those whom he knew to have escaped the massacre there. A handful of them had reached his own station of Mohumdi on June 1, where he and the Commissioner, Thomason, had been doing all in their power to pacify their own native troops and guard the Treasury, but, on the arrival of a detachment of fifty mutineers from Sitapur, his men had joined them. They had, however, sworn solemn oaths that if the treasure—amounting to over a *lac* of rupees—was given up to them, they would spare the lives of the European officers and their families.

"We left Mohumdi at half-past five p.m. on Thursday," Patrick Orr's narrative continued. "After the men had secured the treasure and released the prisoners, I put as many ladies as I could into the buggy and others on the baggage-carts and we reached

Burwar at 10:30 p.m. Next morning, Friday fifth, we marched toward Aurungabad and had gone about two *koss* when we saw a party following us. We pushed on with all our might, but when we were within a mile of Aurungabad, some of the sepoys rushed us. One snatched Key's gun from him, another shot down poor old Sheils . . . and then the most fearful carnage began. We collected beneath a tree and endeavored to protect the ladies and children, but shots were being fired from all directions and soon most of the men were disabled. The poor ladies knelt in prayer, undauntedly awaiting their fate.

"I rushed out toward the insurgents, thinking to end my life thus rather than be shot down, but one of my men, Goordhun of the 6th Company, called out to me to throw down my pistol and he would save me. I had sent Annie, my wife, to Mithowlee with our child and, thinking of them, I endeavored to save my life for their sakes. I yielded my pistol to Goordhun, and he and several others put themselves between me and the rest of the mutineers.

"In about ten minutes more, while I was three hundred yards off, they completed their hellish work. The cowardly wretches would not go near the tree until they had shot poor Lysaght who, to the last, was attempting to defend the ladies. He fell and, rushing up, they killed the wounded and children, butchering them in the most cruel and savage manner, including poor, good Thomason . . . after which they denuded the bodies of their clothes, for the sake of plunder. Everyone on the attached list . . . was killed, with the exception of the drummer boy, whom they took with them."

Alex studied the list with mounting dismay and then read the terrible account of what the fugitives had suffered at the hands of Rajah Lonee Singh, to whom Goordhun and a few faithful sepoys had finally delivered the man whose life they had saved. At Mithowlee, Orr had been reunited with his wife and child, and had joined Mountstuart Jackson, his sister Madeline, and Burns and Morton of the 10th Oudh Irregulars, whose escape from Sitapur had been no less remarkable than his own. One party, which had left Sitapur prior to the mutiny of the native troops, had reached Lucknow safely, escorted by thirty men of the 41st Native Infantry and met by a small detachment of Volunteer Horse whom Sir Henry Lawrence had sent to their aid. The others, who had waited too long, had been butchered as brutally as those from Mohumdi and Shahjehanpur, and the few who had managed to escape had divided into two parties—Burns, the two young Jacksons, and little Sophie Christian being, to the best of Orr's knowledge, the only survivors.

"We reached Mithowlee exhausted and in rags," Patrick Orr's letter went on. "The others had wandered for five days in the jungle . . . their feet were bare and lacerated, they were almost driven mad by thirst, and Lonee Singh lodged us in a cowshed, sending us on next day to a desolate, unfurnished fort at Katchiani. Subsequently, on the excuse that there were mutineers in the district and he could not shelter our whole party, the Rajah sent me out, with my wife and the child, into the jungle. We were there for a week, without food, having to burn fires at night to ward off prowling tigers and continually in dread of discovery by the rebels.

"Finally, the mutineers having dispersed, Lonee Singh permitted us to return to the fort, in which wretched place we existed in helpless misery, for he supplied us with only sufficient food to ward off starvation. Such news as reached us from the outside world told of the sufferings of our countrymen and the triumphs of the mutineers, so that we were close to despair. Then, early in August, on the excuse that more bands of rebels were searching for us, the Rajah sent all of us forth into the jungle to hide as best we could from those who sought to destroy us. We hid ourselves successfully but at the cost of our health and strength, being in turn scorched by a pitiless sun and half-drowned by torrents of rain, from neither of which had we any shelter. All of us were attacked by fever; how we sustained life during those weeks I do not know.

"Once a message reached us, to say that help would be sent from Lucknow and our hopes were revived, only to be dashed when no help came. Finally, Lonee Singh—evidently deciding that the British star had set—sent a large party of his retainers to search for us. On finding us, they put us into bullock carts, and the Rajah's *vakeel*—a man who owed his advancement in Lonee Singh's service to me—ordered us to be fettered, and thus we were brought to Lucknow. On reaching the city, they forced us to walk to the Kaiser Bagh, where we are now confined, and a mob collected to laugh and jeer at us. Poor George Burns went out of his mind and has not yet recovered his senses; Sergeant Major Morton collapsed in a convulsive fit, and when we gained our prison at last, Mountstuart Jackson and my dear wife fell down swooning from weakness. When I pleaded for water—for we were suffering agonies of thirst—it was brought to us, but in a vessel so foul that we could not bring ourselves to touch it.

"Since our arrival, however, a man named Wajid Ali had done all in his power to lighten the burden of our suffering. Even so, we are so sick and emaciated that I fear we shall not survive if help is not sent to us soon."

Alex set down the letter and turned to Ananta Ram, white to the lips with bitter, impotent fury.

"Have you read this letter?" he demanded harshly.

The stout Brahmin inclined his head, avoiding the Englishman's accusing gaze. "I read it, Sheridan Sahib, and my heart bleeds for these poor people. But—"

"It must be shown to your master at once. At once, do you hear? The Rajah Sahib must bring them to his camp, he—"

"Truly, that is impossible, Sahib. I shall have the letter translated immediately, and I will myself bring it to my master's attention, but more I cannot do. The Rajah will help them as much as lies in his power—he has caused Wajid Ali to be put in charge of them, Sahib, but he cannot bring them here without placing himself and his entire camp in great danger. The Moulvi has forbidden that they be moved and it is death to go against the Moulvi's commands."

Conscious, as never before of his own helplessness, Alex made a effort to control the futile anger that swept over him. To rant and rail at Ananta Ram would do no good, he told himself, and might even antagonize the man who, after all, had done the best he could in the circumstances. He decided on an appeal. "Ask the Rajah Sahib to release me. I will take this letter to General Outram and—"

"You would never reach the Residency, Sahib. Even our *cossids* have difficulty. They are only permitted to pass because it is believed that they are spying for the rebels. They—"

"Then I will go to Cawnpore," Alex put in impatiently. "With your help, I could get there, Ananta Ram. Did you not go and return safely?"

"I had a permit, signed by the Begum herself, and an escort

of my master's horsemen," the *vakeel* explained. He expelled his breath in a weary sigh. "It was believed that I, too, went as a spy, Sheridan Sahib. I cannot ask to go again, so soon—that would be to arouse suspicion."

Alex stared at him in bitter frustration. Wrack his brains as he might, he could think of no way to bring aid to the unhappy prisoners in the Kaiser Bagh, who . . . he glanced down again at the letter from Patrick Orr and reread its closing lines. *"Even so, we are so sick and emaciated that I fear we shall not survive if help is not sent to us soon . . ."* But what help and how could it be sent? Even if the appeal reached Outram and he answered it, an attempt by a raiding party from the Residency would cost lives, and it might well fail to gain its objective . . . in desperation, he turned to Ananta Ram.

"Ask your master, Ananta Ram, if he would consider offering to exchange *me* for the Sitapur prisoners."

The *vakeel* smothered a startled exclamation. *"You,* Sahib? But you would go to certain death! The Moulvi offered a reward for you, he has a great hatred of you . . . indeed, he would have you blown from a cannon were you to become his prisoner!"

"The Moulvi is well known to me and I to him," Alex conceded guardedly. "That is why I think he would agree to the exchange. He—"

"My master would not agree to it," Ananta Ram objected.

"Ask him, Ananta Ram."

"If you insist, Sheridan Sahib, I will tell my master of your proposition," the *vakeel* agreed, with visible reluctance. "But he will not agree to it, of that I am sure." He added, with a wry smile, "Would he not be exchanging you, Sahib—a colonel and a man in excellent physical health—for some sahibs of junior rank who, with their *mems* and *baba-log,* are so sick that they are like to die? Were they to do so, my master would have no witness to the loyalty he has shown to the British cause—he might be accused of having aided the rebels and be unable to prove that he did not!"

His reasoning was typically Oriental, Alex thought resentfully, but . . . it was logical, and it confirmed the warning Letty Wheeler had offered him. Man Singh had no intention of releasing him; he was too valuable a hostage.

"Nevertheless, mention my proposal to the Rajah Sahib," he said firmly. "And give him this without delay." He picked up the letter, folded it, and watched Ananta Ram tuck it into his cummerbund before dismissing him.

That night, driven to recklessness by the thought of the Kaiser Bagh prisoners, he made three attempts to escape from Man Singh's camp, only to be detected on each occasion by watchful sentries. After the third attempt, a guard was placed on his tent and the old subedar, Kedar Nath, brought in his bedding roll and laid it, reproachfully, in front of the tent-flap.

"It is useless, Colonel Sahib," the old man told him, settling himself down, cross-legged, on the bedding roll, a pistol in his hand. "They will not let you go. I am ordered to fire my pistol at your legs if you try to leave your tent."

Next morning, toward midday, he had another brief and ostensibly friendly interview with Man Singh, who warned him, under the cloak of concern for his safety, to stay within the confines of the camp.

"Have patience, Sheridan Sahib," he urged. "My *vakeel* has told you of the preparations that are afoot in Cawnpore. The column from Delhi wins victory after victory, and, I am informed, is making its way here. Soon the British commander-in-chief will lead a strong force to General Outram's relief and, with

Lucknow once more in British hands, there will be no further need for you to remain under my protection. As to your proposal . . ." he spread his hands in a gesture of mingled mockery and despair. "While it does you credit, my friend, I cannot accept it. The prisoners whose release you seek so anxiously are safe. The Begum has herself promised that no harm shall come to the *mems* and children, and Wajid Ali will remove them all to his own house at the first opportunity. You need not concern yourself for them." He added, smiling, "And Captain Orr's letter will be sent to General Outram tonight."

As before, Alex had to be satisfied with these assurances. He retired unwillingly to his tent to wait, with what patience he could muster, for the return of Letty Wheeler's husband but, to his intense disappointment, 24 hours passed and there was no sign of the *daffadar*. Old Kedar Nath—now his constant shadow— denied all knowledge of the man's whereabouts but, in a kindly attempt to distract him, brought a pretty, demure young girl to his tent and was hurt and astonished when Alex bade him return her whence she had come.

It was late the following evening when the sound of voices outside his tent roused him from the uneasy doze into which he had sunk. He sat up, his heart quickening its beat as he recognized one of the voices as that of the tall Sikh cavalryman who had come so providentially to his rescue at the Kaiser Bagh . . . the Sikh with blue eyes and the features of a European. The other voice, although it was lowered to a whisper, was unmistakably Man Singh's.

"He is a brave man—he will do as you ask," Man Singh said softly.

Alex slid silently from his *charpoy*, all thought of sleep banished from his mind, his hand groping for the lamp on the table beside him. He had not heard Kedar Nath leave the tent, but the old native officer, fully dressed and wakeful, took the lamp from him, lit it, and then assisted him to don the shirt and trousers he had earlier discarded.

"You have a visitor, Sahib," he announced.

"The Rajah Sahib, at this hour?" Alex challenged, feigning surprise.

Kedar Nath shook his head. "Oh, no, Sahib, you are mistaken. The Rajah Sahib is not here—it is Colonel Kaur Singh who wishes to speak with you." He crossed to the tent flap and held it open, coming stiffly to attention as Kaur Singh entered. He was alone and, after a quick glance about him, he dismissed the old subedar and turned to Alex, his bearded lips curving into a warm and friendly smile.

"My salaams, Colonel Sheridan," he said in English. "And my apologies for having disturbed you at so late an hour. You were asleep, I fear—"

"I have little else to do but sleep," Alex answered wryly. "So any disturbance is welcome. Indeed, I had hoped that I might see you before this, Colonel Singh."

Kaur Singh's smile faded. "I too had cherished that hope but, in my present circumstances, I have to be careful. Visits to this camp, by one of the Moulvi's staff, would have been misunderstood—perhaps even suspect. I have paid only one other, a few days ago, when you were taking your evening exercise and were not to be found."

"Then what brings you here now?" Alex demanded bluntly. "Have you come to arrange for my release?"

There was an odd, steely glint in the incongruous blue eyes as they met his, and Alex felt his throat muscles tighten with the instinctive awareness of danger. "That . . . and other things,"

Kaur Singh confirmed. "You find your captivity irksome?"

"Unbearably irksome, Colonel Singh. The more so, when some of my fellow countrymen—and women—who have already endured appalling suffering, are held in conditions so much worse than my own. They—"

"And yet you offered yourself in exchange for them? Or so the Rajah told me." Kaur Singh shrugged, as if incredulous, but Alex sensed that, in fact, he was neither surprised nor in any doubt as to the reasons that had prompted his offer.

He said stiffly, "I did. War should not be waged against women and children."

"Their lives are in no immediate danger, save from the effects of the weeks they have spent in the jungle, and they are now being well cared for, I assure you. But had you yielded yourself up to the Moulvi, he would have had you put to death instantly. Did the Rajah not warn you?"

"I was warned, yes. But I—"

"Are you still willing to risk your life?" Kaur Singh put in swiftly.

"In exchange for theirs, do you mean?" Alex asked, somewhat at a loss. "If it can be arranged to their advantage, then I am, yes."

"Good," Kaur Singh approved. "I can have them placed under the Rajah's protection—granted one thing, Colonel Sheridan."

"And what is that?"

"That the Moulvi is not left alive to prevent it."

"For God's sake!" Alex was shocked out of his calm. Recalling his earlier suspicions, he demanded incredulously, "You are surely not suggesting that I should put an end to him, are you?"

"You were ready enough to do so that night in the Kaiser

Bagh, were you not?" the Sikh challenged. "And you would have made the attempt, had I not intervened to stop you."

"The circumstances were quite different—he had just ordered me shot. Colonel Singh, I am no assassin . . . in heaven's name, I—"

"Nor, come to that, am I," the rebel officer countered cynically. "But needs must when the devil drives, my friend, and we are both soldiers, are we not, pledged to fight and kill our country's enemies?"

"In battle, not in cold blood," Alex qualified.

"Is there really such a distinction?"

"I've always believed so. If you think otherwise, why do you not play the role of assassin yourself?"

"Because," Kaur Singh answered quietly, "I am in a position of trust, which I must continue to occupy until my work here is completed. You understand I—"

"No, Colonel Singh, I do *not* understand!" Alex interrupted forcefully. "Who the devil are you?"

"It is better that you do not know. Truly, my friend, it is better . . . and safer for us both."

"You are a European. Tell me this at least—are you a British officer?"

The bearded lips parted in an amused smile. "No, I am French. That is to say, I am half French—my father was one of Ranjit Singh's generals, my mother the daughter of a Sikh chief. I fought against you in the Punjab, Colonel Sheridan, and I have no love for your countrymen . . . with one or two exceptions." Kaur Singh's smile widened. "This much is known to those I now serve, so I am telling you no secrets. My father's name was Henri Court."

Alex studied his face with quickened interest but learned little from his scrutiny. General Court's reputation had stood high in the Punjab; Sir Henry Lawrence, he recalled, had spoken of him with respect. "Then you are a soldier of fortune?" he suggested, his tone intentionally provocative. "A mercenary, selling your sword to the highest bidder?"

To his chagrin, Kaur Singh refused to be provoked. "If you like," he conceded, still smiling. "But I sell my loyalty with my sword." His tone changed, becoming urgent. "Colonel Sheridan, you have offered to exchange yourself for the British prisoners held in the Kaiser Bagh. Suppose I accept your offer, which course would you prefer to pursue—to yield yourself up to the Moulvi, who will instantly order your execution? Or to have yourself taken into his presence, ostensibly a prisoner, but armed and guarded by men—*my* men, chosen by me—who, when you have fired the fatal shot, will take you to a safe place from where you will be returned to your own people? Come, my friend—time presses and I must have your answer. Which is it to be?"

Alex shrugged. "Do I have a choice, Colonel?"

Kaur Singh laughed. "Certainly—you may stay and rot here, if you wish, as the Rajah's hostage. But if you are the man I think you are, you will take the chance I can give you. It is not without risks—the best-laid plans can go wrong and one cannot guard against the unexpected—but rest assured that I shall do all in my power to ensure your survival. And there is no doubt that you will be ridding your country of a dangerous enemy."

"And yours?" Alex asked coldly. "Of whom shall I be ridding yours, Colonel Singh?"

"Of a would-be tyrant," Kaur Singh answered, with the first sign of real feeling he had displayed. "And of one of the most evil men that ever drew breath. Believe me, I know the depths of that evil."

As indeed did he, Alex reflected grimly. He again subjected the man standing opposite him to a searching scrutiny, wondering for a moment if this were some bizarre trick or, perhaps, a test of his integrity that would be the prelude to an offer for his services as a mercenary. Stranger things had happened, he was aware; a number of mutinied regiments had endeavored to persuade popular and trusted officers to continue to command them, and even to lead them to Delhi to enlist in the service of the Mogul emperor. But . . . Kaur Singh—or Court—was, he realized, in deadly earnest, and there was now no flicker of amusement in his eyes.

He asked warily, "What guarantee have I, if I accede to this extraordinary proposal of yours, that the Sitapur captives will be placed under Man Singh's protection?"

"You will have my word and his. If the Moulvi dies, nothing will stand in the way of such an outcome." The tall cavalryman spread his hands in a typically Gallic gesture. "It may assist you to reach a decision, Colonel, if I tell you that the Moulvi has given orders that the male members of the party are to be taken out and shot, should Sir Colin Campbell's troops gain the Residency. And since I imagine they will, if they fight like Havelock's did, then . . ." he left the sentence unfinished, hanging in the air between them like a threat.

Alex sighed. "Where will the assassination take place and when—is that decided?"

"Oh, yes, that is decided. It will take place, by coincidence, where the idea first occurred to you—in the audience chamber at the Kaiser Bagh. The *talukdars* have been summoned there

tomorrow evening, so that they may be told what strategy the
Moulvi and his generals intend to employ to counter Campbell's
expected advance from Cawnpore. It offers the perfect opportunity, and I have made my plans in such a manner as to take full
advantage of the situation. As I told you, Colonel Sheridan, the
men on guard there will be men I have chosen, who will obey
my orders implicitly." Kaur Singh's smile was once again in evidence. "The chamber will be crowded and, in the confusion that
will inevitably follow an attack on the Moulvi, the attacker will
be hustled out and horses will be waiting in the courtyard. The
guard will, of course, claim to have fired on and wounded a
British spy . . . and they will be very positive about that, since
their own lives will depend on it. Although, in fact, few of those
present will mourn the Moulvi of Fyzabad."

"I see." Alex was conscious of a sick sensation in the pit of
his stomach. This was treachery of the basest kind, and he wanted
no hand in it, even if the alternative should be, as Kaur Singh
had put it, that he must rot here as the Rajah's hostage. There
was Mohammed Kahn; when he returned, there would surely
be a chance to escape. If he returned . . . He said, his voice
grating harshly in his throat, "You seem to have laid your plans
very skillfully. All that remains to be settled is the identity of the
assassin . . ."

"That is so. But I am counting on you and—"

"If I refuse to play the part you have assigned to me, have
you anyone willing to take my place?"

"I am not a fool, Colonel Sheridan. Captain Orr has already
agreed to my proposition, in order to save his fellow captives."
Kaur Singh had played his trump card and it was evident, from
his expression, that he knew it. He added blandly, "I did not
think, in the circumstances, that you would wish to relinquish

the role to him. He is a brave man, of that there is no doubt, but
. . . he is weak and ill. Arranging his escape would present diffi-
culties."

Aware that he had been outmaneuvered, Alex bowed stiffly,
controlling the bitter rage he felt. "Very well, Colonel Singh, I
will be your assassin. I take it I shall be given precise instructions
as to what I am to do?"

"The subedar, Kedar Nath, will give them to you before you
leave here."

"And Man Singh—is he privy to this plot?"

Kaur Singh shrugged. "He is aware of it, but he will take no
active part. He cannot afford to show his hand as yet. I shall be
with you, of course." He waited, and, when Alex did not speak,
he moved toward the entrance to the tent. Reaching it, he saluted
gravely and was gone.

CHAPTER SEVEN

➤➤➤ • ❤❤❤

AS KAUR SINGH had predicted, the vast audience chamber was crowded, richly robed *talukdars* jostling with scarlet-jacketed sepoy officers for a position near the dining table in the center of the room, which, this time, instead of the remnants of a meal, was spread with papers and maps.

Alex, entering with his guards, paused for a moment unnoticed in the curtained archway and, looking about him, experienced the uncanny sensation that history was repeating itself as he saw and recognized many of the faces he had seen there on the occasion of his first perilous incursion into the rebel stronghold. Old General Mirza Guffur Khan was standing by the table, with Man Singh—as he had done previously, holding himself aloof—a few paces away, Ananta Ram watchfully by his side. Two other high-ranking native officers, one wearing the uniform of the 11th Native Infantry—a regiment that had mutinied in Meerut—and the other that of the 22nd, were talking to a group of Rajput chiefs, while a stout, gray-haired Hindu in a general's sash hovered nervously on the edge of the crowd, as if uncertain of his welcome.

"General Gomundi Singh," Kaur Singh whispered, his tone contemptuous. "Elected by the sepoys and as useless as he looks! The Moulvi is over there. In a moment, I shall go to him . . . be ready to strike, for you will have only one chance!"

As before, the Moulvi, a tall, unmistakable figure in his flowing white robe, stood before the open window on the far side of the room, his back turned with arrogant indifference to the rest of its occupants. This time, however, he was not alone, and Alex stiffened as he recognized the slim, elegantly attired young man with whom he was conversing. It was Azimullah Khan, the Nana's Moslem aide—it could be no one else—and, at the sight of him, memory returned, with all its long suppressed anguish . . . the memory of Cawnpore and of the siege of the crumbling, mud-walled entrenchment in which poor old General Wheeler had pinned his faith, and which Azimullah had called so derisively the Fort of Despair.

To his right, slumped in one of the leather armchairs that had once furnished a British officers' mess house, sat a third man, whose squat, corpulent body was clothed in a resplendent, pea-cock-blue robe and whose shaven head was surmounted by a Mahratta-style turban, ablaze with jewels. His face was in shadow and he was taking no part—and seemingly little interest—in the earnest conversation of his two companions, but Alex did not need to look at him twice to know who he was. The image of the Nana Sahib, self-styled Maharajah of Bithur, was printed indelibly on his mind and only death would erase it—his own death or the Nana's. For all the iron control he had imposed on himself, Alex shivered, taken momentarily off guard by the sheer unexpectedness of the Nana's presence among this gathering of the Begum's martial supporters.

And yet, he reproached himself, he ought to have been aware of the possibility, even if Kaur Singh had said nothing. Had not Letty Wheeler warned him that the Nana intended to visit Luck-now—had not both she and Mohammed Khan insisted repeatedly that the Moulvi had not yet forsaken his old, unholy alliance? He passed a shaking hand across his brow, wiping the sweat from it and wincing with pain, for his escort—to make the story of his capture seem more plausible—had, on the instructions of Kaur Singh, dealt with him none too gently on the way to the Kaiser Bagh. His hand, when he lowered it, was sticky with congealed blood, and he cursed them silently, realizing that a chance blow had opened up the old wound across his cheek. But at least he looked the part, he thought ironically. In the filthy, mud-spattered uniform in which, weeks before, he had fought for his life in the square where the *doolies* had been abandoned, he was already attracting curious glances from some of the sepoy officers standing nearby and . . . Kaur Singh moved forward, thrusting his way through the crowd with well-simulated urgency.

"Moulvi Sahib!" His voice carried across the room, causing heads to turn and the hum of conversation to die down and gradually to cease, as something of his excitement communicated itself to those about him. "We have taken a prisoner of some importance—one who is well known to you, I have reason to believe!"

"In Allah's name, Colonel Singh!" Clearly disconcerted, the Moulvi glared back at him, beetling dark brows drawn together in a resentful scowl. "Your prisoner must be of great importance for you to disrupt this council by bringing him here."

"Indeed he is," Kaur Singh assured him. "He holds the rank of Colonel, Moulvi Sahib, and is a survivor of Wheeler's garrison at Cawnpore. Look on his face, I beg you, and prove my words. He . . ."

Alex could make out no more from the noisy hubbub of voices that followed this announcement. In obedience to Kaur Singh's impatiently beckoning hand, his guards dragged him roughly toward the center of the room and the startled crowd stood aside to make way for him. The Nana, he saw, had risen to his feet, his round moon-face drained of color and his voice querulous as he demanded to know the identity of the prisoner, but, in the general uproar, his question went unanswered.

"There were no survivors of Wheeler's garrison!" Azimullah shouted furiously. "All are dead—men, women and children, every last one of them! The Peishwa witnessed their slaughter with his own eyes, as did I. Those who did not die at the Suttee Chowra Ghat were executed before Havelock entered Cawnpore . . . that I will swear to! The claim is false, Colonel Bahadur." He ranged himself in front of Kaur Singh as if to dispute his passage. His attitude was challenging, yet the expression on his handsome face was anything but hostile, and Alex, struggling with his guards a few feet away, realized to his intense astonishment that, far from enmity between the two men, there was understanding of some kind, perhaps in the shared awareness of what was afoot. Certainly there was recognition—or more probably a warning—in the mute signal they exchanged.

Dear heaven, he thought, stunned by what he had just witnessed, was it possible that Azimullah, too, was a party to the Moulvi's planned assassination? Had the young Moslem so far forgotten his religious allegiance as to throw in his lot unreservedly with the Nana of Bithur . . . the Nana, whose ambitions had been directed, from the outset, to the restoration of the Hindu kingdom of the Mahrattas, with himself as Peishwa? If that were so, then Kaur Singh must also be the Nana's man, and it was the Moulvi's loyalty to the cause of his erstwhile ally that was in doubt—this and no one else's. Kaur Singh had spoken of him as a would-be tyrant, but the Moulvi, to give him at least his due, had always fought for his Faith with single-minded fanaticism and the prospect of a Mahratta-dominated Oudh would be anathema to him. As indeed it would for the Begum and her newly crowned son . . .

Alex stared into Azimullah's smiling face, his brain racing as he attempted to test his reasoning for flaws. There were many, since much of it was guesswork—he had no real basis for his assumption, nothing to go on save the look he had seen on that face a moment ago. Had he read too much into it, he wondered, or even imagined that he had seen it at all? That he himself was a pawn in some tortuous political maneuver he did not doubt; he had had no illusions concerning the role he was expected to play, but to contemplate killing a man in cold blood still troubled his conscience, and he had come with no very clear idea as to how—or even whether—when the moment came, he would act. Until now, though, he had not doubted Kaur Singh. He had believed that, provided he kept his part of the bargain, the Sikh would arrange for his escape, as well as for the transfer of the Sitapur fugitives to Man Singh's camp, but now he was not sure . . . and he could not be sure, until he put the matter to the test.

He drew in his breath sharply, risking a swift glance around the audience chamber. There were the *talukdars* to pacify and the Mohammedan officers, few of whom could be expected to connive at the murder of their leader. They would demand vengeance on his killer and might well exact it, here in this room, before Kaur Singh could order the guards to remove him. And if he were, in fact, the Nana's man, what need had he to give the order? Better for him, surely—and safer by far for Azimullah—if the assassin were disposed of without the formality of a trial and execution. Alex shivered, despite the heat of the lamplit room. He knew now that his chances of leaving it alive were slim, if they existed at all, and with that knowledge came calm and an end to uncertainty.

He heard Kaur Singh answer Azimullah's taunt and then the young Mohammedan approached him, his smile no longer in evidence and his eyes glittering with excitement as he brushed the guards contemptuously aside.

"Stand back, dogs!" he ordered. "And let us see who you have here, since I doubt that . . . ah!" His pause was dramatic, as was the gesture he made when he turned toward the Moulvi. "The Colonel speaks truly, Moulvi Sahib . . . here is a prize indeed. Come, see for thyself who it is that Allah has delivered into our hands!"

The Moulvi moved to join him, his way momentarily impeded by the crowd. He was angry, scowling his displeasure at what he clearly considered a time-consuming interruption to an important meeting, but he was unsuspicious, and his tone, as he bade Azimullah curb his tongue, was no more than impatient.

"What foolishness is this?" he demanded. "We have matters of greater moment than the identity of a *feringhi* prisoner to discuss, Azimullah."

"Only see," Azimullah retorted, unabashed. He had been positioned between Alex and the group by the window, and now he moved, so as to permit them a clear view. "On your knees, *feringhi* cur!" he ordered harshly and Kedar Nath grasped Alex by the shoulders, as if to force him to kneel.

"Now, Sahib," he hissed. "Now . . ." the Adams, as prearranged, was thrust into his cummerbund, the butt protruding, and in the brief struggle that ensued, Alex's hand closed about it. He retained his balance as the old subedar, his part successfully accomplished, went through the clumsy motions of tripping, to collapse helplessly at his feet.

Revolver in hand, Alex hesitated only for an instant. The Moulvi was facing him, momentarily frozen into immobility, and, as startled recognition dawned in his eyes, he presented the perfect target at point-blank range. A dozen paces behind him stood the Nana, the expression of fiendish anticipation on his face proof—if proof were needed—that he, too, was privy to the plot. In his eagerness to witness the eclipse of his rival, he pressed closer and Alex's lingering doubts vanished as if they had never been.

This was the man who had ordered his guns to fire on the unprotected boats at the Suttee Chowra Ghat, he told himself bitterly, this was the would-be tyrant . . . this his enemy, the one man he could kill without pity or compunction in any circumstances. He remembered poor young Saunders, whom the Nana had tortured to death, he remembered General Wheeler and the rest of the brave garrison of Cawnpore, male and female, adult and child. Above all he remembered Emmy, his wife, sinking below the blood-red water of the Ganges with a sepoy musket-ball in her breast.

He raised the pistol, making no attempt to aim it at the Moulvi. Steadily and unerringly, he pointed it at the Nana's heart, but, just as he pulled the trigger, Azimullah, divining his intention, made a desperate grab at his arm. The bullet was deflected; it struck the Nana's right thigh and he went down, screaming with pain, to be surrounded instantly by members of his staff who bore him, still screaming, to a couch.

"He is alive!" one of them shouted. "The Peishwa is wounded, but he lives!"

There was no chance for a second shot. Alex stood, the smoking revolver in his hand, waiting for death when the mob closed on him as, inevitably, they must the moment their panic subsided, his sole regret the fact that he had failed to take his enemy with him. He considered turning the Adams on himself, to cut short the ordeal, but before he could do so, Azimullah seized it from his grasp, to spin round with startling suddenness, the weapon leveled at Kaur Singh.

"Traitor!" he accused, his voice high-pitched and brittle with strain. "*Feringhi* traitor! I should have known thee for what thou wert!" With no more hesitation than he would have shown in crushing a fly, he fired two shots into Kaur Singh's stomach and the tall cavalryman fell gasping to his knees, his cry of agony drowned by a deep-throated, angry roar from the assembled *taluk-dars*. Now the *tulwars* were out, the demands for retribution shouted aloud as old religious feuds and differences—held temporarily in abeyance—were savagely recalled, and men, who had allied themselves in rebellion, forgot their allegiance and remembered only past grievances against their neighbors.

All sensed that there had been a conspiracy, and none, it seemed, doubted that this had been aimed against his own Faith, in a struggle for power that could have had far-reaching consequences. The voices that were raised to vow death to the *feringhis* were fewer and less insistent than those that hurled accusations of treachery at the Moulvi and the Begum, until they, in turn, were shouted down by a chorus of protests from loyal Oudh officers, led thunderously by General Mirza Guffur.

Alex, surrounded by his sepoy guard, was saved by their cowering bodies from attack. Paralyzed with fear, they clustered about him, too frightened to attempt to break away and, ironically, looking to him for protection when a menacing group of the Nana's followers approached, led by Azimullah, howling like animals for his head. He ordered the sepoys to fix bayonets and to Azimullah's fury, they obeyed him, to form a bristling steel hedge between them, behind which, greatly daring, old Kedar Nath contrived to drag the wounded Kaur Singh.

The Moulvi, finally, restored order. White with rage, he harangued the whole assembly, hurling back their accusations with biting contempt and, with all the eloquence at his command, reminding them of the danger of divided loyalties. They heard him shamefacedly, their anger fading as swiftly as it had been aroused, and when the Nana was carried out in a *doolie* and two hastily summoned physicians assured them that his wound was painful but not dangerous, no other voices were raised in dispute.

"A British officer, who has been known to me since the time when he was the deposed government's commissioner for Adjodhabad, was brought as a prisoner into this room," the Moulvi told them. "He was under strong guard, yet he contrived, somehow, to arm himself and, with the pistol he had seized, he fired a shot at the Peishwa—fortunately, as you have heard, without causing him serious injury. I do not know for what purpose he was brought here, nor do I yet know with whose connivance . . . but I intend to find out. The Englishman will not escape punishment, my brothers—his life is forfeit and you shall witness his execution at the cannon's mouth. Before he goes to his death, however, he shall be compelled to tell the truth concerning this night's happenings and to name any with whom he conspired." His gaze rested on Azimullah's face for a long moment, as if challenging him to speak, but he said nothing and the Moulvi went on, his heavy-lidded eyes bright with malice, "I am not entirely convinced that His Highness the Peishwa was the chosen victim of this abortive attempt at assassination . . . indeed, the thought has entered my mind that *I* was the one who was marked for death."

This claim caused angry murmurs from a number of his own adherents, but the Moulvi silenced them with a raised hand. "The truth shall be made known to you all," he promised. "Colonel Sheridan shall be made to speak before he dies."

His words, pregnant with menace, struck chill into Alex's heart. Fool that he had been, he thought wretchedly, to have had any qualms about shooting the Moulvi of Fyzabad in cold blood . . . and greater fool, not to have placed the muzzle of the Adams to his own temple when his first shot had been deflected! It would have been better, even, to have died under the *tulwars* of Azimullah's creatures than to have survived in order to fall into the hands of the Moulvi's torturers. He glanced at Kedar Nath, ashen with terror, and from him to the unconscious Kaur Singh, over whose prostrate form one of the physicians was now bending, in a vain endeavor to staunch the blood that had dyed the lower part of his *chapkan* a hideous scarlet.

"What of Kaur Singh?" a voice from the crowd questioned accusingly. "He whom you yourself appointed to high rank, Moulvi Sahib? Did he not bring the accursed *feringhi* into our midst?"

The Moulvi quelled his accuser with an angry, "Ask Azimullah Khan on whose recommendation he was appointed!" And then, still angry, he demanded of the physician, "How fares he?"

"He lives, but his wound is mortal, Moulvi Sahib. I can do no more for him, alas." The old native doctor rose slowly to his feet, his hands stained with the blood of the injured man. Nervously he wiped them on a corner of his voluminous white robe, awed by the Moulvi's smoldering anger and fearful lest he become the brunt of it. "He has, perhaps, a few hours."

"Then he, too, shall be made to speak before death claims him," the Moulvi vowed. "Put him into a *doolie*."

The old physician hastened to obey him. The Moulvi pushed his way arrogantly through the crowd, waving to them to stand aside. He came to a halt facing Alex and his frightened escort who, in response to an order from Kedar Nath, grounded their muskets and shambled to attention as he approached, their faces as ashen as that of their commander. The Moulvi gestured to the gleaming bayonets and observed sardonically, "You guarded your prisoner well with these, did you not? Quite in the old tradition—a sahib commanded and you obeyed! Did he order you to yield up your pistol to him, Subedar-ji?"

Kedar Nath shook his head. "He wrested it from me, Moulvi Sahib. Truly, I could not prevent it, he—" the Moulvi brutally cut him short with a stinging blow across the mouth.

"You are either a cowardly dog or a traitor. Whichever you are, you will be no loss to Her Highness's army." The Moulvi's voice cut like a whiplash. Turning to the havildar of the escort, he ordered harshly, "Place this misbegotten cur under arrest! And guard him well, for you will answer to me with your life if he escapes."

"He is no traitor," Alex asserted, moved to pity by the old subedar's abject terror. It was, he thought, within the bounds of possibility that he might save both the old man and the dying Kaur Singh from further torment if he dissociated himself from them, and he had little to lose if he made the attempt. Like himself, these two had merely been pawns; the real traitors were too powerful to be called to account for their part in the conspiracy and, even if he learned the truth, the Moulvi could not touch them, save at the risk of losing their alliance. He was a shrewd and clever man and, almost certainly, was as well aware of this as he was of the identity of those who had sought to destroy him. His speech to the *talukdars* had proved it—on the surface, it had not been placatory, but he had gone as far as he dared, with heavy emphasis on the need for mutual loyalty to the cause. No doubt he would bide his time and then . . .

"What say you of the subedar?" the Moulvi demanded.

Alex drew himself up to his full, impressive height. Standing thus he was taller than his interrogator and able to look down on him, and he said, with a calm that belied his inner tension, "What I did, I did alone, Ahmad Ullah. If you seek one on whom to fasten the guilt, you need look no further than my face."

"I see your face, Sheridan Sahib," the Moulvi answered softly. "It is the face of a brave man and a good soldier—would that I knew the faces of all my enemies as well as I know yours! Nevertheless you will have cause to regret that you did not put a bullet into me when you had the opportunity." He gestured to the havildar. "Take the sahib, with the other two, to my palace and remember—I will have your head if you fail in your duty!"

Alex had expected that his escort would be replaced or at least augmented, and his hopes rose, when he realized that this was not to be done, only to fade when the havildar—anxious to demonstrate his reliability—thrust the butt of a musket painfully into the small of his back and ordered him to march. With two of the escort carrying Kaur Singh's *doolie* and old Kedar Nath stumbling unhappily at his side, he descended the wide stone staircase into the lamplit hall, his hopes sinking lower with every step. There was a guard in the hall, under a jemadar, and two sentries posted at the iron-bound wooden door, only the postern of which was open. The escort and the sepoys guarding the palace were his men, Kaur Singh had claimed—his men, who would obey his orders in the commotion that would follow the Moulvi's death—but it was Kaur Singh who was dying, not the Moulvi, and Kaur Singh would give them no orders. Alex expelled his breath in a sigh of frustration. If the worst came to the worst, he thought, he would make a dash for it, into the darkness, and let the sentries shoot him down . . .

The jemadar of the guard approached the chattering escort suspiciously. He had already seen one *doolie* pass, with the wounded Nana in it, and he paused, pulling back the curtain of the second, to exclaim in horror as he recognized its occupant.

"It is Colonel Singh!" he said, addressing Kedar Nath. "What is happening, Subedar-ji? And"—he caught sight then of Alex—"where are you taking the sahib?"

The havildar answered him, eager to assert his new authority. He gave a garbled and highly colored account of all he had witnessed in the audience chamber, ending with the order he had received from the Moulvi.

"Is this true, Subedar Sahib?" the jemadar asked, his jaw dropping. "Surely it cannot be! Surely—" he was interrupted by a warning shout from one of the sentries.

"Jemadar Sahib, there are armed men in the courtyard—many of them! Mounted men, they—"

"Our men?"

"*Nahin,* they are not ours. Mahratta horsemen, they—it seems they are waiting for someone. But the Nana Sahib has already departed."

Alex was conscious of a coldness about his heart. It was not hard to guess for whom the Nana's Irregulars were waiting or for what purpose, and he said, as the jemadar agitatedly made for the open postern gate, "Do not show yourself, Jemadar-ji. They wait for us."

The native officer took heed of his warning. He peered cautiously out into the moonlit courtyard and returned, visibly shaken. "There are nearly a hundred of them—Mahrattas, without a doubt.

Sahib," he appealed to Alex, "why do they wait for you?"

"That they may kill us," Alex told him bluntly. "You also, if you enter the courtyard."

Kedar Nath confirmed his assertion, an edge to his voice.

"Will they seek to force their way into the palace?" the jemadar asked. "If they do, we are too few to oppose them. We—" apprehensively, he ordered the postern closed but before the order could be obeyed, the havildar pushed officiously past him. "You seek to trick me!" he complained. "There are no horsemen, there . . ." they were the last words he spoke. Scarcely had he emerged into the courtyard than the horsemen closed about him and the two sentries, posted at the head of the steps, came rushing back into the dimly lit hall, impeding each other in their frantic efforts to close the gate behind them.

"They have borne the havildar off," one of them screamed. "Like a sack of rice, flung across the saddlebow of their leader!" The jemadar cursed him automatically and again appealed to Alex. "What are we to do, Sahib? It seems you speak truly and they are indeed waiting for you. That misbegotten dog of a havildar will tell them that you are here and . . . whose head do they seek, Sahib? Yours or the subedar's or," his gaze went uneasily to the *doolie,* "that of Colonel Singh, who is surely even now breathing his last?"

Kedar Nath attempted to speak, but Alex laid a restraining hand on his arm. "I fancy they may be satisfied with mine alone," he answered grimly. "And they shall have it, if there is no other way."

It would be quick, he told himself, buoyed up by a fatalistic resignation that banished fear. If he resisted them, the *tulwars* would strike swiftly, since all the plotters required was to ensure his silence. Azimullah had virtually made sure of Kaur Singh's and the word of an old native officer, unsupported, would carry little weight, even with the Moulvi . . . insufficient, in any event, to harm the Nana or Man Singh.

"Sahib," Kedar Nath whispered urgently. "It was arranged that we should make our escape by the west gate. Our horses wait there and an *ekka,* in the charge of *Daffadar* Mohammed Khan. The passageway behind us leads to the west gate."

"Then go, Subedar-ji," Alex bade him, "when you see your opportunity."

"Not without you, Sahib. I—"

"They will not let me go," Alex returned flatly. He crossed to the door, the jemadar, as he had expected, in anxious attendance and, bending his head, studied the well-mounted horsemen in the courtyard beyond, his eye to one of the loopholed apertures. They were the Nana's men—his personal bodyguard, judging by their accouterments—and undoubtedly he had sent them back to waylay the havildar's small escort of sepoys as they left the Kaiser Bagh with their prisoners. Probably their orders had been to leave none alive to tell of it or place the blame where it belonged but, due to overeagerness, perhaps—or even arrogance— they had exceeded their orders and allowed themselves to be seen. Soon they would realize their folly and withdraw from the courtyard, to wait in the darkness at the roadside, as, had they been well commanded, they should have done initially . . . Alex breathed a silent prayer of thankfulness, blessing their unknown leader for his mistake. It gave him a chance, he thought, albeit a slim one, but he would have to grasp it quickly, before the horse-men withdrew. And certainly before the meeting in the audience chamber came to an end . . . he made a swift inspection of the massive, iron-bound door and, turning to the jemadar, said crisply, "Post every man you have at the loopholes, Jemadar Sahib!"

"The loopholes? Will they attack us, then?" The jemadar's apprehension was in his eyes. "I will send for reinforcements and a gun. A six-pounder, Sahib, loaded with grape."

Alex shook his head. "I do not think they will attack, but if they do, you can hold them off without difficulty from here. Twice the number of mounted men could not force a door as stout as this against your men's muskets."

"Perhaps not," the jemadar conceded, only half-convinced. But he posted his men in accordance with Alex's advice and again mentioned the possibility of sending for a gun.

"That would be unwise, Jemadar Sahib. Those men are Mahrattas in the service of the Nana of Bithur . . . they are your allies, are they not?"

"Supposedly, Sahib. They escorted the Nana from here, but why have they come back, if not to attack my post?"

"I tell you, they seek for us," Alex said impatiently. "If they believe we have gone, they will withdraw and seek us elsewhere. There are many other ways out of here—they cannot guard all the exits. You will have to send us by another way, Jemadar-ji, and, when we have gone, open the gate to their commander, so that he may see with his own eyes that we are no longer under your guard. Then they will do you no harm."

The jemadar hesitated, torn between the desire to save his own skin and the fear that he might be held responsible for the loss of his prisoners. "I can spare you no escort—" he began uncertainly. A shout from one of the musketeers cut him short.

"They are sending Havildar Dass to the foot of the steps, Jemadar Sahib! He demands that his prisoners be released to him."

Again the jemadar hesitated in an agony of indecision, fear flickering in his eyes, and Alex, sensing that he was tempted to accede to the havildar's demand, sought desperately for some means to prevent him from doing so. It was Kedar Nath who made up his mind for him. The old subedar had waited, kneeling beside the *doolie* and refusing to take his chance of escape alone, and now he got to his feet and said, a note of authority in his voice, "Colonel Singh is dead. Yield his body to the Mahrattas, my brother, and should you be called upon to account for your actions, say that all three of us passed, with our escort, through your post and into their hands. Thus no blame will fall upon you. Direct the Mahrattas to the south gate in pursuit of us and they will leave you in peace."

Thankfully the jemadar accepted this solution. "Go, Subedar Sahib!" he urged, his voice trembling on the edge of panic. "Go with all speed, you and the Sahib. I will delay the pursuit as long as I can."

Kedar Nath grasped Alex's arm. He ran, with surprising speed for a man of his age, finding his way unerringly through the maze of passages and corridors, some of which were unlit. They were not challenged; no sentries appeared, and it was not until they reached the rear of the palace that Kedar Nath turned aside. "The door is guarded," he said breathlessly and led the way into a dank, cellar-like room, from which a window opened onto the courtyard beyond. Pulling back the shutters, he invited Alex to precede him. They climbed silently through the window and crossed the courtyard cautiously, keeping in the shadows, to pass through a series of unguarded godowns and finally, to Alex's heartfelt relief, a familiar voice hailed them. Ananta Ram, Man Singh's *vakeel,* sounded worried as he greeted them.

"We had despaired of your coming, Sahib, and were on the point of departure, fearing that you had been taken. Indeed, had it not been for the *baba sahiba,* panic must have seized us and we should have gone an hour ago."

"*Baba sahiba?*" Alex questioned, doubting the evidence of his own ears. "Not one of the Sitapur *babas,* Ananta Ram?"

"*Ji-han,* Sahib—she lies sleeping in the *ekka.*" The stout Brahmin gestured ahead of them to a clump of trees and broke into a shambling run. "Hurry, Sahib, I beg you, for it will soon be light and you must set off at once for the Residency. The *daffadar,* Mohammed Khan, waits to escort you and with him a *cossid,* who will go ahead to warn the British sentries of your coming."

They gained the shelter of the trees, Alex having to assist Kedar Nath now, for the old man was spent and breathless, stumbling with exhaustion. The *ekka,* drawn by a single, raw-boned horse, stood waiting, with Mohammed Khan at its head, a dark-faced man in the garb of a servant at his side, holding three saddled horses, his gaze anxiously on the already lightening sky. But he said nothing, and, on receiving a nod from Ananta Ram, he relinquished the horses' reins to his companion and padded off into the darkness without a backward glance. The *cossid,* Alex's mind registered, grateful for the forethought of whoever had provided him. He returned Mohammed Khan's *salaam* with genuine warmth and then asked, as Ananta Ram approached him, "You spoke of a child, *Vakeel* Sahib—a British child. But what of her parents?"

"She is the child of the Sitapur commissioner, Sahib. Both her parents are dead. That is why Orr Sahib asked me to take her . . . I carried her here myself, covered by my robe." The *vakeel's* plump face was wreathed in smiles. "She is a beautiful, golden-haired child who, despite all she has suffered, beguiled the anxious time of waiting with her laughter. And now, as I told you, she sleeps in the *ekka*. She will give you no trouble, Sahib." He drew back the curtain of the *ekka* and a knife twisted in Alex's heart as he looked down at the sleeping child, thin to the point of emaciation in her ragged dress, yet still—as Ananta Ram had said—a beautiful child, who reminded him poignantly of little Jessica Vibart.

"What of the other Sitapur prisoners, Ananta Ram?" he asked huskily.

"Sahib, it was impossible to bring them also," the *vakeel* answered regretfully. "We had thought to do so but, with the exception of Orr Sahib, they are so weak and ill, they cannot walk. And he would not leave them. 'Take the child,' he bade me. 'Take only the child' . . . and I did as he asked. I was to tell you that her name is Sophie Christian and that Orr Sahib has every trust in Wajid Ali, who is doing all in his power to care for and protect them. Sahib . . . you must start on your way. To delay here longer will be dangerous. Conceal yourself in the *ekka,* I pray you . . . and once inside, keep the curtains closed and do not show yourself. The *daffadar* has a permit to convey his wife to his village and that will suffice to get you past the sentries, so long as they do not see your face."

Alex was about to do as he suggested when he remembered Kedar Nath. "Do you come also, Subedar Sahib?" he asked. "Will you return to the Company's service?"

The old subedar hesitated and then shook his head. "I remain, Sheridan Sahib. I shall take service with the Rajah Man Singh."

"That is your last word?"

"Yes, Sahib, it is. Like you, I must say that I fight for a cause. Would that it were *your* cause, but, since it is not, we must go our separate ways." He drew himself up and saluted, and only then did he utter a reproach. "You fired your pistol at the wrong man, Sheridan Sahib," he added softly. "Had your bullet found the heart of him for whom it was intended, many lives would have been spared."

Alex could give him no answer. He wrung the hand of Ananta Ram and climbed into the *ekka* in silence. The child did not stir as the shabby vehicle creaked on its way through the darkened streets. They had barely a quarter of a mile to go, but Mohammed Khan took a circuitous route, approaching their destination cautiously. Twice he was challenged, but each time was permitted to pass, his claim that the *ekka* contained the women of his *zenana* unquestioned and seemingly too commonplace to be doubted. A detour took them across a patch of open ground and the sound of galloping hooves set Alex's taut nerves jangling, but the horsemen swept past, ignoring the slow-moving *ekka,* and Mohammed Khan called back contemptuously, "Irregulars, Sahib—riding like madmen who chase the wind!"

The Nana's bodyguard, Alex thought, still engaged on their vengeful search—the jemadar, for all his indecision, had evidently delayed and successfully misdirected them. He breathed a sigh of relief as the pounding hooves receded and the *daffadar* whipped up his laboring horse. Little Sophie Christian wakened with the swaying of the ill-sprung *ekka* and began to sob, terrified at finding herself alone in the company of a stranger, but Alex took her gently on his knee and after a while, her fears subsided and she slept again, her head trustingly on his shoulder and her hand clasping his.

She was still sleeping when a patrol of the 78th Highlanders came to meet them, issuing like ghosts from behind their defensive perimeter to surround and bring them to a halt. Their commander drew back the curtain of the *ekka* and grinned delightedly as he held out his arms to relieve Alex of the sleeping child.

"Colonel Sheridan? I'm Lockhart, sir, in command of this post. We were warned to expect you . . . but not this poor, sleepy little angel." He jerked his head in the direction of the sandbagged perimeter wall. "Be so good as to follow me and your *daffadar* also. I have instructions to take you at once to General Havelock, who wishes to congratulate you personally on your escape. Er . . ." he paused, his smile widening. "One of my fellows is anxious to offer his congratulations, too, sir—*before* the general has that privilege. Sarn't Hollowell!"

The small, wiry figure that came running toward him was instantly recognizable, despite the addition of sergeant's stripes to the tunic. Alex held out his hand, but Hollowell, correct as always, swung him an impeccable salute before grasping it.

"Welcome back, sir," the Highlander said, beaming. "We'd almost gie'n you up, but I kenned you'd make it if you could. Ye're no' the kind to gie up hope, are you, sir, ever?"

Perhaps he wasn't, Alex thought, feeling suddenly weary. Or perhaps he was living for the day when, at last, he would see the Nana of Bithur brought to justice. *"Some of us must live,"* poor Vibart had said, after the massacre at the Suttee Chowra Ghat. *"Our betrayal has to be avenged. We've no choice but to fight on . . ."*

"No," he said, wringing Hollowell's hand. "I don't give up hope, Sergeant Hollowell—ever."

EPILOGUE

➤➤➤ • ⫷⫷⫷

SIR COLIN CAMPBELL left Cawnpore on the afternoon of November 10 and reached Buntera that evening, having covered 35 miles in a little over three hours. Waiting eagerly for his arrival were Hope Grant's column from Delhi and his own small Lucknow Relief Force.

Next morning, Henry Kavanagh, the government clerk turned volunteer soldier—whose services as guide had proved so valuable to Sir James Outram's officers, when making their various sorties to extend the Residency defenses—miraculously appeared in camp. The big Irishman was disguised as a native, having made his perilous way through the enemy lines during the night, accompanied by a *cossid* named Kananji Lal. The two men had waded naked across the Gomti River, their clothes carried in bundles on their heads, Kavanagh losing much of the lampblack with which he had daubed his face and arms, but they emerged unobserved, dressed, and threaded their way right through the heart of the city without mishap. Once an officer questioned them and let them go; twice they lost themselves in the open country and were within twenty yards of an enemy gun battery in the Dilkusha Park before getting their bearings, and later Kavanagh's efforts to persuade a peasant to guide them resulted in the man's alarming his whole village. Pursued by the village dogs, he and his companion blundered into a swamp, in which they waded waist deep for two hours, but eventually some fleeing villagers put them on the right track and they made contact, at last, with a British picket, and the Sikh officer in charge passed them through to the camp.

Kavanagh described his arrival in graphic words. *"The day was coming swiftly brighter when I approached the tent of the Commander-in-Chief. An elderly gentleman with a stern face came out and going up to him, I asked for Sir Colin Campbell. 'I am Sir Colin Campbell,' was the sharp reply. 'Who are you?' I pulled off my turban and, opening its folds, took out the short note of introduction from Sir James Outram."* *

Aided by Kavanagh's intimate knowledge of the terrain and by the dispatches and plans sent to the Alam Bagh by Outram, Sir Colin Campbell put the final touches to his plan of action, which had been partially worked out while he was still in Calcutta. He knew what severe casualties Havelock's advance through the narrow, heavily defended streets of Lucknow had entailed and was therefore determined to give the city a wide berth. He decided to make a flank march across country to the Dilkusha Park and the Martiniere, rest his troops overnight, and then cross the canal. After this, he would seize the Sikander Bagh and the old barracks of the 32nd from open ground, with the river covering his flank, advance under cover of batteries to be opened on the Kaiser Bagh—the rebels' key position—and carry the intermediate buildings, after these had been subjected to a preliminary bombardment by Peel's naval guns and rockets.

Finally, after effecting a junction with the Residency, he would

---

* Henry Kavanagh was the first civilian to be awarded the Victoria Cross. In addition, his courage was rewarded by promotion to assistant commissioner's rank and a donation of 20,000 rupees, made by the Government of India.

withdraw the garrison—commencing with the women and the sick and wounded—first to the Martiniere and the Dilkusha and then to the Alam Bagh, which would enable him to make a rapid dash to Windham's aid in Cawnpore, should this be necessary in the event of an attack by the Gwalior Contingent . . . an attack he was fully expecting.

The British commander-in-chief had a total force of 4,500, and opposed to him in Lucknow were, at the most conservative estimate, 60,000 trained sepoy troops but, his operational plan decided upon, he did not hesitate. The advance was ordered for daybreak on November 12 and, on the afternoon of the 11th, he reviewed his troops, who were drawn up in quarter-distance columns in the center of a vast brown plain, surrounded by trees.

Mounted on a small white hack, the old general rode through the ranks. Divided into three nominal brigades of infantry and one of cavalry, with artillery, the *Shannon* seamen and marines and a small detachment of engineers, the force scarcely numbered one strong brigade. The infantry, consisting of the 93rd Highlanders, a wing of the 23rd, and one of the 53rd, the 8th, and the 75th—the last two much weakened by Delhi casualties—two companies of the 82nd, detachments of Lucknow regiments, and the 2nd and 4th Punjab infantry did not exceed 3,000. The cavalry brigade was, by comparison, stronger. Commanded by Brigadier Little, it was composed of two squadrons of the 9th Lancers, detachments of the 1st, 2nd, and 5th Punjab Cavalry and Hodson's Horse, supplemented by two squadrons of the Military Train.

The artillery included two companies of Garrison Artillery equipped with eighteen-pounder guns and mortars, one Royal, one Madras, two Bengal Horse Artillery batteries, and a Bengal Field Battery. The 250-strong Naval Brigade manned six 24-pounder guns and two howitzers with bullock draft and two rocket-tubes, mounted on light carts, with their own rifle company to act as escort.

The commander-in-chief addressed each brigade in turn and he was received with thunderous cheers by the 93rd, the regiment he had so nobly commanded in the defense of Balaclava. Brave in their bonnets and tartan, the Highlanders welcomed their veteran commander as chief of their clan. All were in good heart and none needed to be reminded that the fate of the gallant Residency garrison now depended on their fighting prowess.

Next morning, the main body began the advance and pitched camp that evening within sight of the Alam Bagh, after a spirited engagement with a two thousand-strong force of rebels, which ended when Hugh Gough—commanding the scarlet-turbaned Sikhs of Hodson's Horse—charged and captured two guns. On the morning of the thirteenth, the fort of Jellalabad was seized and blown up, the Alam Bagh garrison relieved by the 75th to enable them to join the Relief Force and a strong reconnaissance made of the Char Bagh bridge. At 9 a.m. on the fourteenth the main column continued the advance, striking almost due east across a flat, cultivated plain, dotted with extensive clumps of trees and bordered on the north by the canal and flanked on the northeast by the River Gomti. They met no opposition until they reached the Dilkusha, the rebels having evidently expected them to follow Havelock's route across the Char Bagh Bridge. After some heavy fighting, the Dilkusha Park was occupied and by noon the leading British troops had entered and cleared the great pile of buildings known as the Martiniere, from the roof of which a hurriedly erected semaphore signaled this news to the Lucknow Residency.

Next day, these two positions were consolidated and, under constant enemy attack, the canal bank was cleared and supplies of ammunition and food brought up. Just before dark, the anxious defenders in the Residency saw the arms of the semaphore moving to spell out the welcome message from the commander-in-chief: *"We shall advance tomorrow."* Their prayers, it seemed, were about to be answered . . .

Early on the morning of Monday, November 16, the two generals, Outram and Havelock, with their staffs, ascended to the upper story of the Chutter Munzil Palace. From there, with the aid of telescopes, they were able to make out bodies of red-coated infantry moving toward the formidable walls of the Sikander Bagh, while the British artillery opened a heavy bombardment on the palace and its surrounding courtyards and gardens, which were crowded with rebel musketeers and matchlock men.

To assist the relieving force, Sir James Outram had ordered the defenders to occupy and hold the Hirun Khana and a building known as the Engine House, moving forward from their advanced position on the north-east side of the defensive perimeter. Mines had been laid beneath the wall separating the Hirun Khana from the British-held advance post, behind which two batteries of guns had been set up and these—with the destruction of the masking wall—would have a clear field of fire. While a fierce battle was being waged for possession of the Sikander Bagh, these mines were detonated, but the powder had become damp and only part of the wall was destroyed. Eventually a breach had to be blown in it by fire from Olpherts' own guns, while Francis Maude—commanding a battery of six mortars and, like "Mad Jack" Olpherts, a veteran of Havelock's Force—shelled the enemy's opposing gun positions from the quadrangle of the Chutter Munzil.

At last the wall crumbled under the pounding of Olpherts's

round shot and he was able to bring both the new batteries into action with telling effect, driving a number of rebels from the Hirun Khana and replying to fire from the Kaiser Bagh, in the courtyards and walled gardens of which most of the rebels' heavy artillery was concentrated.

By midday the Sikander Bagh had fallen to the furious assault of Campbell's troops, led heroically by the 93rd. Leaving two thousand rebel sepoys dead and dying behind them, the Highlanders, with their Sikh comrades of the Punjab Infantry and the Queen's 53rd, were seen to be advancing toward the one-time Mess House of the 32nd—the Koorshid Munzil—and the Moti Mahal across 1,200 yards of flat, open ground. Less than halfway to their objective, they were met by a withering fire from the Shah Nujaf, a domed mosque 100 yards to the right of the road. Seeing Peel's naval siege train being brought to the front to cover the advance, Havelock obtained Outram's permission to launch the defenders' supporting attack. Descending from his observation post, he entered the quadrangle of the palace, where the storming column was already assembled and, at 3:30 p.m., gave the order for them to move out.

Alex, acting as one of the little general's aides, felt his heart lift as cheer after cheer greeted this most welcome of orders. The men of the old garrison, advancing shoulder to shoulder with the men of the first relief force, were worn out and close to starvation after the months of hardship they had endured; all looked like scarecrows in their tattered summer uniforms, but nothing could dampen their spirits. Bent on retribution and sensing victory, they charged with the bayonet and the mutineers abandoned their loopholes and their gun emplacements before the vengeful fury of their attack. The Hirun Khana, the Engine House, and the king's stables were seized and, as darkness fell, Vincent Eyre's

guns were brought forward and, from newly constructed positions, they opened on the Kaiser Bagh.

The Shah Nujaf had been defended stubbornly, and British
and Sikh casualties were severe but, after Peel's seamen gallantly
dragged one of their twenty-four-pounders to within a few yards
of its outer wall—laying the gun alongside, as if to engage an
enemy frigate—a breach was finally made. The Highlanders, led
by their brigadier, Adrian Hope, poured through it and, urged on
by Sir Colin Campbell himself, they took mosque and garden at
bayonet point, seeing, as they entered in the gathering darkness,
the last of the white-robed rebel defenders fleeing for their lives.

That night Campbell's exhausted troops slept on the open
ground, their old Chief with them, and early next morning they
continued the advance, subjecting the mess house and its adjacent buildings to a three-hour bombardment. Despite strong
enemy resistance and a hail of musketry fire from the roof and
loopholed walls of the Tara Kothee Observatory on the opposite
side of the road, the Mess House was stormed by a company of
the 90th and a picket of the 53rd, supported by the battalion of
detachments from the Alam Bagh garrison. They advanced in
skirmishing order under cover of the naval guns, crossed the 12-
foot-wide ditch and when, minutes later, the British flag was seen
to be flying from one of its towers, the Residency defenders
hailed its appearance with cheers. The flag was shot down, hoisted
again, shot down, and hoisted for a third time and then, from
their vantage point in the Chutter Munzil, Outram and Havelock saw Campbell and his staff—antlike figures at that
distance—cross the road to the Moti Mahal and enter it, as the
Tara Kothee was set on fire and abandoned by the rebels.

Now only a few hundred yards and a series of courts and
passages separated the two British forces and, despite the fact that

the intervening space was under heavy fire from the Kaiser Bagh, Outram decided to cross it in order to welcome the commander-in-chief. Accompanied by a jubilant Havelock, he and Robert Napier, Vincent Eyre, young Harry Havelock—his wounded arm still in its sling—and Alex, with three other members of the staff, ran the gauntlet of fire. They were all on foot, and Henry Moorsom, who had made the perilous crossing a few minutes earlier, guided them to their destination, with the aid of two of Campbell's officers who had returned with him. As they were traversing a narrow passage, with high walls on both sides, a shell burst so close to them that Havelock was thrown to the ground by the concussion.

He picked himself up, smilingly shook his head to the anxious inquiries, and continued on his way, heedless as always of his own danger. Met by Hope Grant in the Moti Mahal, the little general was heartily cheered by men of his old regiment, the 53rd. Moved to tears by the reception they accorded him, he told them huskily, "Soldiers, I am happy to see you. I am happy to think that you have got into this place with a smaller loss than I had."

"No smaller, I fear, sir," Hope Grant informed him regretfully. "Our casualties are estimated at close to five hundred."

Sir Colin Campbell was waiting outside the mess house, separated from them still by 25 yards of rough, open ground. Almost as if they were aware of the presence of the three generals who had defeated them, the rebel gunners and musketeers in the Kaiser Bagh laid down a daunting curtain of fire, but, scorning their efforts to kill him, Sir James Outram led the way across and Havelock followed him at an unhurried walk. His son Harry, Robert Napier, and Outram's A.D.C. Sitwell were hit and all three slightly wounded, but Outram and Havelock emerged unscathed from the barrage. As they approached him, Campbell courteously doffed his cap and extended his hand to each in turn.

"How do you do, Sir James?" he—inquired gravely, and then Alex saw him wring his old Chief's hand. "How do you do, *Sir* Henry?" A smile of singular warmth lit his thin, austere face as he added, "Her Majesty has been pleased to create you a Knight Commander of the Bath and a major general, my dear Havelock . . . may I offer my congratulations?"

The thunder of the guns drowned Havelock's reply, but for Alex the expression of gratified surprise on his was answer enough. It was, he thought, a fitting and well-deserved reward for a brave old soldier who had been prepared, if the service of his country required it, to die sword in hand.

Some minutes later, while the three generals were engaged in earnest consultation, William Hargood of the Madras Fusiliers— Havelock's A.D.C.—dashed across the shell-torn road to fling himself down at its verge, breathless and spent.

"Would you please tell General Havelock that his son's not seriously hurt, sir?" he requested Alex. "He'll be anxious, I know and . . . I can hardly get my breath."

"Very gladly, my dear fellow," Alex assented, and went forward to deliver this reassuring message. "Lieutenant Hargood has just come from your son, sir, and he says that his wound is not serious," he informed Havelock.

The little general permitted himself an exclamation of heart-felt relief. "Thank God for that!" he said, and then went on, his face suddenly tired and despondent. "We're to evacuate the Residency, Sheridan. Tomorrow night, the commander-in-chief has decided, if arrangements can be made in time."

"The whole garrison, sir?" Alex questioned, conscious of a

sinking of his heart. "Are we to abandon Lucknow completely?"

General Havelock inclined his head. "It is a hard decision to accept, after so long and gallant a defense. Hard for us and," he sighed, "harder still for the heroic garrison Sir Henry Lawrence entrusted with the defense of his Residency. But it is harsh necessity, alas! The women and children and the wounded will leave first. They are to be conveyed to the Dilkusha under cover of darkness and thence to the Alam Bagh and Cawnpore. Sir James Outram will remain with a holding force in the Alam Bagh . . . a small force only, to keep our lines of communication open, until we can return. As, please God, some of us will." He repeated his sigh and added, with conscious bitterness, "This city has cost us too many lives to be abandoned completely, Sheridan. But your warning as to the Nana's intentions has, unhappily, been borne out by Sir Colin Campbell's spies. They report that he is moving on Cawnpore with Tantia Topi and the Gwalior troops, in addition to his own levies—which have been virtually doubled by the regiments fleeing from Delhi—and Windham's been left with barely a thousand men. This force *must* return to his aid or we shall lose Cawnpore. Sir Colin himself admits that it is a desperate gamble, but he has no choice—he must take it. And the odds are slightly in our favor—so long as our combined force is not divided, we shall have sufficient troops to guard against any attack made on the column between here and Cawnpore. And if the chief can get there before Tantia Topi and the Gwalior rebels, he should be able to hold the place."

It was the right—indeed, the only—decision, Alex recognized, although for the defenders it would be a bitter and painful one. The commander-in-chief adhered to it, refusing a plea from Brigadier Inglis that he be left, with a single regiment, to continue the defense of the Residency. During the next two days, the route for the withdrawal was reconnoitered and troops and guns posted so as to cover it against attack. At noon on November 19, a long procession of *doolies* containing the disabled and the women and children—many of them on foot—left the Residency through the Bailey Guard gate, and passing through the Furhut Buksh and Chutter Munzil Palaces, crossed the open ground to Martin's House protected by a flying sap, and after a brief halt at the Moti Mahal, tramped wearily on to the Sikander Bagh. They remained there until nightfall and then, under cover of darkness, all were safely conveyed to the Dilkusha Park.

Captain Peel's naval guns kept up a furious bombardment of the Kaiser Bagh, day and night, as if with the aim of breaching its walls preparatory to an attack, while secretly the garrison of the Residency made preparations for their withdrawal. Guns, ordnance stores, grain, and government treasure were all removed to the Dilkusha unobserved by the rebels, whose entire attention was concentrated on defending the Kaiser Bagh against the expected attack. By November 22, three wide breaches yawned in its walls, and at a little after 11 p.m., the order came for the withdrawal of the fourteen outpost garrisons. This was obeyed in disciplined silence, and by midnight, all was in readiness for the evacuation of the Residency itself.

General Outram stood with Brigadier Inglis at the Bailey Guard gate as the garrison marched past; when all were reported to have gone, Inglis closed the gate, and covered by the guns of the rear-guard, the column gained the Sikander Bagh and then moved on to the Dilkusha Park without a shot being fired at them. Absent from the brief ceremony at the Bailey Guard, Havelock was already at the Dilkusha. Stricken by an acute attack of dysentery, he had been carried there in a *doolie* the previous day, and in the ordinary soldier's tent which had been pitched for him, the little general—whose name was already a household word in far-off England—fought his last battle. His small, wiry body had been so weakened by exposure and the near-starvation rations on which the garrison had existed that, inevitably, this was a losing battle. He died on the morning of November 24, and the soldiers he had so often led to victory bore his body to the Main Bagh where, next day, his simple funeral service was conducted.* On Outram's arrival with the rear-guard, the walled palace was occupied by a force of four thousand men of all arms and twenty-five guns, and he was left in command to hold a front of three miles in length and keep Lucknow's rebels in check.

On November 27, in a 10-mile-long convoy, the Residency garrison, with its women and children, and sick and wounded—numbering almost two thousand—and native camp followers, escorted by three thousand troops, set their faces toward Cawnpore. The column reached Bunni that evening, and as camp was made, the sound of prolonged and heavy gunfire was heard, muted by distance but plainly coming from the direction of Cawnpore. The march was resumed next day, and with Cawnpore still thirty miles away, Alex—riding with the cavalry advance guard—was filled with a sense of deep foreboding.

With every mile the thunder of the distant guns grew louder and the speed of the march was increased. Weary and footsore, the infantry pressed doggedly on; the travel-worn *doolie*-bearers and the heavily laden coolies could scarcely stagger under their burdens; men, horses, and bullocks dropped from exhaustion, and the sick and wounded died, tried beyond endurance, their pleas for water ignored, since no halt could be called. News of the

---

* Flags were flown at half-mast in New York when news of Havelock's death was received there.

attack on Cawnpore was received at noon, when a native *cossid* delivered a letter written in Greek characters and addressed to the commander-in-chief. It was dated two days previously and urgently requested assistance; two later messages confirmed that General Windham was under attack by an estimated 20,000 insurgents and being hard pressed, and the last stated baldly that he had been obliged to abandon the city and fall back to his entrenchment.

Sir Colin Campbell waited no longer. Leaving the convoy to follow with its escorting infantry, he led the cavalry and artillery forward. On reaching Havelock's old camping ground at Mungalwar, he left Brigadier Hope Grant to pitch camp there and galloped on, his escort covering the four miles to the river bank in a straggling line, their horses blown and jaded. Alex, plying his spurs remorselessly, reached the river with the general's staff and had to suppress a gasp of dismay when he saw that the city of Cawnpore was an inferno of smoke and flames, clear proof—if proof were needed—that the Nana was showing no mercy to its inhabitants. The swollen Ganges, gilded by the rays of the setting sun, lay before them, and across its wide expanse, a dark shadow could just be seen. He breathed a heartfelt sigh of relief. The bridge of boats was safe . . . they could reach the beleaguered garrison, so long as that remained intact and in British hands.

Tight-lipped, Sir Colin Campbell spurred on. Met on the bridge by the subaltern commanding the guard, the old Chief reprimanded him harshly when he expressed his relief, adding excitedly that the garrison was at its last gasp.

"How dare you suggest, sir," he demanded, "That any of Her Majesty's troops are at their last gasp? Shame on you, sir!" Waving the abashed young officer wrathfully aside, he turned to Alex. "Get yourself a fresh horse and ride back to Mungalwar. Tell

Brigadier Grant I want his heavy guns in position to cover this bridge before daylight—Captain Peel's twenty-four-pounder, too, if it's humanly possible. And warn Grant that I shall require his brigade with the cavalry and horsed batteries, to cross into Cawnpore at first light. I shall go across now to confer with General Windham but tell the Brigadier I'll rejoin him within the hour. Is that clear?"

"Perfectly, sir," Alex acknowledged.

"Then ride as you never rode in your life," the commander-in-chief bade him. "We must have those guns if we're to save Cawnpore!"

It was a nightmare ride in the gathering darkness and on a borrowed infantry officer's charger, but the way was all too familiar, and Alex found Bouchier's battery already limbering up in anticipation of the order to advance. Guns and cavalry moved forward at a gallop as the moon rose, and just before dawn, Peel's seamen reached the river bank, manhandling their great, unwieldy twenty-four-pounder gun along the rutted track behind the line of straining bullocks to which it was yoked.

Enemy gun batteries opened fire on the bridge, but the British guns made instant reply, as Hope Grant's cavalry and light guns clattered across. By mid-day, the column was occupying the plain, facing the city, its left covering the Allahabad road, and the battle to save Cawnpore had begun.

HISTORICAL NOTES

➽➽➽ • ➾➾➾

Events covered in *The Sepoy Mutiny, Massacre at Cawnpore*
and *The Cannons of Lucknow*

THE MUTINY of the sepoy Army of Bengal began on Sunday, May 10, 1857, with the rising of the 3rd Light Cavalry in Meerut. Despite the fact that he had 2,000 British troops under his command, the obese and senile Major General William Hewitt handled the crisis so ineptly that, after an orgy of arson and slaughter, the Light Cavalry and their sepoy comrades of the 11th and 20th Native Infantry were permitted to reach Delhi, with scarcely a shot fired against them.

Here, supported by the native regiments of the garrison, they proclaimed the last of the Moguls, 80-year-old Shah Bahadur, as Emperor of India, and seized the city, murdering British civil and military officers and massacring hundreds of Europeans and Indian Christians, who had been unable to make their escape. Hampered by both lack of British troops and inadequate transport for those available to him, the British commander-in-chief nevertheless contrived to establish a small force on the Ridge by June 8. This force, which consisted of fewer than 3,000 men of all arms—although it had won two pitched battles against the mutineers on the way to Delhi—was so greatly outnumbered and deficient in heavy artillery that it could only wait for reinforcements, unable, until these arrived, to attempt to recapture the city or even to effectively besiege it.

In Oudh—recently annexed by the East India Company and

already, on this account, seething with discontent—the situation rapidly became critical as, in station after station, the native regiments broke out in revolt. A source of grave anxiety was Cawnpore, 53 miles northeast of Lucknow and on the opposite bank of the Ganges River. With some 375 women and children to protect, the commanding General, Sir Hugh Massey Wheeler, pinned his faith on the friendship of a native prince, the Nana Sahib, Maharajah of Bithur. He had only 200 British soldiers in his garrison—among these 70 invalids and convalescent men of Her Majesty's 32nd Regiment—about the same number of officers and civilian males, 40 native Christian drummers, and a handful of loyal native officers and sepoys.

Betrayed by the Nana, the garrison held out for three weeks with epic heroism, in a mud-walled entrenchment at the height of the Indian summer, under constant attack by 9,000 rebels and surrounded by batteries of heavy caliber guns. Compelled finally to surrender when 250 defenders had been killed and with their food and ammunition exhausted, the survivors were treacherously massacred on the river bank, where they had gone, on the promise of safe passage to Allahabad, on June 27. By the time the Nana called a halt to the awful slaughter, all but 125 women and children and some 60 men had been killed. The men were shot; the women and children, many of them wounded, were held as hostages in a small, single-story house known as the Bibigarh, together with female captives from other stations.

When the small, poorly equipped relief force, under Brigadier General Henry Havelock, fought its way upcountry from Allahabad and recaptured Cawnpore, it was learned that all the hostages had been brutally murdered on July 15, when the British column was still engaging the Nana's troops outside the city. Feeling ran high among Havelock's soldiers, when details of the massacre became known, but the stern and deeply religious little General would permit no indiscriminate reprisals against the civilian population of Cawnpore. Barbarism, he told them, must not be met with barbarism. Punishment would be meted out to the guilty, but the most urgent task facing the column was the relief of Lucknow, which was now under siege by an estimated 25,000 to 30,000 rebels.

Due to the foresight of the Chief Commissioner of Oudh Sir Henry Lawrence, his Residency had been provisioned and preparations made for its defense but he, too, had insufficient British troops—a single regiment, the 32nd—and over 1,200 women, children, and noncombatant males, who had all to be sheltered, protected, and fed. At the end of June, Lawrence suffered a disastrous reverse when he led a small force of his defenders to Chinhat, in an attempt to drive off the rebels and was himself mortally wounded when a round shot entered through the window of his upper room at the Residency on July 2. Command was handed over to Colonel Inglis, of the 32nd, who sent urgent messages to Havelock, requesting aid. At Chinhat, 293 men and 5 guns—which included an 8-inch howitzer—had been lost, and a further 78 men were wounded or sick. A 2000-yard-long defensive perimeter had now to be defended by 1,720 fighting men, of whom over 700 were loyal natives who might or might not remain loyal.

General Havelock made his first attempt to relieve the garrison on July 29, when he crossed the Ganges with 1,500 men—1,200 of them British and the rest Sikhs of the Ferozepore Regiment—and 10 light field guns. He took no tents and 20 of his gunners were invalids of the Veteran Battalion; to his scant force of 20 Volunteer Cavalry were added some 40 infantrymen, with experience of riding, whose cavalry training had of necessity been completed in less than a week. His four European regiments—Her Majesty's 64th, 84th, and 78th Highlanders and the Company's 1st Madras Fusiliers—

had already suffered heavy casualties in the four actions they had fought between Allahabad and Cawnpore, and the terrible ravages of cholera, dysentery, and sunstroke daily reduced their number.

To hold Cawnpore and cover their crossing into Oudh, Havelock ordered the construction of an entrenchment, considerably stronger than General Wheeler's had been, sited on a plateau overlooking the river, and well armed with guns. The Commanding Officer of the Madras Fusiliers, James Neill—whose promotion to Brigadier General was the reward for his ruthless suppression of the mutiny in Benares and Allahabad—was left to defend the newly constructed entrenchment with 300 men. No sooner had Havelock departed than Neill set about executing any native who was even remotely suspected of complicity in the mutiny, reserving a terrible vengeance for those believed to have had a hand in the massacre at the Suttee Chowra Ghat or in the Bibigarh. His reign of terror earned him the unenviable title of "Butcher of Cawnpore," and his disloyal and derogatory dispatches to the Governor General and commander-in-chief, in which he blamed Havelock for his failure to relieve Lucknow, considerably tarnished his hitherto fine record.

Havelock's attempt to bring relief to the "heroic garrison of Lucknow" was, from the outset, doomed to failure. He had too few troops, inadequate transport, and sick carriage, and, in the ancient Kingdom of Oudh, every man's hand was against him, the mutineers' ranks swollen by the armed *zamindars* and peasants who flocked to join them in the insurrection. His small force was victorious in every action, fought against overwhelming odds; it attacked with deathless courage, taking fortified and entrenched positions at the point of the bayonet and inflicting twice and three times the number of casualties it suffered. But the rebel losses could be made good—Havelock's could not and, although his column bravely battled its way to within thirty miles of Lucknow, the little general was compelled to retire to his base at Mungalwar, six miles into Oudh from the river crossing, no less than three times. Faced with the alternative of abandoning his sick and wounded at the roadside and continuing the march on Lucknow with fewer than seven hundred men, his ammunition almost exhausted, he made the only decision he could make and withdrew from the advanced position he had so hardly won.

On the third occasion, he was left with no choice. A frantic message from Neill reached him on August 11, with the warning that the Nana Sahib had gathered a large force at Bithur, 16 miles from Cawnpore, with which he was threatening to recapture the city. Havelock again advanced to Busheratgunj, inflicted a salutary defeat on the Oudh rebels, and then led his weary and greatly depleted column back to Cawnpore on August 13th. But there could be no rest for them. Leaving barely a hundred men to hold the entrenchment, the gallant little General marched to Bithur during the night of the 15th and the next day won a resounding victory over the Nana's 4,000 crack sepoy troops. The Nana himself fled across the river into Oudh, and the one-time commander of his bodyguard, Tantia Topi, was reported to have made contact with the mutinied Gwalior Contingent at Kalpi in order to enlist their aid.

Havelock's constantly reiterated plea for reinforcements was, at last, answered. On his return to Cawnpore on August 17, he received news—via the *Calcutta Gazette* of August 5—that command of the Dinapore Division had been given to Major General Sir James Outram, under whom he had served in the recent Persian campaign. Outram's new command was to include that of Cawnpore, and he was reported to be moving with all possible speed up-country with the two regiments for which Havelock had so often begged, the 5th Fusiliers and the 90th Light Infantry. Sir Colin Campbell, of Balaclava fame, had succeeded the somewhat ineffectual Patrick Grant as commander-in-chief, and Havelock's chagrin, caused by his apparent supersession, was tempered by the new hope that the appointment of Colin Campbell engendered. It vanished completely when Outram, with a chivalrous generosity that was typical of him, announced that Havelock was to continue to command the now augmented relief column until Lucknow was entered. He himself, he stated, would accompany the column in his civilian capacity as chief commissioner of Oudh and serve under his junior as a volunteer.

Outram reached Cawnpore on September 15, bringing 1,268 men with him and a battery of heavy, elephant-drawn guns. These reinforcements brought the total number of troops to a little over 3,000 men—2,400 of them British—with three batteries of artillery, commanded respectively by Captains Francis Maude, R.A. (whose bullock-drawn nine-pounders had accompanied the column from Allahabad at the beginning of July and played a gallant part in all its nine victorious actions), William Olpherts (horsed nine-pounders) and Vincent Eyre (two 24-pounders and two 8-inch howitzers). Captain Lousada Barrow's Volunteer Cavalry—a mere 20 strong when they had joined in July—now augmented by more hurriedly trained infantrymen and by 50 loyal sowars of the 12th Irregulars, under the command of Captain William Johnson and the General's nephew, Charles Havelock, led the way across the newly repaired bridge of boats into Oudh. By the evening of September 20, leaving 300 men to hold Cawnpore, the whole force had crossed the Ganges, with General Havelock in official command, and his two brigades under General Neill and Colonel Hamilton, of the 78th.

The rebels opposed them at their old camping ground at Mungalwar and were brushed aside; the column—free at last of the scourge of cholera—advanced through the once fiercely contested battlefields at Unao and Busseratgunj and, in heavy rain, reached the Sai River at Bunni, driving the fleeing enemy before them in disorder.

Here, with Lucknow only sixteen miles distant, a royal salute was fired to announce the column's impending arrival to the garrison. The Sai was crossed on September 23 in fine weather. After a hard-fought battle with some 10,000 rebels two miles from the city, the Alam Bagh Palace was captured, the cavalry and horsed guns pursuing the broken remnants of the enemy force right up to the heavily defended Char Bagh bridge over the canal, whence the mosques, minarets, and domed palaces of Lucknow itself could be seen clearly.

The British column bivouacked in and around the Alam Bagh that night. The next day was spent resting by the troops and in careful reconnaissance by Havelock and Outram and their senior staff officers. The two generals were not in agreement as to the best way in which to gain the Residency, but, owing to the waterlogged state of the ground—which rendered moving the heavy guns well-nigh impossible—Havelock finally consented to abandon his own plan in favor of that put forward by Outram.

This entailed crossing by the Char Bagh bridge and—instead of advancing through a maze of heavily defended streets direct to the Residency—to take a circuitous route along the canal bank to the then undefended Sikander Bagh Palace, from the shelter of which the final advance would be made under cover of two other walled palaces, leaving only 500 yards of the Khas Bazaar between the column and its objective, the Bailey Guard gate of the Residency. Accordingly, all the sick and wounded and half of Eyre's heavy guns were brought within the walls of the captured Alam Bagh, and, leaving 300 men under Major MacIntyre of the 78th to defend it, the final advance on Lucknow began on September 25.

The Char Bagh bridge was taken with great gallantry by a party of Madras Fusiliers and 84th, led by Colonel Tytler, Havelock's chief of staff, and his son Harry, the column's D.A.A.G., but at bitter cost, almost half of Maude's gunners being killed and Outram being wounded in the arm. With infantry volunteers replacing the gunners and led gallantly by Neill, the advance along the canal bank continued. The Sikander Bagh was reached without much opposition, the rebels having been taken by surprise and unprepared for the route chosen by the British column.

Recovering from their surprise, however, they launched an attack on the rear-guard of the 78th Highlanders and the Volunteer Cavalry, then covering the crossing of the baggage and ammunition trains. The attack was beaten off, with severe losses on both sides but in the resultant delay and confusion, the Highlanders and the Volunteers—instead of following the main body to the Sikander Baghtook a more direct route. It was a providential error, for it brought them out at the rear of the Kaiser Bagh Palace, from which fiercely defended stronghold a battery of twenty-four-pounder guns had brought Havelock's column to a halt, forcing them to take refuge in a narrow passageway formed by the walls of the Moti Mahal Palace, still a mile from the Residency. Highlanders and Volunteers charged the rebel guns from the rear and, bayoneting the gunners, put two and the twenty-four-pounders out of action—temporarily at least—before rejoining the main body, which now advanced through the king's stables to halt again under cover of the walls of the Chutter Munzil Palace.

The light was beginning to fade and the men were weary from their exertions and the heavy fighting; the Kaiser Bagh guns and those in the one-time Mess House of the 32nd had caught the leading regiments in a savage cross-fire, causing many casualties as they battled their way into the defended stables. Outram advised a halt during the hours of darkness, to enable the men to rest and the baggage train and rear-guard to catch up, but Havelock—fearful that the garrison of Lucknow might fall to the prolonged artillery attack now being launched against the Residency—was determined to go on. The men, too, despite their weariness, were eager to reach their objective, the memory of the Cawnpore massacre still vivid in their minds. They had been inspired also by the news, which had reached them in camp at the Alam Bagh, that Delhi had been recaptured, and they greeted their little General's decision to "push on and get it over" with heartening cheers when, reluctantly, Outram acceded to it.

Hitherto, although he had officially relinquished command of the relief force to Havelock, Outram's advice had never been ignored and the result had been, all too often, the confusion of a divided command. But now Henry Havelock stood firm. He knew the fighting spirit of the men he led—at Mungalwar, during an inspection, he had claimed that every one deserved the name of "hero" and, in a loud, clear voice reminiscent of the Havelock of old, he gave his orders.

The wounded among them his courageous son Harry—the baggage train, and the two heavy guns were to remain inside the Moti Mahal Palace, with a guard of two companies of the 90th, under their commanding officer, Colonel Campbell. The field batteries, guided by Captain Moorsom and under strong escort, were to seek a different and safer route to the Residency, since the street leading through the Khas Bazaar was obstructed by trenches and therefore impassible for them.

"The rest of the column will reform," Havelock ended, "with the 78th leading. We shall move out through the courtyard and make straight for the Bailey Guard gate of the Residency. God grant that we may succeed in gaining our objective!"

It was to be General Havelock's finest hour. With Outram at his side, he took his place at the head of the column and, thus exposed but bearing charmed lives, the two commanders set an inspiring example as they rode toward their goal. Cheered on by defenders on the Residency ramparts, the 78th emerged from the sheltering walls of the palace and, beneath a tall archway teeming with rebel sharpshooters, into an inferno of cannon and musketry fire. From every housetop, door, and loopholed wall poured a tempest of shot and the well-sited guns to their rear and mounted at every street crossing unleashed a deadly hail of grape and canister and round shot, scything down the ranks of the advancing Highlanders. But they came on, a single piper playing them home, the Sikhs and the Blue Caps—their comrades throughout the long, heartbreaking campaign, close on their heels. The 64th and the 84th prepared to follow them, bayonets glinting as they charged through the smoke and flames now filling the courtyard, the 5th Fusiliers and the remaining companies of the 90th waiting their turn to run the terrible gauntlet of fire.

The leading regiments could not reply to the fire of their enemies, could not wait even to succor or pick up their wounded comrades. Their orders were to advance to the Residency and not halt until it was reached and they obeyed these orders to the letter.

Their casualties were appalling. Out of the 2,000 men who made the assault, 535 fell dead or wounded, among them James Neill, shot through the head at point-blank range by a rebel sniper. Havelock and Outram reached the Residency unscathed—although Outram had earlier suffered a wound in the arm—to find themselves the center of a crowd of cheering, exultant defenders, who sallied forth, rifles at the ready, to assist them over a low mud wall in front of the Bailey Guard gate, just as darkness fell. After five long and anxious months, the Residency at Lucknow had been relieved and, as one of the garrison described it afterward: "From every pit, trench and battery, from behind sandbags piled on shattered houses, from every post still held by a few gallant spirits, rose cheer on cheer—even from the hospital many of the wounded crawled forth to join in the glad shout of welcome to those who had so bravely come to our assistance. It was a moment never to be forgotten. The delight of the ever gallant Highlanders, who had fought twelve battles to enjoy that moment of ecstasy, and in the last four days had lost a third of their number, seemed to know no bounds."

During the night, stragglers from the column and some of the walking wounded gained the safety of the Bailey Guard; Lousada Barrow's Volunteers and young Johnson's Irregular cavalry sowars brought in more of the wounded, making several daring sallies into the pitch-dark streets in order to do so, and the field guns were guided to their destination by Captain Moorsom. With the coining of daylight, several hundred more men of the assault column joined their comrades in the Residency but many of them were wounded and, in the Moti Mahal Palace a mile away, the small rear-guard of 100 men of the 90th commanded by Colonel Campbell, Eyre's two heavy guns, and the bulk of the wounded were in imminent danger of capture. Throughout the night, they had been under a constant bombardment and, with the coming of daylight, they found themselves surrounded and under attack by a large force of rebels.

Major General Sir James Outram, as chief commissioner for Oudh in succession to Sir Henry Lawrence and senior military officer, formally took command of both the relief force and the garrison on the morning of September 26. It was evident even then that the original plan—which had been to evacuate the Residency garrison to Cawnpore—would have to be abandoned. There were 470 women and children and, to the garrison's sick and wounded had now been added those of the relief force, making a total of some 1,500, for whom there was insufficient carriage available. The original defenders had been reduced to 750 gaunt and famished men, of whom half were Sikhs and loyal sepoys but, their ranks swelled by the addition of the relief force, Outram decided that he could hold Lucknow until the troops Sir Colin Campbell was gathering arrived to reinforce him. Food was a major problem; rations, already barely at subsistence level, would have to be still further reduced, although a supply of grain—of which Colonel Inglis had not known—was subsequently found hidden beneath the Residency and considerably eased the problem.

GLOSSARY OF INDIAN TERMS
➽➽➽ • ⊰⊰⊰

Boorkha: all-enveloping cotton garment worn by purdah
women when mixing with the outside world
Brahmin: high-caste Hindu
Chapkan: knee-length tunic
Charpoy: string bed
Daffadar: sergeant, cavalry
Din: faith
Doolie: stretcher or covered litter for conveyance of wounded
Ekka: small, single-horse-drawn cart, often curtained for
conveyance of purdah women
Fakir: itinerant holy man
Feringhi: foreigner (term of disrespect)
Ghat: river bank, landing place, quay
Godown: storeroom, warehouse
Golandaz: gunner, native
Havildar/Havidar Major: sergeant/sergeant major, infantry
Jemadar: native officer, all arms
Ji/Ji-han: yes
Lal-kote: British soldier
Log: people (baba-log: children)
Moulvi: teacher of religion, Moslem
Nahin: no
Nana: lit. grandfather, popular title bestowed on Mahratta chief
Oudh: kingdom of, recently annexed by Hon. East India
Company

Paltan: regiment

Pandy: name for mutineers, taken from the first to revolt, Sepoy Mangal Pandy, 34th Native Infantry

Peishwa: official title of ruler of the Mahratta race

Pugree: turban

Raj: rule

Rajwana: troops and retainers of native chiefs

Rissala: cavalry

Rissaldar: native officer, cavalry

Ryot: peasant landowner, cultivator

Sepoy: infantry soldier

Sowar: cavalry trooper

Subedar: native officer, infantry (equivalent of Captain)

Sweeper: low-caste servant

Talukdar: minor chief

Tulwar: sword or saber

Vakeel: agent

Zamindar: landowner

Zenana: harem